THE KILLING CODE

A DCI JACK LOGAN THRILLER

J.D. KIRK

ZERTEX
CRIME

THE KILLING CODE
ISBN: 978-1-912767-14-4
Published worldwide by Zertex Media Ltd.
First published in 2019.

3

www.jdkirk.com
www.zertexmedia.com

BOOKS BY J.D. KIRK

A Litter of Bones

Thicker Than Water

The Killing Code

Blood & Treachery

The Last Bloody Straw

A Whisper of Sorrows

The Big Man Upstairs

A Death Most Monumental

A Snowball's Chance in Hell

Ahead of the Game

An Isolated Incident

Colder Than the Grave

Northwind: A Robert Hoon Thriller

CHAPTER ONE

It had been twelve hours since Esme Miller had started her shift. Four since she had begun to watch the clock. Two since she had started counting down the minutes until she could finally clock off.

In less than one, she would be dead.

"You still here?"

Esme looked up from the flat-soled shoes she'd been in the process of untying and smiled through her exhaustion at the young man in the doorway. Kel was barely in his twenties and was usually a bouncy-ball of energy, but the shift had been a long one, and the aftermath of a traffic accident earlier in the day had taken its toll on all of them. Now, he just looked like he wanted to be at home, tucked up in bed.

Instead, he leaned on the handle of a mop, trying to hide the fact that he was currently relying on it for support.

"Aye, but not for long, thank God. That's me finished," Esme said. "You?"

"Nah. Been roped into staying on until midnight. A&E can't get cover."

He smiled, but the way he shook his head betrayed his true feelings on the matter.

"Bloody Brexit," Esme said.

Kel laughed at their little running joke and nodded. "Too right. Bloody Brexit."

Esme kicked off her comfies and began the process of wrestling her swollen feet into her regular outdoor shoes. "You must be due a break, though?" she said. "You look awful."

"Cheeky cow!" Kel protested. "Talk about pot and kettle. Have you looked in the mirror lately?"

"I tried, but it shattered."

"No bloody wonder."

Esme placed her work shoes in her locker and took out her jacket. The walk wasn't far, but she'd been reliably informed that the rain had been off and on all day, and she didn't fancy arriving home like a drowned rat.

"Make sure you get that break," she said, closing her locker and turning back to the door.

"Aye, they're giving me an hour to get my head down. But first..." Kel raised the mop and gave it a waggle. "Clean-up in Room Four."

Esme thought for a moment. "Albert?"

"Aye."

"Not again. What end?"

"Both ends. Simultaneously," Kel said.

Esme tried very hard not to laugh but wasn't entirely successful. "Yikes."

"It was actually one of the most impressive things I've ever seen. He was like a human fountain at one point. I was half-expecting Hugh Jackman to jump out in a top hat and start singing *The Greatest Show* at me."

Esme snorted. "You wish."

Kel gave a dreamy little sigh. "A boy can dream."

"Aye," Esme agreed. She jabbed a thumb in the direction of Room Four. "Once you've cleaned up the shitesplosion."

Kel gave a little tut and sagged against his mop again. "Way to bring that fantasy crashing to the ground there."

"You're welcome," Esme said, pulling her jacket on.

Kel stepped aside to let her out. "You back on tomorrow?"

"Nope! Two whole days off," Esme gloated, waggling a two-fingered peace sign in his face as she passed him.

"Two? Jesus. Who did you have to sleep with to make that happen? And, can you give me his number?"

Esme gave a little chuckle. The remark probably deserved more than that, but exhaustion was muting her reactions. She could hear a hot shower and her bed calling to her from a mile up the road.

"Goodnight, Kel," she said. "And make sure you take that break."

"Too bloody right," Kel said. "Night. See you on..." He puffed out his cheeks. "Whatever day is two days from now."

"God knows. I'm sure someone will keep us right," Esme replied. "See you then."

She shambled away from the changing room and along the corridor in the direction of the nurses' station. The usual alarms *bleeped* and *pinged* from the usual doorways as she passed them. The usual snores. The usual groans.

Not her problem. Not tonight, not tomorrow, and not the next day, either. Two whole days off. Even if she slept for one—which felt quite likely at the moment—she still had another spare. That was dream-come-true stuff.

There was no one at the nurses' station when she got there, everyone was off doing the final rounds for evening medication. Somewhere along the corridor behind her, she heard

Kel's voice. It was bright and enthusiastic, stuffed full of fake cheer.

"Nice try on the redecorating in here, Mr French. But maybe best leave it to the experts next time, eh?"

Esme smiled, scrawled her name on the sign-out sheet, then hurried towards the ward exit before anyone could ask her anything. She swore some days a shift at Raigmore was like being Al Pacino in *The Godfather*.

Just when you thought you were out, they pulled you back in.

Tonight though, she made it to the ward door, out into the corridor, and over to the lifts without anyone calling after her. The lifts weren't there, so she took the stairs rather than risk hanging around to wait. It wouldn't be the first time a doctor or one of the senior nurses on duty had caught up with her while she waited for the lift to arrive and she'd found herself talked into working an extra couple of hours.

There were three flights of stairs to get down. Her feet didn't complain. They knew it was in their best interests to get the hell out of there quickly and with as little fuss as possible.

Two days.

More than that, even. Fifty-nine hours until she clocked back in again. Her feet were willing to take the hit.

She took the side door to the outside when she reached the bottom of the stairs, and the cool October air woke her up a little, sharpening her senses.

It was quicker to walk through the hospital and leave by the Outpatients door, but the longer she was inside the building, the greater the chance she'd be dragged into some unpaid overtime.

No, better to take the longer way around the outside of the

building, enjoy the crispness of the air, and—hopefully—not meet another living soul.

Or, at least, none with any direct authority over her working hours.

With thoughts of the next fifty-nine hours filling her head, Esme Miller set off around the outside of the hospital and headed for a home she would never reach.

HE LOVES the way she walks. So fluid. So smooth. She almost looks real.

But then, he loves the way they all *walk. Always different. Unique. Like a fingerprint. And yet, exactly the same in all the ways that count.*

Her gait varies, just like the rest of them. Sometimes it's bright, like when she walks little Chloe to school, or sets off to meet her sister for lunch. Tonight, now, her footsteps are flat. Slow. Plodding. She's battling exhaustion. It isn't real, of course, but she feels it all the same.

She'll sleep soon.

He'll allow her that.

Her movements are so lifelike. Just by looking, it's almost impossible to know that she's on strings. Most people can't see them. Most people don't understand.

He is not most people.

He is different.

And yet, in all the ways that count, he is the same.

She comes around the back of the hospital, slumping her way past the big bins, then thacking *onto the grass. That too seems so real, so alive, so here-and-now. But he sees the truth.*

Or rather, the lies.

He wonders, just briefly, what she's thinking as she pulls her bag higher on her shoulder and sets off across the shaded lawn. Then, he reminds himself of the stark reality of it.

She isn't thinking. None of them are. None of them ever do.

Taking the shortcut across the grass will save her four minutes on her journey home. He knows this. He has timed her often enough.

Four minutes, even accounting for the way she'll pick up speed when she's halfway across, right in the middle of the darkest spot, hidden in the shadows of the trees lining the edges of the hospital grounds.

The trek across the grass will take her less than two minutes. Not long.

But long enough.

Beyond the trees, the evening traffic trundles by. Pointless people leading make-believe lives. Fools. Liars. All of them.

They don't matter. None of them matter. Not now.

Not ever.

She's a third of the way across the grass. The darkness reaches out to embrace her.

The knife is heavy in his hand, its weight yet another deception in a never-ending list.

She is halfway now. Her pace quickens.

He loves the way she walks. She almost looks real.

But he knows different. He knows the truth. And soon, he'll show them.

He'll show them all.

CHAPTER TWO

Detective Chief Inspector Jack Logan plodded up the winding staircase that led to his top floor flat, his boots scuffing on the uneven stone steps. The day had been a long and exhausting one. Not physically, granted, but a stack of paperwork had finally caught up with him, and being stuck behind a desk for hours always took its toll on his energy levels.

Still, he'd broken the back of it, and what had been a stack was now just a couple of small bundles and an overflowing box file. He'd be through it all in a week or so. Sooner, if he could convince DI Forde to chip in. That shouldn't take too much in the way of bribery and corruption.

Ben Forde wasn't exactly a fan of the paperwork—no bugger was—but he didn't hate it in the same way that Logan did. There were even rumours that he'd once said he found it 'relaxing,' but he'd been quick to take that back after everyone in earshot had offered to help him get properly chilled-out by giving him their own to do.

After the paperwork was out of the way, Logan was hoping for a bit of breathing space. He might even take a couple of days off to get settled into the flat properly. He'd been in for almost two months now but was still living out of boxes.

Not many boxes, granted. He hadn't brought a lot with him when he'd left Glasgow. Still, it would be good to get properly set up. Even better to take a couple of days to unwind. Things had been more hectic than expected following his move north, and he felt like he hadn't caught his breath in weeks.

He might even finally get around to putting up that shelf he'd bought the day after moving in, although he wasn't committing himself to it quite yet.

There were eight flats in the block, each one staggered half a floor above the one before, on opposite sides of the stairwell. He was passing the floor before his own—eight steps from his front door—when he heard the shout and the sound of something breaking. A plate, he thought. Possibly a glass.

His desire to get home carried him up a step before a sense of... not duty, exactly, more common decency, stopped him.

"How was that me? Eh? How is that my fault?"

Male voice. Young-ish. Mid-twenties, maybe.

"It's no'. You're no' listening. That's no' what I'm saying!"

A woman. Younger still, he thought. Both voices were raised, albeit in different ways. His was angry. Aggressive. There was a pleading edge to hers. Not quite desperation, but not far off it.

"Well, what *are* you fucking saying then, eh?"

A crash. A thud.

"Come on, then? What are you fucking saying?"

Logan hadn't met any of his neighbours yet.

He stepped down onto the landing.

Now seemed like as good a time as any to introduce himself.

He knocked on the door. It was a policeman's knock, the

type of knock that made it very clear the knuckles responsible for it weren't going to go away without getting an answer.

The man's voice dropped in volume but lost none of its anger. There were a few hissed comments too quiet for Logan to hear, then a series of thudding footfalls.

The door was yanked open. An unshaven twenty-something with crooked teeth and greasy hair scowled at him, chest all puffed out, fist clenched at his side. His eyes were set so far back in their dark hollows they looked like they'd been put there with a Black & Decker.

"The fuck you want?" the scrote demanded. He was shorter than Logan by a whole head, but his system was currently so flooded with testosterone that he didn't appear to notice his height disadvantage.

Logan held the man's gaze long enough to make an impression, then looked past him to where a skinny lassie with a hair colour that could only have come from a bottle stood at the far end of the hall. Her arms were wrapped around her middle, her weight shifting from foot to foot.

Pieces of a broken mug lay on the bare floorboards around her, a dark brown tea or coffee stain on the wall marking the spot where it had first made impact.

"Everything alright?" Logan asked.

"The fuck's that got to do with you?" the scrote demanded.

Logan flicked his gaze to him, just briefly. "Did I look like I was talking to you?" he asked.

The chest puffed out further. Logan could practically hear the *creak* of the bastard's joints as he tightened his fists.

"The fuck you say?"

"Miss?" said Logan, ignoring him. "Everything alright?"

She opened her mouth as if to reply, but then closed it again when the door started to close.

"She's fine. Fuck off."

The door stopped when it hit the toe of Logan's boot. He thought about reaching into his coat for his warrant card, but decided to keep that a surprise for now.

"Gonnae move yer fucking foot?"

"Gonnae shut yer fucking mouth?" Logan countered, eyeballing him.

It was a direct challenge. There were two ways this could go now, Logan knew. Either the scrote would double-down and come at him, or he'd back off. Chicken out. Shite the bed.

"What?" the man said. He seemed to shrink a little as his eyes furtively looked Logan up and down.

Shite the bed, then.

"Miss? Are you OK? I heard shouting," Logan said.

She stopped her shifting and slouched all her weight on one hip. Her face became a sneer. "Piss off, ya nosy bastard. What's it to do with you?"

Emboldened by this, the greasy wee bam started bumping the door against Logan's foot. "You heard her. She's fine. So, off ya fuck, eh?"

Logan looked between them, then sucked in his bottom lip.

"Fair enough," he said.

He was about to withdraw his foot when he spotted the well-trodden pile of mail on the floor. Brown envelopes, mostly, with red 'Final Demand' warnings stamped on the front.

"Tanya," he said, reading the name on one of the address labels. He met the girl's eye again. "I'm just upstairs, alright? If you need me."

She said nothing, just looked down at the floor and tightened her arms around her middle as Logan withdrew his foot. The door closed between them with a *bang*.

"Prick!" the man spat through the wood, and then there

came the thudding of retreating footsteps, some low muttering, and the slamming of a door somewhere further back in the flat.

Logan grunted below his breath. "Welcome to the bloody neighbourhood," he mumbled, then he reached into his pocket for his keys, plodded up the remaining steps, and finally made it home.

With its dirty windows and peeling metal railing, the stairwell that ran up through the block of flats was tired and grim. Much the same could be said for the inside of Logan's flat, too.

He'd originally been set up with a decent place overlooking the river until Bosco Maximuke, a local property developer, drug-dealer, and long-time pain in Logan's arse, had interfered. Three other places had fallen through since then, and Logan was convinced Bosco was behind them all.

After he'd come for a viewing of this place, Logan had partly been hoping that Bosco would cause this deal to collapse, too. Unfortunately, his offer was accepted, his deposit taken, and the keys duly presented to him by a letting agent who had made no attempt to disguise the fact that she could hardly believe her luck.

It had come fully furnished, but Logan had insisted most of the stuff be taken out before he moved in, and preferably destroyed in a big fire somewhere far away. The couch, in particular, had been covered in so many dirty stains it looked like a map of some newly discovered country. And not one anyone in their right mind would ever want to visit.

He'd bought a few pieces of furniture to replace some of the stuff that had been chucked out. A new couch. A coffee table. That sort of thing. He'd since been informed by Ben's wife, Alice, that none of it matched, and that the couch was too big for the room. Annoyingly, she was probably right.

Logan groaned his way out of his coat, tossed it onto one

arm of the couch, then flopped down beside it. The three-seater may well have been too big, but it was comfy. Bloody should be, considering what he'd paid for it.

He'd just kicked off his boots and put his feet up on the coffee table when two things occurred to him. The first, and most important, was that he should've put the kettle on before sitting down. Now, he was going to have to get up again, just as he was getting comfortable. It was a rookie mistake, and he cursed himself for it.

He could *not* have tea, of course.

He contemplated this idea for a moment, but quickly dismissed it as ridiculous. He was tired, aye, but he wasn't so tired that he was willing to forgo the unique pleasure of a post-shift cuppa.

Still, where was DC Neish when you needed him?

The second thing that occurred to Logan was that the red light on his phone was blinking, signalling he had a new message. He'd never had a message on the landline before. He didn't even think anyone had the number. It would be some shite about PPI, or a non-existent traffic accident he'd never been involved in, no doubt, but he had to pass the handset on the way to the kitchen, so decided to check it anyway.

It took him a full forty seconds of staring at buttons to figure out which one played the messages. He let it run as he continued through to the kitchen, jiggled the cord out of the back of the kettle, and began filling it from the tap.

"You have... one new message," the machine declared in an unconvincing female voice. "From... unknown caller. Received today at... six forty-nine... PM."

Logan put the lid back on the kettle and jammed the cord into the socket.

There was nothing more from the phone's base unit. He

clicked the switch on the kettle, idly wondering if the message had started to play yet, or if he had to go and press some other button to set it going.

And then, he heard it. A soft hissing. A near-silence that suggested a void on the other end of the line. A breath. Two. In. Out. Slow and steady.

And then, a *click* as the handset was replaced at the other end, and a half-second of dead tone before the robotic voice piped up again.

"You have no more messages. To play these messages again, press one. To delete them, press—"

Logan leaned around the doorframe and jabbed a button on the base unit, silencing the machine.

He wondered, just briefly, about the message, but then the water in the kettle began rolling to the boil, and he pulled open the cupboard where he kept the mugs.

Then, when he found it empty, he turned his attention to the sink, and to the Jenga-style stack of dirty dishes contained therein.

By the time he'd picked the least dirty mug and swirled it under the tap, he'd stopped thinking about the phone message.

By the time he'd settled back down on his too-big couch with his size twelves up on the coffee table, he'd forgotten it had ever happened.

KEL YAWNED, stretched, and stepped out of the A&E department's makeshift sleeping quarters, directly into the path of an oncoming ambulance stretcher. Two paramedics were rattling off details of the patient to a frantic-looking nurse, their dark green uniforms made darker still by the smears of blood that covered their fronts.

One of the emergency department doctors was bent double beside the trolley, scuttling crab-like as he worked on the patient. He had his back to Kel, blocking the view of the person on the stretcher.

Kel stepped back into the room, making space for them all to pass. One of the older nurses—Cindy—was doing the same sideways scuttle as the doctor, but on the opposite side of the bed. She'd have done this a hundred times before, but there was a panic to her movements and a frantic edge to her voice.

"Esme? Esme? Can you hear me, pet?"

"Wait, what?" said Kel, stepping out as the trolley swept past. "Esme?"

One of the paramedics looked back over her shoulder. Her eyes were wide, her pupils dilated. A smear of crimson was wrapped across her throat like a scarf.

"Aye," she confirmed, recognition flitting across her face when she saw Kel. "It's Esme. She's been attacked."

"*Attacked*? What?" Kel spluttered. "You sure?"

The paramedic's lips went thin and colourless. She glanced down at the woman on the stretcher, then swallowed. "Aye," she said, throat tight, voice hoarse. "I'm sure."

LOGAN'S PHONE RANG, jolting him awake. His arm jerked, tipping the mug he'd been holding balanced on his stomach, and sloshing his shirt in a glug of cold tea.

"Shite," he spat, the cold cutting through the bleariness and peeling his eyelids all the way open.

After dumping the mug on the coffee table, he rummaged

in his coat until he found the phone. He didn't bother to look at the number on the screen. There was no point. Who else would be calling him at this time?

"Logan," he grunted, stifling a yawn. He checked his watch. After eleven. He'd been asleep for over an hour.

He listened to the voice on the other end.

"When?" he asked, once it had finished. He listened for the answer, then checked his watch again. "OK. I'll head right there. Call in DS McQuarrie. Get her to meet me there. Is the scene locked down?"

He nodded at the answer.

"Good. Right, then. Keep me posted."

He hung up, let his head sink back onto the couch, and sighed.

Maybe take a few days off.

He snorted at the very idea of it now.

"Wishful bloody thinking."

CHAPTER THREE

THE ATMOSPHERE IN A&E BROKE THE BAD NEWS TO Logan before anyone could say a word. He caught the eye of a uniformed officer who was standing talking to a nurse, and received a brief shake of the head in response.

Damn it.

The waiting area was fairly small, with mismatched chairs and a table laden with dog-eared magazines. There were two people waiting to be seen, one nursing a swollen wrist, the other holding a cold cloth against her forehead. Neither looked serious, so Logan had no issue with keeping them waiting.

There was a sliding glass hatch in the wall that showed a corner of a little reception room beyond. A nurse spotted him and said something he couldn't hear. DS McQuarrie's face appeared at the glass a moment later, and she gestured to a door just to the left of the window.

"Sir," Caitlyn said, straightening as he entered the room. "Bad news, I'm afraid."

"Aye," said Logan. "What have we got?"

"Victim worked here at the hospital," Caitlyn began.

"Esme," said the nurse sitting at the desk. "Her name was Esme."

Caitlyn glanced back at her. "Esme. Yes. Sorry," she said, then she nodded past Logan to the door at his back. "Should we maybe...?"

"Aye. We'll step outside," Logan said. He smiled grimly at the nurse. "Sorry for your loss."

"It's not our loss. It's Rowan's," the nurse said. Her hand went to her mouth, tears blurring her eyes. "And, oh God, Chloe. Little Chloe."

"Family," Caitlyn said, although Logan had already guessed as much.

The nurse drew in a steadying breath through her nose, shook her head, then raised her gaze to the detectives. "Right. OK. If you need anything else, just... I don't know. Someone will be able to... I'm sure."

"Thank you. We know it's difficult," said Caitlyn. "Are you OK? Would you like us to get someone?"

"I'm fine," the nurse said. "Honestly. It's just a shock. Go do what you have to do."

Logan led the way out of the room, and Caitlyn followed him to a quiet area of the corridor. There were four treatment areas leading off from the corridor ahead. Three of them were open, showing empty beds. A blue curtain was drawn across the fourth, concealing everything within.

A male nurse stood talking to a uniformed female officer over by a window. They kept their voices low, occasionally shooting glances at the curtained-off area.

"So?" Logan prompted.

Caitlyn had a notebook in her hand but rattled off the details without looking at it.

"Esme Miller. Age thirty-three. Nurse here. She was on

her way home from her shift when she was attacked. Right outside on the hospital grounds. Another nurse found her on his way in. He was running late, and it's a common shortcut, apparently."

"Attacked how?"

"Multiple stab wounds," Caitlyn said. "She was alive when they brought her in, but she'd lost too much blood, and some of her organs had been punctured. There was nothing they could do. She died a few minutes before I got here."

There was some commotion from out in reception, and then the double doors that led through into the back area were thrown wide. A red-haired forty-something man with wide eyes and a dishevelled appearance came barrelling through, his movements sharp and agitated.

"Esme? Esme?"

"Rowan, wait," said a nurse, hurrying through the doors behind him.

"Where is she? Where's Esme?" the man demanded, powering along the corridor, head snapping left and right as he searched the area.

"Rowan, wait pet, please!" the nurse pleaded, but he was having none of it.

His eyes fell on the curtained-off area and he broke into a jog. Caitlyn moved quickly to intercept.

"Mr Miller? Mr Miller, stop."

He looked at the woman blocking his path, something like disgust contorting his features. "What? Who are you? Let me through. That's... My wife's in there."

"I understand that, Mr Miller," Caitlyn said. "But I'm afraid you can't go in there. I'm sorry. I know how you must be feeling, but we can't risk you contaminating potential evidence."

"*Evidence*?" Rowan spluttered. "She's not *evidence*, she's my bloody wife! She needs me. I should be in there with her. Who even are you, anyway?"

Logan groaned inwardly. He didn't know. The poor bastard. He had no idea.

But he was catching up quickly.

"Wait. Wait," he said, the force of the realisation forcing him back a step. He shook his head, tears cutting down his cheeks from nowhere. "No. No. She's not..."

He tried to step past Caitlyn, his voice rising. "Esme? Esme, sweetheart, it's... It's..."

"I'm sorry, Mr Miller," said Logan, moving in to stand with DS McQuarrie.

"She's not. She can't be," Rowan said, the words squeaking out of his narrowing throat. He looked from one detective to the other, eyes pleading, like they could somehow change it. Somehow fix it. "Please. *Please*. She's not."

The nurse who had come hurrying through after him put a hand on his arm. He stared down at it, frowning, like he couldn't quite figure out what it was.

"I'm so sorry, pet," she said, her voice almost as shaky as his. "We're all so very sorry. We did everything we could."

Rowan continued to stare at the hand on his arm. His Adam's apple was the only part of him that moved as he swallowed a few times, like he was choking back a mouthful of spew.

"I'm DCI Jack Logan, this is DS Caitlyn McQuarrie," Logan told him. "I won't insult you by saying we understand what you must be going through."

Rowan pulled his arm away from the nurse's hand. "I want to see her. I want to go in. I want to see her."

"I'm afraid that's not possible," said Caitlyn. "Like I said—"

"I heard what you fucking said! But that's my wife! I want to see her. I need to see her!"

"Mr Miller—" Caitlyn began.

Logan put a hand on her shoulder. "I think we can allow it," he said. He met Rowan's eye and held his gaze, drilling the importance of what he was saying into the man. "But I'm afraid we can only let you see her. Any contact will jeopardise our chances of catching the person responsible for this. Is that understood, Mr Miller?"

Rowan nodded without any hesitation. "I just... I just need to see her."

DS McQuarrie shot the DCI a look that suggested she had strong reservations. Logan acknowledged them with a nod, then placed a hand on Rowan's back and guided him to the corner of the curtain.

"Are you sure about this?"

"Yes," Rowan croaked, without an ounce of doubt.

Logan peeled the curtain aside and stepped through first. Caitlyn watched Rowan step through behind him, and the curtain fall back into place.

She met the nurse's gaze, then they both looked away at the sound of Rowan's sobbing. "No. Oh, God, no. Esme. No. No. God, no, please!"

"I'm sorry, Mr Miller. I can't let you go any closer." That was Logan's voice, soft and gentle, yet unmistakably rigid at the same time.

The nurse shifted anxiously, wringing her hands together as she waited by the curtain.

When it was pulled aside a moment later, she was quick to step in close to Rowan and put her arms around him. He let himself be pulled in, his own hands trailing limply at his sides, his face blank and expressionless, like a robot in the middle of a reboot.

"I'm so sorry. I'm so very sorry," the nurse whispered to him. "Come on, let's get you a cup of tea."

She looked to Logan for approval. "That's OK, isn't it?"

"Aye. Of course," Logan said. "Caitlyn, will you...?"

DS McQuarrie nodded. "Yes, sir."

She followed behind as the nurse led the still torpid Rowan towards an office tucked away at the back of A&E.

They were halfway to the door when Rowan stopped abruptly, his brain starting to process the enormity of how his whole life had been irrevocably changed.

"Oh, God. Chloe. What am I going to tell Chloe? What's she going to do without her mum?" he asked. He looked imploringly at the nurse and Caitlyn, like one of them might offer an answer. "What are we going to do?"

"We'll figure it out, pet," the nurse said, squeezing his arm. "Come on. Let's get you that cup of tea."

Logan watched Rowan resume his shell-shocked shuffle. Almost as soon as they'd disappeared into the office and closed the door, there was a tap on his shoulder.

He turned to find a woman in a parka jacket looking up at him, a circle of her face visible inside the synthetic fur edging of the hood.

"Ye alright there, Jack?" she asked, playing up her Irish accent. She looked past him in the direction of the door. "Was that her fella?"

"Uh, aye. Yeah, that was him," Logan said. To his immense annoyance, he caught himself straightening his shoulders a little. For the first time since he'd taken the phone call back at the flat, he wished he'd taken a moment to at least glance in a mirror.

The woman pushed back her hood and gave a little shake of her hair. "Thought so. That's why I hung back. I'm not great with the living ones. Give me the dead ones, any day. Much less small talk required."

She jabbed a thumb over her shoulder in the direction of the curtain. "Body in there?"

It had been a few months since Logan had first met the pathologist, Shona Maguire. He'd been struck then just how unlike the previous pathologists he'd worked with she was, and that opinion had not changed since. It had grown, in fact, to the extent he was now positive he'd never met *anyone* who was quite like she was.

Professionally, he meant.

That was all.

"Aye. She's in there," Logan confirmed.

"Stabbing, I hear."

"So it seems. I'll leave it to you to make the final call."

Shona tucked her thumbs into an imaginary pair of braces and rocked back on her heels. "That's why they pay me the big bucks."

"Do they?" Logan asked.

"Not really," she admitted, letting the non-existent braces *twang* back into place. "Piss poor, actually. I should probably strike."

"Aye, well, if you could leave it until you've dealt with this, that would be handy."

She tapped a finger to her forehead in salute. "Ten-four."

Shona beckoned to the male nurse who stood beside the uniformed officer over by the window. "Is there a porter available who can help me move..."

"Esme," Logan mumbled.

"...Esme around to..." She glanced at the office door, then lowered her voice to a whisper so that Rowan Miller wouldn't hear. "*...you know where?*"

The nurse blinked a few times, like he wasn't quite sure what was being asked of him, then gave a nod. "I think Kel's just taking a minute to himself. I'm sure he'll be able to help. I'll go check. If not, I can do it."

Shona gave the nurse a thumbs-up as he passed her, then turned back to Logan. "Want to come watch?"

"Not even remotely," Logan said.

The pathologist crinkled her nose. "Nah, that line very rarely works," she admitted. She backed away in the direction of the curtain. "You do still owe me lunch, though."

"How about breakfast?" Logan asked her.

Shona's expression became one of genuine surprise. "Detective Chief Inspector! What are you suggesting?"

"That I swing by your office in the morning to see what you've found," Logan said. "I'll bring you a bacon roll."

"Chuck an egg on top and it's a date," Shona told him, opening the curtain at her back. "Enjoy the rest of your night."

"You, too," Logan told her, then he winced.

"Well, it's unlikely to be a barrel of laughs," Shona said, after just a moment of hesitation. "But I'll see what I can do."

Then, with another little salute, she stepped through the curtain and closed it behind her.

Logan stood rooted to the spot for a moment, then shook his head.

"*You, too,*" he muttered. "Jesus."

He caught the Uniform smirking at him. She quickly glanced away when she realised she'd been rumbled.

Logan clicked his fingers and pointed at her. "You."

"Sir?"

"Any idea who found the body?"

The constable shook her head. "No, sir."

"Well, then," Logan grunted. He put a hand on the back of his neck and tilted his head, working out some of the knots. "Maybe you could make yourself useful and go find out."

CHAPTER FOUR

THE DOCTOR'S OFFICE WAS REASONABLY LARGE, BUT THE overflowing bookcases and industrial-looking shelves made it feel claustrophobically small.

The amount of clutter in the place didn't help. There was pointless shite on almost every surface. Stress toys. A *World's Best Surgeon* mug. Three cactuses in little pots.

The doctor who'd donated his office had made a point of telling Logan to, "Watch out for my trophies." Logan had expected them to be some sort of medical awards, but instead had been confronted by a half-dozen-strong army of little tennis figurines made of gold-coloured plastic. Runner-up prizes, mostly, according to the little etched plates on the front, but there were a couple of winners in there, too.

There had only been one chair—a battered old padded number with stuffing spewing out through a tear in the armrest—but one of the porters had brought in another at Logan's request. It was hard plastic on metal legs, and it had taken three attempts before Logan had found a way to fit it in the room in a way that wouldn't leave him playing footsie with the person sitting opposite.

The person sitting opposite at this particular moment was the nurse who had discovered Esme on the hospital grounds. He was older than Logan—mid-fifties or thereabouts—with greying hair, a day or two of stubble, and the demeanour of someone trying very hard to put a brave face on things.

Logan checked the notebook he'd been given by one of the Uniforms. "Mr... Brews, is it?"

"Bob."

"Bob. How are you doing?"

The question seemed to take the nurse by surprise. "Um... Aye. Bit shaken, if I'm honest. But, you know. We see this sort of stuff all the time."

He shook his head like he was annoyed at himself. "Not stabbings. Not really. But, you know, injuries." He swallowed. His bottom jaw juddered. "Death. It's all part of the job."

Bob attempted a smile. "Bit like you lot, I suppose."

"Aye. Different when it's one of your own, though," Logan said.

The nurse exhaled, puffing out his cheeks, and nodded in agreement. He didn't say anything, though, and Logan suspected that, right at that moment, he couldn't.

"Take a minute, Mr Brews. Bob. You've had a shock."

"You can say that again," Bob whispered. He became unable to hold Logan's gaze and looked past him instead, adopting that thousand-yard-stare that the detective knew only too well. He was replaying it in his head. Or rather, it was replaying for him, whether he wanted it to or not.

"Tell me what you saw," Logan encouraged.

"It was... I was late. Again. Fell asleep after dinner and woke up in a panic. The bus stopped at the traffic lights back along the road, so I asked to get off there. It's quicker to cut across the grass than wait for it to pull into..."

He smiled apologetically.

"Sorry. Not relevant."

"Don't worry. Just keep going," Logan told him.

Bob continued, hesitantly at first. The more he said, though, the more freely the words came.

"There's a gap. At the trees, where they meet the fence. There's a path. Aye, not a path, but a... It's been worn in. A track, I suppose. We all use it. Anyway, it's dark until you get closer to the hospital. I had the phone torch on. To see. Only, I didn't. See, I mean. Her."

He shook his head, annoyed at himself.

"I'm not explaining it. I heard her, is what I mean. This... noise. I thought it was an animal at first. I thought maybe a cat or a dog had been hit by a car and had crawled onto the grass. It's happened before."

"The sound was coming from the path ahead of you?" Logan asked.

"No. To the side. Over on the right. Nearer the fence," Bob said, gesturing in that direction. "I was late. Third time this month. I thought about not stopping, but... How couldn't I? I could tell it was in pain, whatever it was. It was suffering. I couldn't just... I wasn't just going to... Late or not, you know? I couldn't."

"I understand. It's to your credit, Mr Brews."

"Bob," he said again.

"It's to your credit, Bob. You couldn't leave it suffering. Then what?"

Bob bit down on his bottom lip, like he couldn't bring himself to say the words. Or maybe he couldn't face hearing them out loud.

"I think I realised before I saw her," he said, his voice a whisper. "Not that it was Esme, I had no idea, but that it wasn't an animal. The noises were... wrong. Different. I felt sick. Even before I saw her, I felt sick. Even before I knew, I *knew*."

He took a series of breaths, like a swimmer preparing to dive down deep. "She'd been gagged. There was tape on her mouth. Her eyes were rolling. She couldn't breathe. I took it off. There was a rag stuffed in there, right down into her throat. I took it out."

Bob's hands were twisting together, the veins on his forearms standing on end. "And the blood. There was so much blood. Too much. Far too much. I knew. She'd lost too much. But I shouted. I shouted and shouted, and then someone came. Paramedics. They'd been doing a drop-off. Luck, really."

Tears fell and *pluh-plinked* onto the front of his uniform. His voice had been wavering through the past few sentences and was now throaty and raw.

"But it was all too late. I knew that. They did everything they could, but I knew. All that blood. I knew."

"I'm sorry," Logan said. "I know how difficult this must be. You're doing really well."

Bob ran a bare forearm across his eyes, smiled weakly, and sat up straighter in the padded chair.

"Did you see or hear anyone else?" Logan asked. "Around where you found Esme, or maybe out on the pavement before you started across the grass?"

"No. I don't think so. I wasn't really paying attention, though. I was... With me being late and everything. I wasn't really looking, so I don't... I'm not... I'm sorry."

"You sure?" Logan pressed. "You didn't hear anything, maybe? When you were with Esme?"

The realisation of what the detective was getting at registered on Bob's face. "You think he was still there?" he gasped. "What, like, watching? You think he was there?"

"Almost certainly not, no," Logan said. "I'd be very surprised. But always worth asking. So, there was nothing that made you think someone else was nearby?"

"No. Nothing."

Bob's voice was flat, his face drained of colour. The initial adrenaline surge of the discovery was passing, and he was heading for a crash. Logan had seen it often enough to recognise the signs.

"I think we'll call it a night, Bob," the DCI said, flipping the notebook closed. "You don't need this right now."

Bob's relief wrote itself in large letters across his face. "Thank you."

"Do you have someone to get you home?" Logan asked.

"Home?"

Logan stood up. "Aye. Do you need a lift?"

"I'm on shift," Bob said. "We're... With Esme... We're short-staffed enough as it is."

"I'm not sure that's such a good idea."

Bob's mouth arranged itself into something that could almost pass for a smile. "No, nor me. But it is what it is."

He put his hands on the armrests as if to stand up, but then stopped.

"I think... If you don't mind, I'll just take another minute in here by myself."

Logan gave him a nod. "Of course. Take care of yourself. We'll be in touch, and if you think of anything else..."

He passed the nurse his card. "Just ask for me by name. Someone will get you through."

Bob took the card, glanced at it, then slipped it into the breast pocket of his tunic. "I will."

Logan side-stepped between the chairs, leaned to avoid a shelf overburdened with box files, then stopped by the door.

"All the best, Mr Brews."

"Bob."

"Bob," Logan corrected. Then, with a final nod of acknowledgement, he slipped out of the room and left the man alone with his grief.

CHAPTER FIVE

THE CRIME SCENE WAS THE STANDARD AFFAIR. Spotlights. Tape. White paper suits.

The usual.

The night was crisp and cold, and even with Raigmore spilling its light pollution towards the sky, Logan could make out a fair crop of stars winking down on the proceedings below.

A tent had been set up over the spot where the body had been discovered. Illuminated from within, its whiteness gave it a ghostly appearance against the dark trees standing guard at the edges of the hospital grounds.

Logan stood just outside the cordon tape, watching one of the paper suits come striding towards him. He didn't know many of the Scene of Crime team particularly well yet, but Logan would recognise Geoff Palmer's graceless lumbering anywhere. It was ironic that the only member of the team he really knew was the one he had the least desire to.

There was something about Palmer that rubbed Logan the wrong way. More than one thing, actually. Mainly, it was the fact that he always seemed annoyed at having been called in to do his bloody job. Even if the shout came in during office hours, he'd huff and grumble like it was all some big inconvenience.

Getting dragged out of his warm bed at this time of night had only served to make his mood worse.

"DCI Logan," Palmer said. The elasticated opening of the paper hood framed his face, turning it into a pudgy circle of flesh. It wasn't a good look on anyone, but Palmer's red cheeks and bulbous nose meant he appeared particularly grotesque and ridiculous in it.

Probably one of the reasons he hated showing up to these things, Logan reckoned.

"Geoff. What have we got?"

"Well, I'm hesitant to say, 'bugger all,'" Palmer spat. "But not far off."

He pushed back his hood and shot a look of distaste up at the hospital. "Maybe if half of NHS Highland hadn't gone trampling all over the place, we'd have been able to get something useful. No attempt made to preserve the crime scene. None at all."

"Well, they were more interested in preserving life at that point," Logan pointed out.

Palmer grunted, like he didn't consider this an acceptable excuse.

"I've seen how much blood she'd lost. They were obviously wasting their time," he said. "They should've known that."

Logan stared at the man in disbelief, grateful for the cordon tape between them.

"Preservation of life is top priority," Logan said.

"Well, it's made our job a lot more bloody difficult."

"Tough shite," the DCI snapped. The tone of his voice was

enough to make Palmer reconsider voicing any further complaints. "What do we have?"

Palmer's suit rustled as he pointed to a spot about ten feet from the tent, where two other SOC officers were doing a fingertip search of the grass.

"We think she was grabbed there. Knocked over, then dragged closer to the fence. Marks suggest she was kicking at the time, so conscious."

His finger moved to the tent itself. "She was stabbed there. From the blood pattern, she was on the ground at the time. Either she tried to roll away, or he flipped her over at one point. He might've stabbed her again. You'll have to look at the body for that."

Palmer made a vague sort of gesture. "Looks like she tried to crawl back in the direction of the hospital after she'd been injured, but she didn't get far."

"What about the tape and the rag?"

Palmer's eyebrows knotted above his bulbous nose. "The what?"

"The nurse who found her, he said she had tape over her mouth. He took it off and took out a rag that had been stuffed in her throat."

"News to me."

"What? You haven't found it?"

"Haw!" Palmer shouted, cupping a hand to his mouth. The other SOC officers *meerkatted* up, all eyes turning his way. "Tape and a rag. We found anything?"

Glances were exchanged. Heads were shaken.

"Doesn't look like it, no," Palmer said, turning back to Logan. "Maybe your man took it. Or one of the paramedics. Not like they didn't fuck it all up enough already."

"Keep your eyes peeled for them," Logan instructed.

Palmer tutted. "Obviously."

For a moment, Logan considered grabbing the cordon tape and wrapping it around the bastard's throat, but common sense prevailed and he settled for glowering at him, instead.

"Anything else you can tell me?"

"Not a lot, no. It's a well-used path, and the scene was heavily compromised."

He pointed to the left of the tent, to where a fence divided the patch of grass from a neater, more landscaped area next door.

"If I had to guess, I'd say your killer went that way, over the fence into the grounds of Maggie's next door."

"Maggie's?"

"Cancer support," Palmer said. "You'll have seen the building. Looks a bit like a boat."

"Right, aye. I've seen it," Logan confirmed. He looked in the direction of the building now, but the view of it was blocked by a row of hospital vehicles.

"That's pretty much a guess, though," Palmer stressed. "There's some depression in the grass leading to the fence, but it could be unconnected." He shrugged. "Still, he had to go somewhere, so that's your best bet."

"He'd be bloody."

"Maybe not as bad as you think. There was no arterial spray, from what we can tell, and she was lying down, so beyond a bit of backsplash, he could've been reasonably clean, provided he was careful."

"And do you think he was?" Logan asked. "Careful, I mean?"

"Pathology would know more than me," Palmer said. "But he had the presence of mind to take her away from the track and, so you tell me, stick an efficient gag on her. No sign of the murder weapon either, so he took that with him. So, based on that, he certainly wasn't reckless."

"Have you got someone searching the grounds next door?"

"Not yet, no."

Logan tutted. "Why not?"

"Oh, hang on, and I'll just give the Magic Manpower Tree a shake, will I?" scoffed Palmer. He mimed shaking a tree. "Oh, look. Fuck all fell out."

He dropped his arms to his sides and scowled. "We're doing what we can with what we've got. If you want to talk to Hoon about getting more resource brought in, great. I won't stop you. Otherwise, it'll have to wait until we're done on this side of the fence."

Logan gave a grunt of annoyance. Mostly because Palmer was right. It was a relatively small department, and they couldn't do everything at once.

"You've cordoned it off, though?"

"Please," Palmer sneered.

"Right. Good."

"Can I get back to it now? Are we done?"

Logan briefly fantasised about throttling him again, then about-turned and started marching back in the direction of the hospital.

"Aye," he said. "We're done."

CHAPTER SIX

The morning sunlight seeped insidiously through the corridor's single window, weak and grey, and about as half-arsed as was to be expected for Scotland in October.

Logan paused outside the door to the mortuary for a moment, knocked twice, then pushed it open. *Ballroom Blitz* by Sweet hammered into him, almost forcing him back a step. He'd heard it from out in the corridor, but the door was heavy, and clearly had some impressive soundproofing qualities.

The volume of it trembled his eardrums and vibrated his internal organs in a deeply unpleasant way. Bracing himself, he stepped into the room just as *the man at the back* was instructing everyone to attack.

The song was blasting out from a cylindrical speaker that sat on a desk in the corner of the mortuary's outer office. There was a pencil holder beside it, the pens and pencils jiggling and dancing in time with the music's vibrations.

The swing door that led through to the actual business part of the mortuary opened, and Shona Maguire shuffled through.

She was in the process of trying to peel off a pair of rubber gloves that seemed intent on making things difficult for her, and let out a little yelp of fright when she spotted Logan standing in the doorway.

"Jesus!"

"No' quite," Logan said, raising his voice to be heard over the racket.

"Alexa. Stop," Shona instructed.

The music kept blaring out.

"Alexa! Stop!" Shona shouted. "Alexa!"

The chorus kicked in, raising the volume in the room even further. Shona shot Logan a sideways look and had another go at shouting over it.

"ALEXA! STOP!"

The blitzing of the ballroom continued uninterrupted.

Logan reached the speaker in three big strides, and yanked the power cable out of the back. Silence fell so suddenly the impact of it almost shook the floor. A spinning blue light on top of the cylinder gave an indignant flash, then faded into darkness.

"Thanks. There's a volume button on top, though," Shona said. "You don't need to rip the cable out."

"It was that or kick it to death," Logan told her.

"It's one of those Amazon things. They're voice-controlled."

"Aye, I saw. Handy, that," Logan remarked. He considered putting the cable back in, then decided it wasn't worth the risk and hooked it in amongst the now stationary stationery.

"The volume might have been on the high side for it to work."

Logan nodded past her at the swing door. "I just assumed

you were trying to wake that lot," he said. "Anyway, what happened to the brain music you usually listen to?"

"Long night," Shona told him. She gave a triumphant little cheer as she finally managed to remove the rubber gloves. "The brain music's good for concentration. It's not so good at keeping you awake."

She pressed a foot down on the pedal of a bin and dropped the gloves inside. "Don't suppose you remembered to bring...?"

Logan held up a white paper bag, and Shona's eyes lit up.

"Did you get an egg on it?"

The DCI smiled. "Don't say I'm not good to you."

A FEW MINUTES LATER, Logan and Shona sat on opposite sides of her desk. The detective was nursing a mug of tea, while the pathologist munched her way through the bacon and fried egg roll. The yolk had burst almost immediately and was in the process of dribbling down onto the paper bag Shona had placed on the desk directly in front of her as a makeshift napkin.

"Mm. 'S good," she said. "Want a bit?"

Logan considered the offered roll, and the puddle of yellow currently congealing in the paper bag.

"You're alright, thanks," he said. "I'm a vegan."

Shona almost choked. "You are not. Are you?"

"No. But I'm seriously considering it after watching you eat that, you clarty bastard," he said.

Shona laughed and dunked the edge of the roll in the pool of egg yolk. "It's the only way to eat it," she said, before cramming in another mouthful.

Logan took a sip of his tea and glanced impatiently at the swing door.

"So, late night, then?" he asked.

"Aye. Fairly. You?"

"Got home about three."

"But let me guess. You didn't sleep," Shona said. She crunched a crispy piece of bacon. "Just lay awake, thinking about how cruel a place the world is."

Her face lit up. "No. Wait. You stood by the window looking out over the twinkling lights of the city, all dramatic-like."

She narrowed her eyes and adopted a Clint Eastwood drawl. "*I'll show those criminal scum that crime doesn't pay. Not in my city.*" She smiled at him. "Am I close?"

"Was out like a light, actually," Logan told her. "Besides, my view's shite." He took another drink of tea. "Also, I'm not Batman."

"That's just what Batman would say," she said, eyeing him with exaggerated suspicion.

"Would he? Doesn't he literally say, 'I'm Batman' in the films?"

"Fair point," Shona conceded.

She finished the last bite of her roll, then brushed her hands together, dusting off the flour. After a glug of her tea, she tilted her head in the direction of the inner mortuary door. "Right. Want a look?"

Logan's eyes flicked very briefly to her stomach. "You not wanting to let that settle first? You know, before..."

"Hmm? Oh, no. It's fine," Shona said. She fished a piece of bread out from the back of her teeth with her tongue. "Wait, is that why you didn't have anything? Were you worried about...?"

She puffed out her cheeks and made a vomiting sound.

Logan gave a dismissive little wave. "If my stomach can handle watching you eating that, it can handle anything."

"Just as well," Shona said, standing up. "Because this one's *really* not pretty."

CHAPTER SEVEN

Shona hadn't been kidding. Esme Miller's body had been covered when they'd entered the mortuary, but when the sheet had been drawn back, Logan had been thankful he'd avoided breakfast.

You got used to them, of course. The corpses.

The first one was rough. No matter how prepared you thought you were, that first body on that first slab always hit you hard.

The apprehension made the second one worse. You built it up in your head beforehand, braced yourself for the horror to the point that you were panicking before you'd even set foot in the place. When you actually saw it, though, it wasn't as bad as your imagination had been preparing you for.

After that, it was easier. After that, it was just part of the job.

He wasn't sure how many down the line he was now. How many bodies had he seen? How many empty shells on cold slabs? How many of them could he remember the names of? Not many.

Not enough.

But then, it wasn't his job to remember them, he told himself. It was his job to avenge them. To get them justice. The remembering—the mourning—that was up to someone else.

Esme Miller lay on her back, naked and fully exposed. Shameless in death. Her torso was a pin-cushion of stab wounds, each dark hole standing out as a bloody affront against her pale, bloodless skin.

A single slit ran from below her sternum to just past her belly button. Logan had seen similar incisions made during the autopsy process, but this one looked ragged and uneven. Either Shona wasn't as good at her job as he thought she was, or the killer had inflicted the wound himself.

"That wasn't me, by the way," the pathologist said, as if reading his mind. "She came in like that."

Logan nodded. Grunted. Said nothing.

"I'll run you through what I think happened," Shona continued. "Any questions, just ask."

She walked around the table until she was beside Esme's head. "There was an impact to the back of her head. A hard one, too. I reckon your man brained her from behind as she was walking across the path. Hilt of the knife, before you ask. Judging by the shape of it."

Shona took a pen from her pocket and indicated a couple of points on the top of the victim's skull. "There's hair missing and some damage to the scalp. I reckon he dragged her by the hair. Going by the state of her hands, she tried to resist being pulled. There's a lot of dirt under the fingernails. She dug in. Does that fit the scene?"

Logan nodded, and Shona made a satisfied little *click* sound with her tongue. At the same time, her face crumpled a little, like she hadn't really wanted to be right.

"Moving further down the body, there are some burst capillaries on the cheeks and elsewhere on the face that suggest asphyxiation. Nothing on the throat to indicate strangulation, though, and there's sticky residue on the cheeks that—"

"She was gagged. He put a rag in her mouth then taped it shut," Logan said.

Shona looked impressed.

"The witness told me."

"Oh. Right. Well, yeah, that's the conclusion I came to. I found some fibres in the throat and passed them to the Forensics lot, but I'd imagine they've already found the rag itself."

"Aye. You'd imagine," Logan said.

Shona raised an eyebrow. "They haven't?"

"No. We thought maybe the paramedics took it, but they say not. The nurse who discovered the body reckons he tossed it on the ground after he took it off her. Nobody has seen it since."

"So... what does that mean?" Shona wondered. "He came back for it? The killer, I mean?"

"That's the best I've got at the moment," Logan confirmed.

"He hung around, then? Nearby. While they were working on her. He didn't just run."

Logan shook his head. "He didn't just run."

"Bold," Shona said, then she continued down the body to where most of the obvious action had occurred. "And then, we have this. Fourteen stab wounds, various depths, mostly confined to the chest area. There's a lot of laceration on the forearms, too."

"She put up a fight."

"Tried to, anyway," the pathologist confirmed. "There are six other wounds on her back, but we'll come to that in a minute."

"Any thoughts on the knife?"

"Big bastard of a thing," Shona said. She held her index fingers about eight inches apart. "That size, roughly. Serrated. It's got a hilt. Is that the right word? Like a two-pronged little hand shield, an inch or so long on each side. They left an imprint next to some of the wounds."

"Jesus."

"Yeah. He put some force into it."

"Definitely 'he,' you think?"

"I tend to avoid definites so there's less chance of me looking bad later if I turn out to be wrong," Shona confessed. "But I'd say so. Could a woman put the same amount of force behind it? Probably. But—and I'm aware this isn't really my department—a knife that size? An attack like this? That's a man trying to compensate for something."

Logan couldn't really argue. Statistically, they were almost certainly looking for a man. He'd keep an open mind, of course, but right now he was just happy to narrow the search a little.

"Anything else you can tell me about him?"

"Nothing overly useful. Right-handed, I think, judging by the angle of the wounds. Probably a bit taller than the victim. The head impact was a downward strike from higher up."

"So why just 'probably' taller?"

Shona shrugged. "He could've jumped."

"Jumped?"

"He expended a lot of energy in the attack. Those stab wounds were pretty frenzied. And the head blow was hard. I mean, like, *hard*. Either he's big and *very* strong, or he didn't do it from a standing start," Shona explained.

Logan stepped through this in his head. "So, he runs up behind her, jumps, knife raised, and—"

"Bang. Cracks her on the skull," said Shona. "It's a theory, anyway. But, like I say, maybe he's just a big fella."

"And this?" Logan asked, indicating the slit in the stomach.

"Nasty one. I wish I could say it was done post-mortem, but judging by the wound, I think he cut her open while she was conscious."

"Why would he do that?" Logan asked. The question was more for himself than the pathologist, but she answered anyway.

"Not my area of expertise, I'm afraid," Shona said. She puffed out her cheeks. "He was mental, maybe? Probably one for the psychologists if you want a more thorough diagnosis than that. All I can tell you is that he cut her open, but her insides are all present and correct, if a little worse for wear. He didn't take anything, I mean."

"That's... good," Logan said.

"You know when 'she didn't have her organs harvested' is the most positive thing you can take away from a conversation that it's going to be a shitty day, don't you?" Shona said.

"Just the latest in a long line," Jack replied. He looked the victim up and down, then raised his eyes to meet Shona's. "Any sign of sexual assault?"

"No. Nothing. Although, from what the A&E guys tell me, her jacket and tunic had been removed," Shona said. "But I think that was so he could get to her back."

"Her back?"

"Yeah. Don't really want to turn her over again until I stitch her up, but I took some photos."

Logan followed her over to a large screen that was mounted vertically on the wall. A keyboard and mouse sat perched on a shelf that could've done with being a few inches longer and wider directly below the display. Shona gave the mouse a little dunt and the screen blinked into life.

Esme's body lay face-down on the slab in the image that appeared, several more puncture marks clearly visible around the middle of her back. They were bunched close together, like bullet holes clustered around a bull's-eye.

"I don't know if she turned herself over, or if the killer did it," Shona said. "I'd be surprised if she'd have had the strength, but it's not beyond the realms of possibility. Adrenaline would have been flowing pretty freely at that point." She indicated the stab wounds. "Obviously, these were him. As was this."

She clicked the mouse. The picture changed to show a closer shot of the upper back. Logan leaned in closer to the screen, his brow furrowing.

"What the hell's that?" he asked, peering at two marks on her skin just below and to the right of her left shoulder. "Not more bloody voodoo symbols?"

"Hmm? Oh, the Loch Ness woman? No. More straightforward than that."

She clicked the mouse again, and a similar image appeared. In this one, the wounds had been cleaned, and the markings were clearly visible.

"F A," Logan said, reading the letters aloud. He looked from the screen to Shona and back again. "What's that? F A?"

"Football Association? Folk Awards? Fuck All?" Shona guessed. She shrugged. "Could be anything."

"Aye. I suppose."

"Although..."

"What?"

Shona indicated the photo. "Look at the positioning of it on her back. It's all over on the left."

Logan studied the photo again. He was about to ask what she was getting at when the penny dropped.

"It's not finished."

"That's what I reckon. He was interrupted. Whatever he was writing, it's not finished. It's half a message."

"But what's the other half?"

Shona patted him on the shoulder. "I think that's your job, not mine," she said. She started to turn away, then stopped. "Oh, but one thing that might be useful?"

"Yes?"

"The knife he used? It couldn't have made those letters. Too big, there's no way your killer could've formed the shapes the way he did. Not using that thing."

"So, he had a smaller knife with him, too, then?"

Shona shook her head. "Not a knife, exactly," she told him.

She took a short metal rod from a tray and held it up. The overhead lights glinted off its thin blade.

"A scalpel."

CHAPTER EIGHT

"You should've phoned me, Jack."

Logan finished shrugging off his coat, then gave a dismissive wave in DI Ben Forde's direction. "You hadn't stopped in days. You needed to catch up with yourself," he said. "Guys your age, you need your rest."

"I'll 'guys your age' you, you cheeky bastard," Ben retorted. "Anyway, I was hardly relaxing. Alice had me in the bedroom all bloody evening. You should see the state of my knees."

Logan blinked, momentarily lost for words.

"No' like that. Get your mind out of the gutter, man," Ben told him. "We're putting laminate flooring down."

"Oh, thank God," Logan said.

"Well, I say, 'we,' but she assumed a strictly supervisory role," Ben continued. "I told her I'd happily pay for some other bugger to come in and do it, but oh no. 'Why waste money when we can do it ourselves?' she says. Then she just stands there in the doorway with a mug of cocoa and a judgemental bloody look on her face."

Logan gave a chuckle, then dumped his coat on the back of his chair.

"Sorry, if I'd have known, I'd have sent an Armed Response Unit to come get you out," he said. "Caitlyn was there though, so we got by without you." He looked around the Incident Room. "She in yet?"

"In and back out, boss."

DC Tyler Neish sat at his desk, the mouthpiece of a phone handset pressed against his shoulder so whoever was on the other end couldn't hear him.

"She said she was going back to the hospital to pick up some paperwork. Shift changes, or something."

The junior detective returned the phone to his ear and jumped back into the conversation. "Sorry about that."

"I'm just back from the hospital myself. I could've done it," Logan said.

Ben couldn't hide his smirk. His bushy eyebrows danced as he waggled them up and down. "Oh, aye? Hoping for a check-up with a certain Irish doctor, were we?"

"Well, considering all her other patients are all mutilated corpses, no. No' really," Logan said. "But aye, she took me through what she'd found on the body."

"Bad one?" Ben asked, noting the slight change in Logan's tone, and the way the lines of his face altered. Anyone else would've missed both, but Ben had known Logan longer than most.

"Aren't they all?" Logan asked, then he jabbed a thumb in Tyler's direction. "Who's Bawchops talking to?"

"The family liaison over at the Miller's house. He offered to be the point of contact."

"Did he now?" Logan asked. "And who's the liaison, out of interest?"

Ben glanced over at DC Neish, then shrugged. "Not sure, actually. Why?"

Tyler raised his eyes as Logan approached the desk with hand extended.

"Uh, boss?"

Logan made a beckoning motion. Tyler managed almost a full second of resistance, before caving in and passing the handset to the DCI.

"You alright there, Constable Bell?" Logan said into the phone.

For a moment, there was nothing but a soft hiss of static and a suggestion of surprise. Then, the voice of Constable Sinead Bell returned to him down the line.

"All good here, sir," she said, a little sheepishly.

"Great. Glad to hear that," Logan said, staring down at Tyler as he spoke. The DC wilted under his gaze and started flicking through his notebook like it was suddenly the most interesting thing in the world. "How's Mr Miller doing?"

"Um, not bad, actually, sir. He's got someone from Victim Support in with him now. A counsellor. Think they know each other through the hospital. I, uh, thought I'd take the opportunity to call and report in. They're talking to Chloe now. The daughter."

The daughter. Damn. He'd known about her from conversations at the hospital, of course, but there had been so much else going on, so much else to do, to think about.

"What age is she?" he asked.

"She's six."

Logan pinched the bridge of his nose. "Shite. And how is she coping?"

"Upset, obviously. But more sort of... confused, really. I don't think she quite understands."

Of course, she didn't. How could she?

"Poor wee bugger."

"She's that alright, sir," Sinead agreed.

"I'll get over this morning. Let me know when Vic Support's finished."

"Right, sir. Will do," Sinead said. He heard her take a breath before she continued. "Um, is that everything?"

Logan's eyes narrowed. "Aye. Why?"

"Can you... Would you mind putting me back onto Tyler? Onto DC Neish, I mean? I just... I need to check something with him."

Logan muttered something unintelligible, then held the phone out to Tyler. "You have thirty seconds. Make it quick."

Tyler regarded the phone with suspicion, like it might be some sort of trap.

"Twenty-five seconds."

Lunging, the DC took the phone, cradled it to his ear, and turned in his chair so he was facing away from the rest of the room. "Hey... Yeah, I know."

He flicked a wary glance in Logan's direction. "Uh, yes. That sounds like a plan, um, constable."

Tyler listened. Logan continued to loom over him, tapping his watch.

"Yes. I agree. Half-seven," Tyler said. He was clearly enunciating every word, like it somehow made the conversation he was having more legitimate. "That sounds fine."

"Five. Four," Logan announced.

"OK. You, too. Bye!"

"Three. Two."

Tyler pressed the 'end call' button and dropped the phone on the desk like it was suddenly too hot for him to hold. He cleared his throat and then gestured to the abandoned handset. "Work stuff."

"My arse," Logan said. He cast his gaze across the Incident Room, as if only just noticing how empty it was. "Where's Hamza?"

"He's still on that HOLMES course up in Aberdeen," said Ben. "They're doing a new update, apparently. Just as I was getting used to the last one."

Logan grunted. HOLMES—or, to be more precise, HOLMES 2—was a computer system that linked up all the UK police forces, allowed the sharing of information, and helped keep track of ongoing cases. The acronym stood for 'Home Office Large Major Enquiry System,' and it had been put together for the sole purpose of being an all-in-one crime investigation tool.

Unfortunately, it was a heap of shite. It had been barely usable when it had first come online, and every subsequent update had somehow found new and interesting ways of making it worse.

"When does it finish? Can we get him back?" Logan asked.

"We've already called him back in. He's on his way over."

"Right. Good. We're going to need all hands on deck for this one."

"Aye, reckon you're right there," Ben agreed. "And I say that as someone who's seen the Forensics report this morning."

Logan nodded grimly. "They didn't have a lot when I left last night."

"Things didn't improve much after you left, either," Ben said. "Not a lot to go on."

"Any mention of them finding the gag?"

Ben frowned. "Not that I saw, no. What gag?"

"There was a rag shoved in her mouth, then taped over the

top," Logan explained. "The fella that found her took it off, but there's been no sign of it since. If we haven't found it, we have to work on the assumption the killer took it."

"You reckon he came back to the scene then, boss? Bit ballsy, that," Tyler said.

"Aye. But ballsy's good. We want ballsy."

"Means he's more likely to give himself away," Ben added.

"Exactly."

"Suppose," Tyler conceded.

"Forensics have anything else?" Logan asked.

Ben gave a non-committal shrug. "Not really, no. Said they couldn't be sure if he went over the fence or not but reckon it's the most likely escape route."

"Except he didn't escape. He waited until the victim had been taken away, then went back and cleared the scene."

"Worrying," Ben said, and Logan gave a grunt of agreement.

DC Neish looked from Logan to Ben and back again. "Why's that worrying? I thought it was a good thing? I thought we wanted him ballsy."

"There's ballsy and there's calculated," Logan said. "He attacked her yards from the hospital on a relatively busy path, dragged her a short distance away, then waited nearby while paramedics worked on her. The stab wounds were hard. Frenzied. And yet, he didn't run or panic after being discovered. He waited. Patiently. Then, he tidied up after himself."

"Calculated," Ben emphasised.

"And to be *that* calculated–to not panic like that–suggests it's not his first time," Logan continued. "There may be other victims."

"What, like a serial killer?" Tyler gasped, his eyes going wide.

"Look at the state of that," Ben said, glowering at the younger detective. "Like a kid in a bloody sweetie shop."

Tyler tried to dampen down his excitement. "What? I mean, obviously, it's terrible and everything. It's just... I've never been on a serial killer case before."

"Aye, well we don't know that's what this is," Logan pointed out. "It's only a hunch at this point. So, we keep an open mind."

"It almost certainly *won't* be," Ben said, shooting Tyler a chastising look. "So, try not to get your hopes up."

"I wasn't getting my hopes up! I don't *want* it to be," the DC protested. "I'm just saying, I've never worked one before. That's all."

"Aye, while frothing at the bloody mouth," Ben said. "It's a one-off. Let's hope so, anyway."

"No arguments there," Logan said.

He sat down at his desk. It was in the middle of the room, with the others circling it like wild west wagons. He had an office tucked away at the back of the Incident Room, but he had never been one for lurking around the edges. Much better to be slap-bang in the centre of it, even if that meant subjecting himself to Tyler's attempts at banter.

"Dr Maguire was going to email over the Pathology report when I left. I'll send it on and you can both have a read," Logan said, powering up his computer. "The big headline though, is that our killer had started to carve something into the victim's back, but we think he was interrupted."

Tyler groaned. "Not another occult thing?"

"That was my first instinct, but no. These were letters."

"Great. Just a good old *bog-standard* headcase then," said Tyler. "That's a relief."

Ben's brow furrowed. "Letters? What letters?"

"An F and an A," Logan said.

Ben sat on the edge of his desk. "F A?"

"Football Association?" Tyler guessed.

Logan shook his head. "We don't think it was an acronym. We think it's the start of a word. A short word. Like 'fat,' or 'fast,' or—"

"Fake," Ben said.

Logan looked at the DI over the top of his computer monitor. "Eh?"

"It says 'Fake.' Or would've done, anyway."

Tyler jumped in with the question before Logan could ask it. "How'd you know that, boss?"

"Because," Ben began. He exhaled through his nose, briefly glanced at the ceiling, then continued. "I've seen it before."

CHAPTER NINE

DS Caitlyn McQuarrie looked pointedly at her watch, then eyeballed the door across from where she had been sitting for the past fifteen minutes. One of the senior clerical staff members had vanished into the room to run off the shift schedules she'd asked for, and there had been a conspicuous lack of printer whirring sounds since.

Had it been a waiting room, there would at least have been a few magazines for her to flick through. Instead, all she had to look at was a stack of leaflets pointing out the warning signs of bowel cancer and stroke, and a chart showing the hospital's cleanliness rating over the past week. (Silver star: Room for Improvement.)

She didn't even have a signal on her phone, so couldn't check to see if the Forensics or Pathology reports had come in.

More to kill time than any desire to actually know what it said, she checked her watch again.

Sixteen minutes. Long enough.

Standing, she crossed to the door and gave a knock. The same member of clerical staff opened it immediately, like she'd been poised with her hand on the handle on the other side. The woman was short and stocky, and was rocking the classic half-moon-glasses-on-a-length-of-cord look favoured by women of a certain age and station.

"Yes?" she asked, peering up at Caitlyn like they'd never previously met.

"You were going to get me that printout."

"And I'm getting it," the woman said, bookending the sentence with a couple of tuts. "What does it look like I'm doing?"

Caitlyn resisted the urge to say, "Not a whole fucking lot, actually," and instead flashed something that could generously be described as a smile.

"Any idea how long it'll be?"

"I need to get clearance. Data protection," the woman replied.

"And how long will that take?"

"How long's a piece of string?"

"Roughly?" Caitlyn said, valiantly clinging to the last vestiges of her patience. "How long will it be, *roughly*?"

"Is there a problem here?"

Caitlyn turned to find a tall man with hawk-like features striding over to her. He wore a stethoscope around his neck, suggesting not only that he was a doctor, but that he wanted everyone to know it. She pegged him to be in his early fifties, with some grey streaks in his hair that gave him the sort of 'distinguished' look that would immediately see a woman of the same age consigned to the scrapheap.

"DS McQuarrie," Caitlyn said, producing her warrant card. She savoured the way the doctor's surly approach stuttered and came to an abrupt halt.

"Oh. Is this about Esme?"

Caitlyn nodded. "It is. We've requested shift records for who was on duty last night."

"I was just getting them," said the woman in the office, practically curtseying when the doctor turned her way.

"Good. Let's speed it up. We don't want to keep this young lady waiting."

Caitlyn decided to let the 'this young lady' bit go, and instead just enjoyed the expression of defeat on the admin woman's face.

"Of course. I'll chase it up right away."

"Yes. Do that."

The doctor waited until the door closed, then smiled apologetically. "Sorry. They can be sticklers for procedure." He gestured to another door a little way along the corridor. "Here. You can wait in my office."

"I'm fine here, thank you," Caitlyn said.

"I'd like to talk to you, actually," the doctor told her. "Plus, I was on duty last night, so chances are you're going to want to talk to me at some point, anyway."

He made another gesture in the direction of the door.

"Shall we?"

"HERE, let me shift those for you," said the doctor, moving a couple of tennis trophies that hadn't been even remotely in Caitlyn's way. He placed them in the middle of his desk, then motioned for Caitlyn to sit on the plastic seat Logan had dragged in the night before.

"Please," he urged, smiling encouragingly. He looked happy when Caitlyn sat, and lowered himself into the padded chair with the ripped arms. "Colin."

"I'm sorry?"

"Colin. Fletcher. *Doctor* Colin Fletcher."

"Right. Yes. DS McQuarrie. Caitlyn."

"Caitlyn!" he said, clasping his hands together. "Lovely. And 'DS,' that's Detective...?"

"Sergeant."

"Detective Sergeant!" Colin echoed. "Well done."

Caitlyn hesitated, not quite sure how to respond to that. She decided not to bother.

"You were on duty last night when Esme Miller was brought in?"

Colin's face became sombre. He pinched his chin between thumb and forefinger like a man deep in thought. "Indeed. Yes. Terrible business. Poor Esme. We did all we could, of course, but we were fighting a losing battle. Whoever attacked her, he made a bloody good job of it."

He caught the look on Caitlyn's face, and hurriedly clarified. "Not *good*. I'm not condoning it in any way, of course. I'm just saying. If he'd been trying to kill her, then he went the right way about it. Mission accomplished."

"Right," said Caitlyn, making a mental note of all that. She fished in her pocket and took out her actual notebook, then flipped it open. "What can you tell me about when she came in?"

"What would you like to know?"

"Was she conscious?"

"Barely. She'd lost a lot of blood by that point. Everything was in the process of shutting down."

"Did she say anything?"

"Nothing coherent. The odd mumble, maybe. Nothing I caught." Colin shrugged. "She may have said something to the paramedics prior to her arrival, but by the time I saw her she was almost gone. There was nothing anyone could've done. I did everything I could."

"I'm sure you did, Mr Fletcher."

Colin smiled. "Please. 'Doctor.' It's petty, I know, but six years of medical school and a mountain of student debt. I have to justify it somehow."

Caitlyn doubted the mountain of debt part. The guy would've been educated back in the student grant days, and his plummy accent—Oxford area, she thought—suggested Mummy and Daddy probably helped with the bills.

"Doctor. My apologies," she said, going along with it. "I'm sure nobody blames you for what happened."

"Well, they shouldn't. She was too far gone," Colin reiterated, and Caitlyn wondered just whose benefit he was saying it for. "I did all I could."

"Did you know Esme well?"

"Hmm? Oh, no. Not really. We've been short-staffed of late, so everyone has been moving around. I knew her, but only vaguely. Always seemed nice, though. Excellent at her job. Really excellent. Well thought of by everyone. An asset to the NHS. She'll be sorely missed."

It sounded, Caitlyn thought, more like a press statement than an honest account of his actual feelings on the matter. She made a note of it and clocked him watching her when she looked up from her pad.

"Is everything alright?" he asked.

"Of course. Just making a few notes."

"Important to keep records," said Colin. He gestured to the box files on the shelves surrounding them. His eyes went to the pad again. "Do I get to see?"

"Why would you want to see?"

The doctor shrugged and smiled. "Freedom of Information."

Caitlyn didn't return the smile. "You're free to put in a request through the official channels," she told him.

"Ouch," Colin said, then he gave a little chuckle. "I jest. Of course, you need to take notes. Feel free."

"I will," Caitlyn told him, her tone making it clear that she had no need for, nor interest in, his permission. "You said there was something you wanted to talk to me about."

"Hmm. Oh. Yes. Yes, I did," Colin said. He tapped idly on the head of one of his trophies. It was a little tennis player in the middle of a serve. "It's nothing, really."

Caitlyn waited for him to continue. Unfortunately, patience had never really been her strong point, and she urged him on with a, "Well?"

"I'm hoping this doesn't strike you as too forward, but, well..."

He stopped fiddling with the trophy and clasped his hands in his lap. "I can't believe I'm asking this. It's not entirely appropriate, given the... You know. With everything?"

Caitlyn frowned. "I don't follow. What are you trying to say?"

"OK. I'm just going to... I'll just say it," Colin said. He took a breath. "Would you like to go out sometime?"

Caitlyn blinked. Stared. Felt her jaw dropping open.

"Go out? You mean, like...? What?"

"Dinner. The cinema. Whatever people do these days."

"Mr Fletcher, are you... Are you asking me on a date?"

"Doctor," Colin auto-piloted. He winced, annoyed at himself. "I mean, yes. Yes. A date. Or just... You know. As friends?"

"Friends? I literally met you five minutes ago."

"No, I know. I know. But, I mean... And forgive me if this sounds..."

Colin shook his head, clearly getting flustered. "I saw you last night. And, well, I thought... You're quite striking, and I thought..."

"A woman was murdered, Mr Fletcher," Caitlyn said, putting emphasis on the 'mister' part. "A woman was stabbed to death. A woman you know. I hardly think this is appropriate, do you?"

"Well, I mean... But we deal with it all the time, don't we? Death. We're hardly strangers to that. And life doesn't just stop when someone dies, does it? I mean, it does for them, obviously, but not... That's not what I'm trying to..."

He sighed and seemed to deflate. He dropped his head, then raised his eyes to meet Caitlyn's.

"Is that a no, then?"

"Yes, Mr Fletcher," Caitlyn said. She got to her feet and stood above him, looking down. "It's very much a no."

"I really do... I know it sounds silly, but I really do prefer 'Doctor,'" he said.

"Aye," Caitlyn said. She closed her notebook and shoved it back down into her pocket. "I know you do."

CHAPTER TEN

Logan sat forward in his chair, studying the image on his computer screen. It showed a woman's chest, from midway up her breasts to the bottom of her chin. She had some well-defined tan lines from a bikini, and a smattering of freckles blooming up from her cleavage.

He noticed neither, his attention instead focused fully on the four letters sliced into the woman's skin.

FAKE.

"Danni Gillespie," said Ben. He stood behind Logan's chair, leaning in so the glare of the overhead lights wasn't blocking his view of the screen. "CID case from a couple of years ago. I got asked to give them a hand."

"Oof. Looks nasty," said Tyler, who had rolled his own chair over to Logan's desk.

"That's not the half of it. She was attacked on the way home from a night out. Sexual assault. Bad one," Ben said. "I mean, they're all bad, but this one was different."

"Different how?" Logan asked.

"Just... God. I don't know. The things he said to her. The

things he did. I don't really want to..." Ben gestured to the screen. "There's a report. But it doesn't make for pleasant reading, I'll warn you now."

Logan glanced over his shoulder at the DI. One look at the older officer's face told him not to push for the gory details.

He turned back to the screen and clicked through to the next image. It gave a closer look at the first letter.

Fishing out his phone, he opened up the images Shona Maguire had emailed over and pinch-zoomed in. The shapes of the F and the A weren't identical, but they were close enough to suggest that the same person was responsible for both.

"Bollocks," he muttered. "I'm assuming we never caught whoever was behind it?"

"They had a suspect. Donald... something. Sloane. Weird fella. He looked a dead cert, but it fell through. He came up with an alibi. Pretty cast iron, if I remember rightly," Ben said. "Victim's brother and a couple of his mates leathered shite out of him soon after we'd let him go."

"Oh! I remember that!" Tyler said. "I was still in uniform. I remember the brother being brought in. Shaun Gillespie."

The way he said it suggested Logan should know who he was.

"Made a fortune writing apps for the iPhone when he was a teenager, boss. He now owns Osmosis."

"What's Osmosis?" Logan asked.

"The nightclub."

Logan scowled at the very thought of it. "No' really my cup of tea."

"You'd love it. They do retro nights every Wednesday. For the old—"

Tyler stopped himself just a little too late, and tried valiantly to salvage the situation.

"—er music fans. Fans of older music, I mean," he said, then he flashed a smile that showed too many teeth, cleared his throat, and went back to looking at the screen. "Anyway. You think it's the same guy? Both attacks, I mean."

"Hell of a coincidence, if not," Logan said, fixing Tyler with a glare. "The suspect. Sloane. Is he still living locally?"

"Don't know, boss," the DC said.

"I wasn't expecting you to know. I was expecting you to find out," Logan told him. When this elicited no immediate response, he clapped his hands together. "Chop chop."

"Oh! Right, boss. On it!" Tyler said, wheeling himself hurriedly back to his desk.

Logan turned and looked up at Ben. "You've spoken to the guy before?"

The DI puffed out his cheeks. "Aye. Briefly. And it was a while back."

"What was your instinct?"

"My instinct? My instinct was that he was a big creepy bastard. I was surprised when he came up with the alibi. We all were," Ben said. "But he did. There was nothing we could pin on him."

"Aye, well, we'll see if he has one for last night," Logan said. He returned to the screen, closed down the image and double-clicked the first of the reports attached to the case file in HOLMES.

"If you're going to read that, let me at least get you a coffee first," Ben told him. He drew in a breath as his eyes went to the file just as it opened. "Trust me. You're going to need it."

BEN HAD NOT BEEN EXAGGERATING. Logan clicked the X in the top corner of the document and felt a palpable sense of relief when the report vanished.

"Jesus."

DI Forde was back sitting at his own desk, hidden by Logan's monitor.

"Told you. If you'd still been on the drink, I'd have suggested something stronger than the coffee."

"Tempted, after that," Logan said. "And we never caught the bastard?"

Ben stood up so Logan could see him. "Technically, it's still an open case, but doesn't look like there's been any movement on it in a good year or so."

He was ashen-faced, and looked a few years older than he had when he'd sat down. Clearly, he'd been refamiliarising himself with the case while Logan had been digging through the details for the first time.

The details of the actual attack had been bad, but not the worst Logan had ever heard. It was a sexual assault and, like most, seemed to have been all about the power trip, rather than anything resembling actual desire.

The victim had been beaten, humiliated, and degraded over the course of almost three hours, but no attempt had been made on her life. After subjecting her to all the things he'd put her through, her attacker simply let her go.

It doesn't matter.

That was the phrase that kept coming up. One of the things he said to her, over and over, as he assaulted her. Beat her. Raped her.

It doesn't matter. You don't matter. None of it matters.

Because none of this is real.

Logan rocked back and forth in his chair, chewing on his

bottom lip. "I'd like to talk to her. Danni Gillespie. I think we should talk to her."

Ben looked unsure. "It's... I mean, aye. Of course," he said. "But I can't say I relish the thought of making the poor lassie relive it all again. He did a real number on her. Mentally, as well as physically."

"I'm no' exactly jumping for joy at the prospect of it either, but if it helps us catch the bastard."

"Donald Sloane is still in town, boss," Tyler said, rolling himself back from his desk so he had a direct line of sight on the DCI. "Works at the butcher's on Queensgate. He was in the paper last month. They made a big sausage."

The furrowing of Logan's brow said it all.

"It was some charity thing. He's mentioned in the online version of the article," Tyler clarified. "It's how I found him. He's not on the electoral register."

"OK. Good work. We'll talk to him, too," Logan said.

"On what pretence?" Ben asked. "He threatened to sue us after everything was dropped the last time. Came close after Danni's brother gave him the kicking, too. There's nothing to tie him to this attack. We'd need a good excuse."

Logan stood and picked up his coat. "We're three bright lads," he said, then he shot DC Neish a sideways look. "Well, two and a half, maybe. I'm sure we'll come up with something."

"I know that was meant to be a dig, boss, but it's probably the nicest thing you've ever said to me," Tyler said, grinning from ear to ear. "Thank you."

"Well, don't get used to it," Logan warned. He pulled on his coat, then motioned for Tyler to get to his feet. "And hurry up."

"What? Oh? Am I coming?" Tyler asked, springing to his feet.

"Only because Ben's running the room and there's no other bugger around," Logan said.

"Good enough for me, boss!" Tyler said, looking pleased with himself.

The door to the Incident Room opened, and DS McQuarrie stepped through.

"Change of plan," Logan said.

Tyler tutted and flopped back into his chair. "Sake," he muttered.

"Quit your whinging. You'll get your chance. Caitlyn, keep your jacket on," Logan instructed, stalking towards the door. "You're coming with me."

CHAPTER ELEVEN

THE MAN WHO ANSWERED THE DOOR DIDN'T LOOK HAPPY to see them. He was in his early thirties and managed to look irritatingly handsome despite the fact he had clearly just been woken up.

"What do you want? Do you know what time it is?" he grunted.

"It's five to eleven," Caitlyn said.

"Yes. What's your point? Some of us work nights, you know?"

"Aye. That's true. We didn't think of that, right enough. Sorry if we woke you, Mr Gillespie," said Logan, demonstrating a surprising amount of restraint. "We were hoping to speak to your sister, Danni."

Shaun Gillespie looked both of them up and down in turn. "Are you cops?" he asked. "What am I saying? Look at you. You're cops, aren't you? What do you want?"

"Detective Chief Inspector Logan. This is DS McQuarrie. We're with the Major Investigations Team. Is Danni available? We have this down as her address."

Shaun had already been partially obstructing the doorway, but now he put a hand on the doorframe, fully blocking the way. "What do you want to see Danni for? You finally got your fingers out of your arses and caught the bastard?"

"We're hoping she might be able to help us with another investigation. We think there may be a connection," Logan explained.

Shaun didn't show any sign of budging.

"A woman was murdered," Logan told him.

"Stop being a dick and let them in," a female voice instructed from somewhere behind Gillespie.

Shaun didn't look happy about it, but dropped his arm and stepped back, letting the front door swing open.

A woman stood in the hallway, dressed in oversized pyjamas and Homer Simpson slippers. Her hair was cut into a boyish bob, her eyes wide and worried behind the tips of her fringe. There was a weariness to the way she stood, like a weight was pushing down on her, and Logan got the impression she'd been waiting for this day to come.

"When?" she asked.

"Last night. Near the hospital," Logan told her. "A nurse."

Danni looked down and locked eyes with Homer Simpson. She shook her head, muttered something, then drew herself back up to her full height.

"Well then," she said, her voice flat and controlled. "I suppose you'd best come in."

"YOU HAVE A LOVELY HOUSE," said Caitlyn, as she and Logan sat on an L-shaped leather sofa positioned in front of a wood-burning stove. A large television was mounted on the wall above it, so thin and sleek it could almost have been painted on.

"It's not hers. It's mine," said Shaun. He caught the look Danni shot his way, tutted his annoyance, then slumped on through the open-plan living room and dining area. "Fine. I'll be in the kitchen."

They waited until he'd disappeared through the door at the far end of the dining area, then Danni smiled apologetically. "He's not great in the mornings."

"I know the feeling," Logan said. "Sorry. Did we get you both up?"

"What? No," said Danni, confused by the question. She glanced down at her pyjamas, then pulled her slippered feet up onto the armchair beside her. "Oh. Yeah. I don't really go out much these days."

There was a moment of slightly awkward silence at that, which Danni rushed to fill.

"What is it you think I can help you with?" she asked.

"Right. Aye. Well, as I said, a woman was murdered last night. We have reason to believe the individual who attacked her may be the same one who attacked you."

Danni nodded and raised a hand to her chest bone, her fingertips idly tracing her scars through the fabric of her pyjamas.

"You don't seem surprised," Caitlyn remarked.

"Surprised? No. I'm surprised it's taken this long, if anything," Danni said. She dropped her hand down into her lap. The other hand kneaded it, as if offering comfort. "Did he... Did he mark her?"

"He started to, yes," Logan said. "But he was interrupted."

"Was it the same?"

"It was," Logan confirmed.

Tears sprang to Danni's eyes. She looked away, out through the French doors that led to a long garden at the back of the house. "Did he... Was she..."

"There was no sexual element to the attack," Caitlyn said.

The look that flitted across Danni's face was impossible to read. Relief? Resentment? It passed too quickly for Logan to be able to identify. Whichever it was, he couldn't blame the woman.

"That's something," she said.

"I know this must be very difficult for you, Miss Gillespie. I've gone over the case files, and the statements you made at the time of the assault, so we won't take up much of your time," Logan said. "But I wanted to talk to you directly. See if there's anything you can tell us that might help us identify your attacker."

"I already told the police everything," Danni said. "There's nothing else to say."

She rubbed the heels of her hands on her thighs, like they had suddenly become unbearably itchy. "I don't want to go over it again."

"I appreciate that, Miss Gillespie. I really do," said Logan. He leaned forward on the couch. The sudden movement made Danni gasp and grab for her armchair, like the floor had started to fall away beneath her.

Logan froze, not wanting to make any other movement in case he panicked her further.

"Sir, why don't you go get us a cup of tea?" Caitlyn suggested. She looked to Danni for confirmation. "Would that be alright?"

Danni was quick to give her agreement. "Fine. Yes."

Caitlyn caught Logan's eye. A nod was exchanged between them, then the DCI got to his feet, taking his time about it so as not to further startle the woman in the pyjamas.

"What do you take in it?" Logan asked.

Caitlyn rolled her eyes and smiled in Danni's direction. "Months we've been working together now. Shows how often he makes the tea, eh? Milk, no sugar."

"And yourself, Miss Gillespie?"

"I'm fine," she replied, then she tagged a slightly reluctant, "Thanks," onto the end.

"Right. One tea coming up," Logan said.

"Thanks, sir," Caitlyn replied. She looked up at him from where she sat on the couch. "And take your time."

SHAUN GILLESPIE WAS SITTING at the breakfast bar, flicking through a copy of *Computer Shopper* magazine when Logan entered.

The kitchen, like the rest of the house, looked expensive, with smooth handleless cabinets, thick wooden worktops, and an island that would've taken up most of Logan's flat.

"What do you want?" Shaun asked, not looking up from the magazine.

"I've been sent to make the tea," Logan said.

Shaun grunted. "Girl talk then, is it?"

"Aye. Something like that."

Waving a hand, Shaun indicated the kettle. "Knock yourself out."

"Thanks. You having one yourself?" Logan asked.

Shaun tapped the edge of the magazine against a mostly-full mug of coffee. "I'm fine."

"Probably wise. Can't say it's my strong point," said Logan.

The kettle was tall, silver, and with a confusing array of buttons on the side of the handle. A light flashed orange on the side, like it was trying to tell him something. He had no idea what it was though, so he bashed on and pressed the button that looked most likely to turn it on.

Nothing happened. He leaned in, squinted at the controls, then tried the same button again. The result was exactly the same.

He was about to press it for a third time when Shaun intervened.

"It needs water," he said. Then, with a sigh he put down his magazine, got up off his stool, and nudged the DCI aside. "Here. I'll get it."

"Maybe for the best," Logan agreed. "Gadgets have never really been my strong point, either."

"It's not a gadget. It's a kettle," Shaun said, opening the top and sloshing some water into it from the tap. "Water in. Power on. It's not difficult."

"Aye. Well. When you put it like that," Logan said, watching as Shaun sat the kettle back on its base. The orange light turned green, and almost as soon as the button was pressed Logan could hear the water start to come to life. "I hear you make... games, was it? For the phone."

"Apps," Shaun corrected, appearing irritated by the mistake. He sat back at the breakfast bar and picked up his magazine. "I used to. Market got flooded. Have you arrested him yet?"

"Who?" Logan asked.

"You know who. Sloane."

"Mr Sloane was dismissed as a suspect in your sister's assault," Logan told him. "We've no reason to believe he was involved in this latest attack."

"Bollocks," Shaun barked, slamming the magazine down. "He did it. To Danni, I mean. I know he fucking did it. Creepy bastard. Everyone knows he fucking did it, and yet he gets off scot-free."

"No' quite scot-free. You did go round there with your pals and leather shite out of him, did you not?" Logan asked.

"What, and you think we shouldn't have, like?"

"I *know* you shouldn't have, Mr Gillespie. That's why you were arrested," Logan said. "That's how it works, you see? You're fortunate that Mr Sloane decided not to press charges. Although, I do wonder what brought on his sudden change of heart."

Shaun seemed like he might be about to say something, then thought better of it. "No comment."

"Fair enough. Look, I wasn't involved in the case, but from what I read, he had an alibi that proved it couldn't have been him," Logan said. "He was literally doing a show live on the radio at the time your sister was attacked."

"Aye, like he couldn't have recorded the whole show in advance?" Shaun said, sneering like this should've been obvious. "Two in the morning on Moray Firth? Not like anyone would even be listening."

"From what I understand, there were other people with him in the station at the time," Logan said. "He ran a phone-in. I can appreciate your frustration, but as alibis go, it's one of the better ones."

"It's bullshit, is what it is!" Shaun barked. His face had reddened, and a vein on the side of his neck was practically pulsing. "I don't know how he fucking did it, but he did it. It was him. I'm telling you. And if that weirdo fuck has gone and killed someone, that's on you lot. That's on you."

"I'll bear that in mind," Logan said. The kettle rolled

towards the boil beside him, and he unhooked a couple of mugs from hooks on the wall. "What makes you so sure it was him?"

"Because he's a creepy bastard," Shaun said.

"There's plenty of other creepy bastards out there," Logan reasoned.

"Not like him. He was in Danni's year in school. Fucking obsessed with her, he was."

Logan set the mugs down on the worktop and looked back over his shoulder. "Were they in a relationship?"

"Fuck off! With Sloane? With *Mr Nobody*? No. She didn't give him the time of day. No one did."

"Mr Nobody? Is that what they called him?"

Shaun shook his head. "No. That'd be fair enough. That'd be *normal*. But no."

He glanced at the kitchen door, then leaned forward.

"That's what the bastard called *himself*."

"Himself?"

"Aye. 'Just call me Mr Nobody,' he'd say. 'Just act like I'm no' here. I don't even exist.'" Shaun shook his head. "Total fucking weirdo."

Snatches of Danni's statement replayed in Logan's head. The things her attacker had told her. The words he'd whispered in her ear.

It doesn't matter. None of it matters.

Because none of this is real.

"Now he gets it," Shaun said, smirking to himself as he watched the realisation dawning on the DCI's face. He picked up his magazine and flicked to a random page. "Alibi or no alibi, Donald Sloane was the one who raped my sister, and your lot did nothing about it."

The kettle reached the boil with a *click*.

"And now, he's gone and upped his game."

CHAPTER TWELVE

Logan closed the door of his car and waited for Caitlyn to get into the passenger seat beside him.

He'd been sad to see the back of the Ford Focus that had served him so well over the past couple of years, but the fact it had been comprehensively smashed to pieces by a big truck meant hanging onto it hadn't really been an option.

The blow had been softened somewhat when the car had been replaced with a Volvo XC90 seven-seater SUV. And, while the fact it was a hybrid electric model had given him some cause for concern to begin with, he'd quickly come to see the appeal.

The passenger door gave a satisfying *thunk* as Caitlyn pulled it shut. She stared ahead, not yet reaching for her seat-belt. She looked stunned. Haunted, perhaps.

"Well?" Logan asked. "Thoughts?"

Caitlyn blinked, as if coming out of a trance.

"She's, uh, I don't think she's convinced it was Donald Sloane who attacked her," the DS said. "Not as convinced as her brother is, anyway."

Logan nodded. He'd got the same impression while he'd gulped down his tea. Not a bad cuppa, if he said so himself.

As they pulled away from the house, Caitlyn recounted what Danni had discussed while Logan had been in the kitchen. Most of it, he already knew from her original victim statements.

The attacker had stepped out of an alleyway as she'd been walking home from her brother's club. He'd worn a smooth, featureless white mask, and had hit her before she could open her mouth to scream.

She'd regained consciousness during the sexual assault. He'd taken her into the shell of a shop that had been closed due to fire damage, the boarded windows hiding them from the late-night revellers passing by just outside.

Her attempts to cry for help had been thwarted by the tape across her mouth. Her hands had been bound together while she was unconscious, the trousers around her ankles keeping her from kicking out.

That feeling of helplessness had been one of the worst parts, she'd told Caitlyn. One of the many.

"What about the 'you're not real,' stuff?" Logan asked, as he nudged the car out of a junction, forcing traffic coming from the right to stop to let him out. He waved his thanks and received an angry raised finger in response.

"Charming."

"She couldn't remember what the attacker said word for word, obviously, but the gist of it was that he could do what he liked because she wasn't real. Because nothing was real," Caitlyn said. "He was... She thought he was laughing about it, but at one point she thought maybe he was crying."

Logan shot her a quizzical look. "Crying?"

"That's what she said, sir. Like he was hysterical or something, but she couldn't say for sure. Anyway, he kept telling her that she didn't matter. Told her to get over it. That none of it was actually happening."

"The hell was he saying that for?"

Caitlyn shrugged. "He said there were no rules anymore. That no one could punish him."

"Big bloody talk for a man wearing a mask," Logan grunted.

"Are we going to go and talk to Donald Sloane?" Caitlyn asked.

Logan flexed his fingers on the steering wheel, weighing this up.

"It's just... We seem to be heading in that direction," Caitlyn pointed out.

Logan glanced from the road to the DS and back again. When he'd driven away from Shaun Gillespie's house, he hadn't been consciously setting out in any particular direction, but sure enough, they were almost at Queensgate. It was slap bang in the centre of the city's main shopping area, and one of a handful of places he knew how to find without having to consult the GPS.

After a moment's thought, he swung the Volvo into a bus stop. "No. We've no reason to talk to him yet. If it is him, we don't want to spook him. Let's wait and see if we get anything DNA-wise from Pathology first. If we can make a connection, we bring him in then. If we can't... We'll think of something."

Caitlyn nodded. "Makes sense. And in the meantime?"

Logan rubbed his chin. The growth had gone beyond stubble and into the beginnings of a beard that, a quick glance in the rear-view mirror confirmed, made him look like he had been sleeping rough for the past several days.

"You got that list, right? Everyone who was on duty at the hospital last night?"

"I did. I was going to hand it off to Hamza and Tyler to go over. Don't expect we'll get much from it."

"Right, aye," Logan agreed. That made sense. Uniform could probably handle it even, and report in anything of interest.

"Except..." Caitlyn took her notebook from her pocket and flicked through a couple of pages. "Kel Conlyn. He was the last person to see her alive. Or talk to her, anyway. Before she left. He was also there when they brought her back in. They were apparently pretty friendly. Thought he might be worth us talking to directly. Maybe she mentioned something to him."

"About how she was planning to get murdered?" Logan asked.

Caitlyn managed a grim smile. "Maybe she'd fallen out with someone, or noticed anyone acting suspicious."

Logan clicked the indicator and began forcing his way out into the traffic. "You got the address?"

"Aye, sir, it's twenty-two—"

"No point telling me," Logan said. He tapped the satnav on the dash. "Stick it in there, or I'll never bloody find it."

KEL CONLYN LIVED JUST a little out from the city centre, in a ground floor flat just a stone's throw from Aldi. Logan was vaguely familiar with the area, partly because of the aforementioned Aldi, and partly because one of the flats he'd had stolen out from under him by Bosco Maximuke was just around the corner.

There was no driveway for the flats, so Logan pulled the

car in at the side of the road. The big Volvo stuck out like a sore thumb between an '05 plate Clio and an '07 Honda Civic with a mismatched driver's door, and he had a nagging suspicion that some bastard would come along and key it while they were in talking to Conlyn. Still, at least the repairs wouldn't be coming out of his pocket.

The hospital hadn't given much away about any of the names who'd been on the rota the night before, and DS McQuarrie hadn't yet had time to do any research, so they were going in blind.

There were half a dozen identical maisonettes along the street, each with four flats—two ground floor, two above. Each flat had its own entrance, and after Caitlyn had double-checked the address, they'd approached Conlyn's front door.

There was a metal nameplate holder fixed just above a spyhole in the door, but it was empty. Judging by the way the edges had rusted, it had been empty for quite some time.

The paint on the door would once have been a vibrant red, but a rectangle where the sun must regularly hit had faded to a salmon pink. The step was shoogly and uneven, with moss growing in a few thin cracks, and along the join where it met the bottom of the doorframe.

There was a button fixed to the wall beside the frame. It looked like it had been a recent addition, and was jarringly out of place amongst the otherwise tired exterior.

Almost immediately after Logan gave the button a press, a man's voice came from somewhere in its plastic housing.

"Yes?"

"Mr Conlyn?"

A hesitation, then: "Yes?"

"We're from the Police Scotland Major Investigations Team. If you have a few minutes, we'd like to talk to you."

There was another moment of silence, then the *clack* of a lock being turned. The door opened halfway, revealing a young man in a red silk dressing gown. There was a weariness in his eyes as he stepped aside and gave a beckoning tilt of his head.

"You'd best come in," Kel said.

"Thank you," Logan replied, then he stepped into the flat and onto a floor made of bare, unsanded boards.

"I've not long moved in," Kel explained. He gestured almost apologetically at the Magnolia-coloured walls, the paint faded and peeling in places, and peppered with drawing pinholes. "Excuse the state of the place."

"I'm in the same boat myself," Logan said. He waited for Kel to shut the door, then followed him along the narrow hallway towards an open door at the far end. "Hard to find the time to unpack everything."

"Not really a problem for me," Kel said, leading them into the living room.

At least, Logan assumed that was its purpose. Then again, it could've been anything. There was no furniture to speak of, no carpet on the floor, or curtains on the windows. It was an empty space, with a single folding camping chair and four Banana boxes stacked up in the corner.

"My parents kept most of my stuff when they kicked me out," Kel said.

He anticipated the next question before either of the detectives could ask.

"Didn't approve of my..." Kel mimed air-quotes with his fingers, "lifestyle choices."

"I'm sorry to hear that," Logan told him.

"Yeah, well, there's something to be said for minimalism, I suppose," Kel said. He shrugged and smiled, but there was nothing convincing about either. "Once I get a few more payslips behind me, I'll start... you know. Furniture, or whatever normal people have."

He pointed in the direction of another door that led through to a small galley kitchen. "I do have a fridge, though. Coke? Fanta?"

"You're fine, thanks," Logan told him.

Kel turned to Caitlyn. "Ma'am? I mean... Miss?" He blushed slightly. "I don't... Sorry. What do I call you both?"

"Sorry, son. Detective Chief Inspector Logan. Call me Jack. This is Detective Sergeant McQuarrie."

"Caitlyn."

"Caitlyn. Jack. Right," said Kel. He tapped himself on the side of the head, as if locking it in. "You sure I can't get either of you anything? I'd offer you tea, but I haven't got a kettle yet."

"We're grand. Thank you," Logan said.

Kel tightened the belt of his kimono-style dressing gown, then put his hands on his hips. "Well?" he asked, glancing between them both. "Did you get someone?"

"Not yet, I'm afraid. We're still working on it," Logan said. "I understand you and Esme were close."

"Yeah. I mean, not... *close* close, but she was good fun. We had a laugh. When I first started, she looked after me. I'd tell her about my parents, she'd tell me what a pair of bastards they were and how I was better off without them, and... Yeah. She's... *was* great."

"You spoke to her before she left last night," Caitlyn said. "Did she say anything unusual?"

"Like what?"

"Anything that seemed out of the ordinary?"

Kel thought back, his eyes darting left to right as if replaying the events of the night before in his head. "No. She said she was tired, but that's par for the course. She seemed happy, though. In fact, she was gloating about having two days off in a row."

Logan raised an eyebrow. "Gloating?"

"No, not like... She wasn't actually gloating. Joking, I mean. She wasn't like that. We were having a laugh."

"She hadn't mentioned anything that might be giving her cause for concern?" Caitlyn pressed.

"Last night?"

"Or recently?"

Another moment of silence as Kel gave this some consideration. "No. I don't think so. Chloe had Chicken Pox a few weeks back. Her daughter. Is that the sort of thing you mean?"

"Any information you can give us is useful," Caitlyn said, but she hadn't yet bothered to write anything down.

"What about people?" Logan asked, looking out of the living room window at the gardens below. There were two of them, side by side, both long and narrow, running straight back from the house. One half was neat and well-kept, the other was one sunny afternoon away from becoming a jungle.

"People? What do you mean?"

Logan turned from the window. "Had she spoken about anyone new recently? Had she fallen out with anyone?"

"Esme? Fall out with someone?" Kel said, reacting with a sort of disbelief that suggested such a thing wasn't possible. "No. Not that she told me about, anyway."

Kel's voice trailed off as he neared the end of the sentence. A frown briefly troubled his face, then he curtly shook his head, chasing it away.

"Mr Conlyn?" Logan asked. "Is there something you can tell us? Had Esme fallen out with someone recently?"

"Not fallen out, exactly, no. It was nothing. She laughed it off."

"Laughed what off?" Logan asked.

Beside him, Caitlyn instinctively reached for her notebook.

"One of the doctors. He was... not trying his hand, exactly, but he'd asked her out a few times recently. She told him she wasn't interested. He knew she was married, but..."

He caught the look that passed between the detectives.

"I'm sure it's nothing. Honestly. She laughed about it. She thought it was funny. We both did."

"Aye, I'm sure you're right, and it won't be anything," Logan agreed. "Out of interest, though, what was his name, this doctor?"

Kel looked worried, like he'd said too much.

"Just for our records," Logan urged.

"Like I say, I really don't think he'd... He's not..." Kel gave a sigh. He tightened the belt of his kimono again. "Fletcher," he said. "His name is Doctor Colin Fletcher."

CHAPTER THIRTEEN

"Colin Fletcher. Consultant at Raigmore. On duty last night around the time Esme Miller was murdered."

Caitlyn pinned a printout of a photo she'd found of the doctor online. It was from an academic website, and was a perfect head and shoulders shot. A couple of years out of date, maybe, but good enough.

"He was also the doctor who worked on the victim when she was brought in," she continued. "A colleague reports he'd been making advances towards the victim over the past few weeks. This doesn't come as a surprise, given that he tried cracking on to me earlier today."

"*You*?" ejected DC Hamza Khaled from behind his desk. He'd stumbled in the door just a few minutes before Logan and Caitlyn had returned to the office, and was still in the process of getting caught up. "He tried his hand with *you*?"

"Aye, me. What are you saying it like that for, you cheeky bastard?" Caitlyn asked him.

"Oh. No. That's not what I meant. I meant... I mean..." Hamza babbled, his panic making his Aberdonian twang that bit stronger. He shot Tyler a sideways look. "What do I mean?"

"You're on your own with this one, pal," DC Neish replied, holding his hands up to show he was having nothing to do with it.

Ben Forde cleared his throat. "I'm sure what the Detective Constable is trying to say is that making an advance on the investigating officer in the recent murder of one of your colleagues is a bit on the crass side."

Hamza clicked his fingers and pointed at the Detective Inspector. "Aye. Exactly. That's exactly what I was meaning," he said.

"Aye. Well," Caitlyn sniffed. "It's a lot on the crass side. I told him as much, but I don't think it bothered him."

"He's a sleaze, then?" asked Ben.

"And then some, sir," Caitlyn confirmed.

"So, he asks her out, she shoots him down. Pretty weak as motives go," said Tyler. "I mean, if I killed every woman who'd ever turned me down, I'd be Jack the Ripper."

Ben raised an eyebrow. "Good looking lad like you? You surprise me, son."

"Aw. Cheers, boss!"

"Must be your personality," Ben continued.

"Haha. Yeah," Tyler replied, sounding a little less thrilled.

"Or his voice, maybe," suggested Hamza. "That *meemeemeemee*. Like one of the Chipmunks shagged a Muppet."

"What's wrong with my voice? There's nothing wrong with my voice," Tyler protested. He tried it out a few times. "Hello? Hello! What's wrong with that?"

"Nothing's wrong with it. It's fine," Ben told him. "If you like that sort of thing."

At the back of the room, Logan cleared his throat. He was sitting on the rearmost desk, trying to watch DS McQuarrie's presentation as a detached observer. Much as he liked to be right in the middle of things, sometimes taking a step or two back could help bring things into focus.

"Can we get on with it, do we think?" he asked.

"Aye, let's all grow up a bit and get on with it, shall we?" Tyler agreed, smiling smugly at the others.

"We can discuss DC Neish's awful personality and voice another time," Logan concluded. "Caitlyn. Go on. What else do we have on Fletcher?"

Caitlyn referred to the notes she'd pulled together on the doctor. "Not a huge amount yet, sir. His marriage broke down a couple of years back. Divorce is still a work in progress. Two kids, both boys in their teens. They live with their mother in Elgin."

"I've just found him on a couple of dating sites," Tyler volunteered. He clicked his mouse a few times, flicking between tabs on his browser. "Looks like he's really been putting himself out there."

"Send those to print," Caitlyn said. Even before she'd finished speaking, the noisy inkjet was clanking into life.

"Done."

"That's most of what I've got at the moment, sir," Caitlyn said. "DC Khaled and I can pull together a proper profile this afternoon."

Hamza looked up from where he'd been leafing through a printout of the current case file. "Right. Aye. Just... Did I see something in here about a scalpel being used on the victim?"

"You did," Logan confirmed. "Pathology report. The letters carved into her back were done with a thin blade. A scalpel's the best bet."

"On Fletcher's desk. One of the mugs," Caitlyn began. "It said 'World's—'"

"'Best Surgeon.' Aye, I saw that."

"What's a surgeon doing working A&E?" Ben wondered.

"They're short-staffed," Caitlyn said. "Maybe there was no one else?"

Hamza looked up from the report. "I've got a 'World's Best Lover' mug at home somewhere, and that is *far* from accurate. Believe me."

He caught the bewildered look on Tyler's face.

"My point is, do we know he's actually a surgeon? Besides the fact he had it printed on a mug, I mean? You can get those mugs for anything these days, can't you?"

A few blank glances were exchanged.

"OK, that's something for us to find out," Logan said. "What is he trained in? What's his speciality?"

"We bringing him in, Jack?" asked Ben.

Logan regarded the face in the photo for a while, then shook his head. "Not yet. Let's build a better picture of him first. No point alerting him when we've got hee-haw to pin on him yet. We need to know if it was possible for him to be behind the attack. Did anyone see him on the ward before the victim was brought in? If so, how long before? She wasn't out there long, so timing would've been tight."

"And there's the gag, sir," Caitlyn reminded him.

"Shite. Aye," Logan muttered. "If he was working on her, how did he manage to go back and pick up the gag? He'd have to have attacked her, been disturbed, run back to the hospital, worked on Esme, gone *back* to the crime scene, gather up the evidence, then return to the hospital again without anyone noticing."

"Uniform was already on the scene when I arrived, sir,"

Caitlyn said. "Not sure how he could've picked up the gag after returning to the hospital. I don't see how that's possible."

Logan felt his heart sink down into his stomach. It had given a flutter when the hospital porter had told them about Fletcher's romantic interest in the victim. He had fit. Scorned alpha male, based near the scene of the crime at the time of the attack. He had the means and the motive, but unless there was something wrong with the timeline of events, probably not the opportunity.

Still, it was the best lead they had.

"Stick to the plan. Caitlyn, you and Hamza keep pursuing this. Get me everything we can on Fletcher, and let's see if we can make the timeline work," Logan instructed. "But let's not put all our eggs in one basket. What else do we have?"

"Forensics report should be in this afternoon on the victim's clothes," Ben said. "Hopefully, we'll get something off them, because we've got a distinct lack of anything resembling evidence at the minute."

He gestured to the desk Logan was sitting on. "Hoon's given us a Uniform Sergeant to handle Exhibits, but I sent her away again for now, since we've got bugger all for her to do. Once the clothes come back, I'll get her to check them in."

"Uniform's been doing door-to-door around the scene, boss," said Tyler. "The houses are pretty far away, though, through the trees and over the road. Doubt we'll get anything. Appeal for witnesses going out on Moray Firth this afternoon, and we're putting a call out on social media, too. Wider Police Scotland network is going to give us a bump."

Logan gave a nod. These things were important, of course. Many's a case had been cracked by the nosy bastard at number forty-three who'd witnessed the whole thing from the kitchen window.

But it was busy-work. It was grasping. This was a relatively isolated crime scene, hidden from view. Aye, sure, someone might have heard the victim scream, but so what? What did that tell them that they didn't already know? Unless the killer had blurted out his full name and address, all the door-knocking and social media shout-outs in the world were unlikely to get them any closer to solving the case.

"How are things with the family?" Logan asked Tyler. He cut the younger detective off before he could play innocent. "Don't pretend you don't know. I've seen you texting."

Tyler glanced instinctively at his mobile on the desk, then back to the DCI. "Pretty much as you'd expect, sir. Lots of family and friends coming and going. The husband and daughter are planning to go stay with his parents. They've a big house out near Dingwall. Don't think he can face being at home right now."

"Understandable," Logan said. He stood up. "I'll go round and see him before they head off."

"Want me to come, boss?"

"No, I do not. You and your bloody hormones are the last thing I need," Logan retorted. "I want you going over the Gillespie case again."

"The rape case, boss?"

"Aye. Caitlyn will fill you in on everything she told us today."

Logan reached for his coat, then hesitated.

"Oh, and look into the brother, will you? Shaun Gillespie. Something about him got on my tits. Besides him being a mouthy bastard, I mean. There was something... I don't know. See if anything jumps out. It might be nothing."

"Will do, boss."

The phone on Logan's desk *burred* into life. It was, he

thought, the first time it had ever rung, and he wasted a few moments staring at it in surprise before picking up the handset.

"DCI Logan."

There was silence from the other end. Or *near* silence, anyway.

"Hello?" Logan asked, and he heard the faint whine of an echo, as if his voice was feeding back on a speaker. "Hello? Who's this?"

The silence continued, but there was something more to it. Something different. An edge. A weight. An expectation, like the person on the other end was waiting for him to say just the right words.

A suggestion of static hissed at him down the line, soft and faint.

Or... no. Not a hiss. Not exactly.

A whisper.

The word leapt into Logan's throat and slipped out before he could stop it.

"Petrie?"

A *click*. A tone. The line went dead.

"Who was that?" asked Ben, when Logan replaced the handset.

"What?" Logan frowned, his gaze flitting between DI Forde and the phone. "Oh. I don't... I'm not sure. Hamza, try to find out, will you? See if you can get a number."

DC Khaled blew out his cheeks. "I'll see what I can do, sir, but if they withheld it then—"

"I don't need the technical details, just see what you can get," Logan said.

He stole another look at the phone, then shook his head. A bad line, that was all. A call centre trying to sell him something, no doubt. That was all.

Aye. That was all.

"Actually, you're fine. Forget it."

"You sure, sir?"

"Aye. Cold callers. Don't bother with it."

Hamza gave a nod. "Will do, sir."

"Won't do, you mean," Tyler corrected. He grinned, like he'd just made the greatest joke in the world, then shrugged when nobody else laughed. "Suit yourself."

"Right, that's me off," Logan announced. He had his coat on and was halfway to the door when he stopped again and turned. "Oh, but one more thing. Anyone needing any sausages?"

Ben looked the DCI warily up and down, like he was concerned he'd lost his mind. "Sausages?"

"Aye. Thought I might swing by the butcher's on the way back," Logan said. He pulled the collar of his coat up, bracing himself for the October chill. "I hear the one on Queensgate is worth a look."

CHAPTER FOURTEEN

He'd done it. He'd actually done it. After all this time, after all his observation, he'd actually done it.

It had been harder than he'd thought at first. The sound the knife had made, the way her body had offered that momentary resistance to the blade before succumbing—those had both been... unexpected.

She'd felt real. Solid. For a moment, he'd forgotten. For a moment, he'd believed the lies. She'd gargled and gasped behind the gag, almost like she was alive. Like she was real.

And her eyes. Her eyes. Pleading, begging, accusing him, all at once. So vibrant and alive, even as death rushed towards her. He'd doubted, then. He'd wavered. Those eyes. That expression. How could something so intricate and detailed be fake? How could she not *be real?*

But, that was why it had worked for so long, he had reasoned. It had to be convincing. Utterly, wholly convincing. It was the only way the whole elaborate plan could work. That was how they had been able to fool all of the people, all of the time.

Almost *all.*

Each plunge of the knife had made it easier. Each thack *of metal piercing flesh. Each weakening grunt and sob. Every stab had been an affirmation. A commitment to the truth. A blow struck not just against this individual lie, but against the liars themselves, wherever they were hiding.*

The interruption had been annoying. He'd thought about waiting there, about revealing himself. What did it matter if they caught him? What did anything matter now?

But, even though he knew the truth of this world, he was still confined by its rules. What good was he in prison? Who'd listen then? One dead body wasn't enough. It wasn't clear enough, loud enough. It didn't say what needed to be said. For that, he'd need more.

Many more.

The first had been difficult to begin with, but it had become easier. The next would be easier still, and the next, and all the ones after that.

He took no pleasure in it. It was necessary, that was all.

Everyone needed to learn the cold, brutal truth of it. It was time they all had their eyes opened to their reality. A message must be sent, to the liars and the blind alike.

And he was the one who would send it.

CHAPTER FIFTEEN

LOGAN HAD JUST OPENED THE FRONT GATE OF ROWAN Miller's house when he heard the sharp rap of knuckles on glass.

He spent a few seconds searching the nearest windows, then clocked a white-haired woman at an upstairs window of the house next door. She made a sharp beckoning motion to Logan when he spotted her, then retreated away into the house.

"OK," he muttered to himself, closing the gate again and heading for the next one along.

The pavement outside the house was laden with flowers. Word of Esme's death had spread quickly through the local area, and neighbours had been quick to pay their respects. Logan picked his way through them, and arrived at the next door gate in time for the front door to open.

"You're with the police," the woman said. A statement, more than a question.

"Aye. That's right."

Bending forward, she glanced left and right along the street, then beckoned for him to come inside.

"There's something you should know," she said. "About..." She mouthed the next two words. "...the murder."

Logan looked back at the Millers' house. Sinead stood at a downstairs window, eyeing him curiously. He raised a couple of fingers to indicate he'd just be two minutes, then strode along the path to where the elderly neighbour was holding the door for him.

"Hello. I'm Detective Inspect—"

"Just come away in," the woman said, shooting furtive looks to the windows of the houses across the road. "Hurry, before anyone sees."

Once inside, it immediately became apparent that this was as far into the house as Logan was going to get. The old woman all but blocked the narrow hallway, holding onto a wooden railing of the staircase with one hand as if to form a barrier.

"Is everything alright, Mrs...?"

"That's not important. My name doesn't matter," she said. She was a little younger than her hair colour suggested, Logan thought, and not as old up close as she'd looked at a distance. Sixties. Maybe even the lower end.

"Well, it does. I need to know your name," Logan told her.

"Oh. Do you? Right," the woman said. "It's... Jane. Jane... Green."

"I'd prefer your real name."

Her shoulder sagged. "Fine. It's Olwyn Prosser. Happy?"

"What can I do for you, Mrs Prosser?" Logan asked.

Olwyn dropped her voice to a whisper. "You didn't hear this from me. Alright? Swear. You didn't hear it from me."

"Didn't hear what from you?" Logan pressed.

"You've got to promise. You keep my name out of it. I don't

want dragged into it. I'm not having people thinking I'm a grass."

"I'll do what I can, Mrs Prosser," Logan assured her. "But I need to know what you have to tell me first."

Olwyn's shoulders sagged even further, so they were practically pointing straight down at the floral carpet. "Alright, alright. Fine."

She took a deep breath, glanced around again as if the place might be bugged, then spat it out in one big breath.

"They were arguing. The day she was murdered. Esme, I mean. Her and Rowan, they were arguing."

She clamped her mouth shut, like she was scared she'd said too much, or possibly worried about what she might blurt out next.

"There. I've said it," she announced. "Now you know."

"What were they arguing about?" Logan asked.

"Well, I don't know, do I? I wasn't listening," Olwyn snapped, although Logan found that hard to believe. He'd only just met the woman, but he was already building a pretty solid picture of her.

"You have no idea at all?"

"Well. I mean, I *may* have heard a few things," Olwyn said, cagily. "Nothing specific, but I think they were having money problems. Esme was going to be working more overtime, and Rowan—well, Rowan's been out of work for a few months now. Not right, that. Young man like that. Prime of his life. He shouldn't be out of work, should he?"

"Well—"

"Bloody shame. And it's not for want of trying, I'll give him that."

Logan smiled thinly. "Could we get back to the argument, Mrs Prosser?"

"Oh. Right. Yes. Well, he wasn't happy about her doing more overtime, and she was pointing out that they had to pay the mortgage—they bought the house a few years ago. Off the council. Just before the rule change. Got it at a bit of a song. Good investment for Chloe's future, I told them. It's where the money is, isn't it? Property."

Logan blinked slowly as he tried to follow the thread of the conversation.

"So I'm told," he said. "They were arguing about Esme doing more overtime. Right. Then what?"

"What do you mean?" Olwyn asked. "Then she was murdered. That very night." She held her hands out, palms upward, as if presenting the case to him on a plate. "Coincidence?"

"Well, I mean... Couples argue, don't they?"

"Not on the day one of them gets murdered they don't!"

Experience told Logan otherwise. He'd lost count of the number of grieving spouses, parents, or children whose final words with their loved ones had been in anger. He'd held mothers who wished, more than anything, they could take back the last thing they'd said to their child before they'd headed on a night out. He'd watched husbands break down, stricken by the lack of affection they'd shown their wives in those final days, haunted by some of the things they'd said or done.

People argued. People died. And the world kept grinding on.

"Did they argue often?" Logan asked.

"No. Very rarely. The odd tiff, but very rare. Very rare. Always seemed such a loving couple," Olwyn said. "That's what made it so strange. Them fighting, I mean. On the day that she... You know. That's not normal, is it? That's suspicious, isn't it?"

"I tend to treat everyone with a degree of suspicion, Mrs Prosser," Logan said. He smiled, showing a lot of teeth. "Even you."

The old woman's mouth dropped open.

"What? I mean... What? What are you saying?"

Logan tapped a finger to his forehead in salute, then opened the front door. "Thanks for the information. I'll be in touch," he told her, stepping down onto the path. "Oh," he said, looking back at her over his shoulder. "And don't leave town. I might be back."

The door closed behind him before he'd reached the gate. He left the garden, tiptoed through the bunches of flowers, then headed up the path of Rowan Miller's house. He saw a twitch of a curtain at one of Olwyn's upstairs windows, caught a fleeting glimpse of someone watching him, and then they were gone, swallowed by the shadows of the room behind them.

Olwyn? She'd have had to move quickly. Someone else in the house? A husband?

Before he could dwell on it, the front door of the Millers' house opened, and Constable Sinead Bell flashed him a warm smile. "Get sidetracked, sir?"

"Aye. Something like that," Logan confirmed, stepping into the house.

"Anything of interest?" Sinead asked, dropping her voice to a murmur.

"No. Just a nosy bastard, I think," Logan replied. "You know how many people live next door?"

"Not a clue. Sure Rowan will know, though. You could ask him."

Logan ran his tongue across the back of his teeth. "Maybe, aye. How's he doing?"

"He's... dealing with it, I think," Sinead said. "Chloe's over at his sister's, and he's getting sorted out to go move in with his parents for a bit."

"So DC Neish tells me. Good that you're keeping him so informed," Logan said. It was meant as a tease, but it came out sounding more confrontational than intended, and Sinead blushed at the implied accusation. "I mean that. It's a good system, you to him to the rest of us. Single point of contact. It works."

Sinead was still blushing but smiled through it. "Thanks. That's good. That it's working, I mean."

"Just as long as it keeps working," Logan said. "We don't want the lines of communication breaking down over... personal reasons."

"Oh, they won't, sir. Tyler... DC Neish and I, we're just... It's nothing. Nothing serious, I mean."

Logan grunted. He didn't seem entirely comfortable with the conversation but was managing to blunder through. "Aye, well. You've no' seen his face when he gets a message from you," he said. "Just... be professional. That's all I'm saying. To both of you. Him more than you."

"Of course, sir. Always," Sinead said.

"Right. Good."

Logan nodded, then rolled his shoulders and cricked his neck, bracing himself for the next part. There were lots of elements to the job he hated. Too many to count, in fact. But this one—what came next—was one of the parts he hated most of all.

"Right, then," he said, the words coming as a heavy sigh. "Let's go talk to Mr Miller."

CHAPTER SIXTEEN

"I THINK I'VE GOT SOMETHING, BOSS."

"It's no' contagious, is it?" asked Ben Forde, not yet looking up from the report that lay flat open on his desk.

DC Neish hovered in front of the desk. It took a moment for the joke to hit home.

"Oh. Aye. Good one. It's about the brother. Shaun Gillespie. I've been looking into him."

Ben leaned back in his chair and looked up from the report. "What have you got?"

"It might be nothing. It's just, well, I was looking through Osmosis' records at Companies House. You know, his nightclub? And there was a new director brought on about a year ago."

"Right. And?"

"Valdis Petronis," Tyler announced.

Ben's nose scrunched up. "Is that no' a spell out of Harry Potter?"

"Uh, no, boss. It's a guy. He works for Bosco Maximuke. You know, the—"

"I'm well aware of who Bosco Maximuke is, son," Ben told him.

"Aye, well. Looks like 'Mr Petronis'—and I'm putting quotation marks around his name there—put in a cash injection last year and took a minority share in the club. Sixty grand. No prizes for guessing who bankrolled that," Tyler continued. "Strange thing is, they weren't struggling for money before that, and they've done nothing with it since, so I don't see why it was needed."

Ben's chair creaked as he clasped his hands behind his head and leaned back. If Gillespie was mixed up with Bosco Maximuke, then it was no wonder Logan's instincts had been nagging at him. He and Maximuke had a long and colourful history, and very little of it good. If Bosco was involved in the nightclub, then chances were the whole set-up was dodgy in some way.

"Good work," Ben said.

"Want me to keep digging, boss?"

Ben shook his head. "No. That's enough for now. The rest can wait. I want you to get on to Uniform, see if the door-to-doors have brought anything in."

He raised his voice so the others could hear.

"And any sign of that Forensics report on the clothing yet?"

"Just came in, sir," said Hamza. "Email's in the inbox, and report is up on HOLMES."

"Good. Have a scout through. See if there's anything we can use."

"Already on it, sir," Hamza replied. "Summary isn't promising, but I'll dig in."

Ben tried not to show his disappointment. "Scrutinise it. Find us something," he instructed.

"HOLMES is playing silly buggers. Think the update is slowing everything down. But, I'll see what I can find, sir."

Ben groaned. HOLMES being on the fritz was the last thing they needed right now.

"Caitlyn, anything new on our doctor friend?"

"I can give you his whole life story if you want it, sir," Caitlyn replied from her desk.

"Just the edited highlights will do."

"Well, he was a surgeon. Cardiac, down in Edinburgh. All good until three years ago, when he received a couple of disciplinaries. Three of his patients died, and NHS Lothian started asking some questions. Turned out he'd been hiding a drinking problem."

"An alkie surgeon? That's no' ideal," Ben remarked.

"No. Looks like they didn't want to make a big fuss about it, though. He went to a drying-out clinic for a few weeks, then applied for a move up here to A&E."

"That's a step down, isn't it?" Tyler asked.

"More like a vertical drop," Caitlyn replied.

"A fall from grace, you might say," said Ben.

"Anyway, his wife came with him. She's from around this way originally. But the marriage seems to have collapsed almost immediately. The dating profiles Tyler found suggest he's been actively seeking... *companionship* pretty much from the day after she moved out."

Ben scribbled a couple of notes on this, then looked up. "And can we make the timeline work? For Esme's murder, I mean."

"We've still to talk to other hospital staff. Until we know if he was seen around at the time of her murder, it's difficult to say. If he wasn't visible on the ward, then it's possible he followed Esme out of the building and attacked her as she took the shortcut across the grass, but it's that missing gag that's the problem," Caitlyn reasoned.

"Aye. The hospital called in the attack right away. Hospital's just down the road from headquarters, so Uniform would've been on the scene practically right away. There's no way he could've dealt with Esme, then gone back out and got the gag without being spotted. No way I can think of, anyway."

"Maybe he had an accomplice, boss," Tyler suggested, slumping back down into his seat.

Ben looked doubtful. "Maybe. Can't see it, though. This feels like a lone wolf thing."

"Maybe it blew away," Hamza suggested. "Or, I don't know, a bird took it."

"A bird?" Tyler scoffed. "Why would a bird swoop in and steal a big bit of gaffer tape."

"Obviously you've never lived in Aberdeen," Hamza told him. "The bastards will take anything. I had a whole bag of chips nicked out of my hands once. A whole bag!"

"Aye, but that's food, isn't it?" Tyler pointed out. "I can believe that. If you'd said it had nicked your shoes or your wallet, I'd be calling bullshit. Chips, yes. Gaffer tape? No."

"Much as it pains me to do so, I have to agree with DC Neish on this one," Ben said. "A bird isn't impossible, but it's helluva unlikely."

"Maybe, sir. But what was it Sherlock Holmes said?" Hamza countered.

"'Elementary, my dear Watson,'" said Tyler, puffing on an imaginary pipe.

"No' that, ye div," Hamza said. "It was, 'Rule out the...' Wait. No. 'Rule out the unlikely...'" He shook his head, annoyed at himself. "Hang on. It was something like..."

Hamza stared into space for a moment, trying to recall the quote.

"Forget it. I don't remember," he admitted.

Ben clicked his tongue against the roof of his mouth. "Well, that's certainly given us pause for thought," he said, drolly. "Now, everyone back to work. Let's have some progress to show by the time himself gets back, or we'll never hear the bloody end of it."

CHAPTER SEVENTEEN

There was a stillness to Rowan Miller. A quiet.

When Logan had last seen the man, he'd been an emotional wreck, all twisted up in anger and in pain. Now, though, he sat straight and upright on a wooden chair he'd turned away from the dining table that sat at one end of the living room.

It was clear from the room that a family lived here. The couch and two armchairs were angled towards a large television, beside which stood a rack of DVDs, mostly pre-school titles with bright, garish colours. A pale blue monstrosity stared out at Logan from the cover of something called *In the Night Garden*, and a soft toy version of the same creature was eyeing him up from the armchair closest to the screen.

Family photographs lined the walls. Mostly, they showed Esme and Chloe, although a very different looking Rowan appeared in a few of them. The main difference being that the version in the photograph was smiling, and didn't look like his whole world was in the process of collapsing around his ears.

"I appreciate you taking the time to talk to me, Mr Miller,"

Logan said. He was still standing by the door and took a moment to consider his seating options.

He decided to join Rowan at the table and took the seat directly across from where he sat. Rowan half-stood, gripping the sides of his own chair, and turned it around until he was directly facing the detective across the table.

"Anyone for tea? Coffee?" asked Sinead, hovering by the door that led through into the kitchen.

"Uh, no. No. Thanks," said Rowan.

Logan quite fancied a cup of tea, if he were being honest, but didn't want to be the only one drinking one, so declined with a wave of his hand. He turned the movement into a beckoning gesture that indicated the seat beside him, and both men waited for Sinead to sit.

"How are you coping, Mr Miller?" Logan asked.

"How do you think?" Rowan answered.

"Aye," was all Logan could really say to that. "I wanted to come round and pass on my condolences before you headed to your... sister, was it?"

"My mum and dad's," Rowan said. His voice was flat and measured, and Logan realised his stillness was not accidental. He was actively controlling himself, fighting the urge to break down and cry, or scream, or smash the place up in rage. "They've got a big place. Plenty of room for the thr—" He swallowed. "For the two of us."

"It'll do you both good. You can come back when you're ready."

Rowan's eyes darted to the pictures on the wall. Right now, Logan knew, he'd be thinking that he'd never be ready. Never be able to come back here, to move on. Right now, his only thought would be to endure. To get by. Somehow, to get by.

And he would get by.

Somehow.

He could tell him that, of course. He could try to give him the benefit of his experience. But it was the last thing the poor bastard needed to hear now. *Don't worry, pal, you'll soon get over your wife's death. Chin up, life goes on.*

Here, now, the man needed his grief. His pain. What right had Logan to try to take that away from him?

"I have to ask you a couple of questions. Standard stuff," Logan said. "But it might help us figure out who murdered Esme."

Rowan flinched at the starkness of it. The truth of it, laid bare like that.

"Fine," he croaked. "Ask away."

"Were you aware of any problems Esme was having? Maybe at work? Anyone she was having issues with?"

The question seemed to catch Mr Miller unawares. His eyes narrowed, the pupils darting between Logan and Sinead. "No. Why? You think it was someone from the hospital who did this?"

"No. Not necessarily, Mr Miller. Like I say, this is all standard stuff."

"So... what? You're just fishing around for suspects at this point? You don't have any leads to follow up?"

"We're pursuing several lines of enquiry, Mr Miller," Logan told him. "But it's important to be as thorough as we can."

That seemed to settle Rowan a little. He nodded his understanding, and offered a whispered apology.

"Right. Yes. Sorry."

"Nothing to be sorry for, Mr Miller," Logan assured him. "So, she hadn't said anything about any disagreements she'd had with anyone recently?"

"At the hospital?"

"Or elsewhere."

The wooden chair squeaked beneath Rowan's weight as he shifted himself around. "No. I don't... Not that I can remember. You should talk to her friend, Kel, though."

"Had they fallen out?" Logan asked.

Rowan's eyes widened in panic, like he'd just said something wrong. "What? No! God. No, they were friends. He's a nice kid. He's already been on the phone offering to help. Offered to drive us up to my parents, if I wasn't up for it. Nice kid."

He crossed his arms on the table and leaned on them for support. "I just meant, if anyone would know about her falling out with anyone, it'd be Kel. Esme and I, we'd barely seen each other in the last few weeks. They're short-staffed. She was doing a lot of overtime."

He put a hand over his eyes, massaging his temples with fingers and thumb. "She wasn't even meant to be on last night, but her shift got swapped. We had an argument about it. We had plans for last night. We were going to go out. Just the two of us, you know? We hadn't done that in so long. A date night."

He dropped his hand into his lap and picked at the skin around his fingernails. "But swapping meant she had two days off in a row. That hasn't happened in... Well. I don't know when. She was going to take today to rest, then we were going to head away somewhere tomorrow. The three of us were going to just pile in the car, choose a direction and—"

His voice wobbled, then betrayed him completely. He lowered his head, his shoulders heaving as big silent sobs came. Sinead reached across the table and squeezed his hand. He didn't react, didn't acknowledge it. He just sat there, too tired to fight back the tears any longer.

"I think maybe I will go get us that cup of tea," Logan suggested, easing himself up out of the chair. He caught Sinead's eye, then tilted his head in Rowan's direction.

"Coffee. Milk and one," she mouthed.

Logan headed through into the kitchen. For the size of the house, it was fairly small, barely larger than galley-style. A brushed-chrome American fridge took up most of one end, the front of it decorated with Chloe's drawings, all attached by magnets.

One of the drawings showed a smiling woman with angel wings and a halo. The word 'Mummy' was scrawled inexpertly beneath it. It was presumably a very recent addition to the gallery. Either that, or little Chloe had one hell of a gift for premonition.

Logan filled the kettle from the tap and clicked the button to switch it on. He could hear Sinead talking to Rowan through in the living room, her voice low and soothing in a way that his own rarely was. Better to leave her to it, and let Rowan get it out of his system.

There was another door that led into a utility room almost the size of the kitchen itself. From that, another door led out into what Logan guessed would be the front hall. He went for a wander while he waited for the kettle to boil.

The house was a mirror image of the one next door, he thought, based on the fact the staircase was on the opposite side. He didn't want to go poking around upstairs without permission, so he stood by the bottom step, checking out some of the framed photos that adorned the wall there.

As with the living room, most of them showed Esme and Chloe. Chloe was smiling in most of them. Esme was smiling, too, albeit far more self-consciously than her more carefree daughter.

One of the pictures showed a large group of people sitting around a table in a pub or club. They were all dressed like they'd stepped out of the 1970s, with big collars and flares all but filling the frame.

There were twenty or so people in the photograph, and it took Logan a moment to spot Esme. She was tucked away near the back of the curved booth, wearing a blonde wig with a gold hairband, and—from what little of her could be seen behind the man next to her—a silver catsuit. A vast array of glasses on the table suggested the group had been drinking quite heavily for some time.

The man sitting next to her, Logan realised, was Kel Conlyn, the porter he'd spoken to earlier. He was kitted out in a brown leather jacket, paisley patterned shirt, and a handlebar moustache that looked comically oversized for his face.

Doctor Fletcher was in the picture, too. His costume was more subdued than everyone else's, consisting of a purple shirt with frills down the front, and a sensible pair of black trousers. It was a token gesture, and judging by the way he sat slightly apart from the rest of the group, everyone knew it.

Logan half-recognised a couple of the other nurses from the hospital the night before. He got the impression that most of the people in the picture were nurses, porters, and cleaning staff, in fact, with Fletcher being the noteworthy exception. Had he invited himself along? Inflicted himself upon the party? Or had someone else suggested he join in?

There was one other face in the photograph that Logan kept returning to. Male. Twenties. He wore a long hippie wig with a garland of flowers just above the fringe. He also had a peace sign painted on one cheek. It wasn't much of a disguise, but it was enough to prove distracting and made it difficult for

Logan to recognise him. He'd seen him before, though. Recently.

At the hospital? Probably, but he couldn't place him there. Still, that had to be it. Where else could he know the face from?

Taking out his phone, Logan snapped off a couple of pictures of the photo, just as the kettle came to the boil back in the kitchen.

Then, with a final glance at the wall of photos, and the many smiling faces of Esme Miller, he headed through the utility room, and got on with the important business of making the tea.

TWENTY MINUTES, and one decent-if-not-spectacular cup of tea later, Logan stood on Rowan Miller's front step, his car keys clutched in one hand.

"You don't think he had anything to do with it, do you?" Sinead asked, her voice hushed and low.

Logan shook his head. "No. Contrary to what the neighbours might say."

"That what you were in next door for?"

"Aye. She'd heard them arguing. Thought it was worth bringing to my attention," Logan said. "I suppose, if nothing else, it corroborates what he told us himself. But no. I don't think he had anything to do with it."

Sinead looked pleased at that. "That's good. I mean, not *good*, but... You know."

"Aye. Well." Logan stepped down onto the path. "You take care of yourself. Let me know if anything comes up."

"Will do, sir," Sinead said. "Oh, and sir?"

Logan stopped. PC Bell stepped out of the house and pulled the door closed behind her. She shuffled a little uneasily, like she was building up to something.

"What is it?"

"It's, um, it's Harris's birthday next week. My wee... My brother. And, he was asking me if you might be coming."

"Me?"

"I think he wants you there, sir."

"What the bloody hell does he want me at his birthday for?" Logan asked.

"I think you made a bit of an impression down in the Fort, sir," Sinead said.

"Did you point out I'm a bit tied up trying to catch a murdering rapist?"

"Funnily enough, no, sir. I neglected to mention that." Sinead gave a reassuring smile. "It's fine, I told him you'd be busy. I just, you know, didn't go into quite that level of detail."

She was disappointed. Despite the smile she was putting on, it was written all over her face.

"I just... I wanted to make it good for him. You know, after everything that happened in the last couple of years? Our mum and dad... He didn't really have much of a birthday last year, and he's not got a lot of friends here yet."

Her eyes widened and the tone of her voice became a little more urgent.

"But that wasn't me trying to guilt-trip you into it, sir!" she said. "It's not a problem. He knows you're busy."

Logan gave a noncommittal sort of grunt. "When did you say it was?"

"Tuesday, but honestly, it's fine. It's just a wee thing for him after school. Four-ish. A couple of the boys from school are coming over. And the girl from next door, much to his horror and disgust," Sinead said. "You don't have to come, though. I just promised him I'd ask."

Logan rubbed his chin and smoothed the jaggy hairs that were sprouting on his top lip. "What's the cake situation?" he asked. "I'm assuming there'll be cake."

"Oh. Yeah. It's a Groot cake, sir."

"I don't know what that is," Logan pointed out.

"From *Guardians of the Galaxy*."

"I don't know what that is, either."

"It's a film, sir."

"Ah. Right. Must've passed me by," Logan said. This did not come as a surprise to either of them. "Four-ish on Tuesday?"

"That's right, sir."

"I'll try. No promises. Depends on what's happening with..."

He looked up at the front of the house.

"Of course, sir. And thanks. He'll be over the moon. If you can make it, I mean. No pressure, obviously."

Logan retreated along the path. "Aye, well. Like I say, I'll see what... Wait." He stopped. "Is DC Neish going to be there?"

Sinead's cheeks reddened just a fraction. "That's the plan, sir."

"Shite," Logan sighed. He considered his options again, then tutted. "Ach, I'll come anyway. I can always order him no' to talk to me."

Sinead smiled. "I'm sure you can try, sir," she told him. "I'm sure you can try."

CHAPTER EIGHTEEN

LOGAN SAT IN THE VOLVO ALONG FROM THE HOUSE AND watched as another well-wisher laid another bunch of flowers on the pavement outside the garden. The woman bowed her head in silent prayer, then scurried off like she was worried someone inside would come out to speak to her.

Rowan Miller had pulled himself together when Logan brought the tea in. They'd made some small talk for a few moments, then Logan had gone back to quizzing him—albeit gently—about his wife's personal life.

She had a few good friends, mostly through work. A sister who also lived in the city, not all that far away. They weren't in touch as often as either of them would like, but made a point of meeting up a couple of times a month for lunch and a good blether.

Logan had got the impression that Rowan wasn't the sister's biggest fan, but there had been nothing about the way he'd said it that had aroused any suspicions. In-laws could just be a pain in the arse sometimes. Logan knew that better than most.

Rowan hadn't been able to identify the man in the hippie outfit in the photograph in the hall. At least, not beyond a vague recollection that he'd worked with Esme at the time. A cleaner, Rowan thought, probably long since moved on.

An itch had been forming somewhere at the back of Logan's head since he'd seen the man in the picture, and Rowan's explanation did nothing to help scratch it. If he didn't work at the hospital, then why did Logan find him familiar? Where did he know him from?

Opening his phone, the DCI brought up the picture, then emailed it to the team's shared inbox, marking it for the attention of Tyler and Hamza with a message that simply read: 'Who's the hippie? Third from the right.'

Once the email was away, he punched 'Queensgate,' into the Maps app, selected the first result, and slotted the phone into the holder on the Volvo's smooth, curved dash.

An email notification appeared at the top of the screen. Tyler.

I think it's a costume, boss.

Muttering, Logan took the phone out of the holder, tapped, 'I know it's a bloody costume. Who's the guy wearing it?' and sent the reply.

Then, with the GPS showing him the way, he fired up the engine, pulled away from the Millers' house, and headed off to buy some sausages.

"IRN BRU?" Logan asked, peering suspiciously at the orange-tinted bangers nestling in a pile behind the glass. He raised his gaze to the portly gent smiling back at him from the other side of the counter. "You're no' serious."

"I am!" the butcher laughed. "It's our own recipe. Pork and Irn Bru. The customers love them!"

Did they though, Logan wondered? Beyond the novelty value, did they *actually* love them, or did they get them home, fry them up, and then spit the bastarding things out after one bite?

"We were going to try beef and Tizer, but... no. Decided against it."

"Aye. Because that would've been mental, I suppose," Logan reasoned.

He shook his head. Irn Bru sausages. What the hell was the world coming to?

"You don't look convinced," the butcher said.

"I can't say that I am, no."

"Do you like Irn Bru?"

Logan confirmed that he was partial to the occasional can.

"Right. Do you like pork?"

"Aye. But—"

"Well, then," said the butcher, holding his hands out at his sides as if presenting a cast iron case.

"Aye, but I like curry and ice cream, too. Doesn't mean I want them on the same plate," Logan replied. He looked down at the bright orange links again, then tutted. "Right. Go on, then. I'll take a dozen," he said. "I'm sure some bugger will eat them."

"Great!" the butcher exclaimed, and from the way he said it, Logan got the impression the man was both relieved and amazed that some gullible bugger had finally bought some. "One thing I should tell you—not sure if you're interested in that sort of thing—but they're four hundred calories each."

"*Each*?" Logan spluttered.

"Aye. I'm thinking of using Diet for the next batch," the

butcher said, wrapping the sausages in a bundle of waxy paper. He deposited the parcel on top of the counter and beamed a big broad smile. "Now. Anything else?"

Logan fished for his wallet. "No. That'll do. But, eh..." He glanced around the shop. Besides himself and the ruddy complexioned guy serving him, there was nobody else to be seen. "Does Donald still work here?"

"He does, aye. He's through the back, prepping for the afternoon." The butcher looked Logan up and down. "You a friend of his?"

"Not exactly, no," Logan said. He glanced at a doorway leading through to the back. There was no door, but a curtain made of hundreds of metal beads blocked the view into the room beyond. "Mind if I have a word?"

"He's got his hands full. Afternoons get busy."

Logan produced his warrant card and held it up. Squinting, the butcher beckoned for him to hand it over for a closer look. Logan watched with growing dismay as the butcher's plastic-gloved fingers left big meaty prints on the wallet.

"Right," he said, handing back a wallet that was considerably stickier than it had been a moment ago. He gave the DCI another once over with his eyes. "He in trouble? What's he done?"

"Nothing that I'm aware of," Logan said. Which was true. "I'd just like a quick word."

The butcher drew in a breath, getting ready to shout.

"In private. If you don't mind."

Whatever the man was going to shout caught somewhere at the back of his throat. He looked over at the shop's front door, then raised a hatch in the counter and beckoned for Logan to come through quickly.

"Come on, come on. Don't want customers seeing randomers piling into the back shop. Health and hygiene."

Logan considered sharing the health and hygiene concerns he now had for his warrant card but decided not to bother. Instead, he stepped through the hatch, ducked through the curtains, and came face-to-face with a man holding a cleaver.

Donald Sloane looked up from where he was doing something unspeakable to a dead pig and locked Logan with a piercing stare. He was dressed in a blood-soaked blue apron that he'd complemented nicely with a matching hairnet and gloves.

There was a white mask over the lower half of his face, spots of blood dotting the material like freckles. The sleeves of his shirt were rolled up, revealing sinewy arms with muscles standing out on them like wraps of rope.

"Donald. This fella's from the police. He wants a quick word," the butcher said, poking his head through the curtain. He eyeballed Logan, emphasised the "*quick*" part again, then retreated to the front shop.

Sloane brought the cleaver down, neatly severing one part of the pig from another. The smell in the room reminded Logan of every mortuary he'd ever been to. It wasn't exactly the same—in fact, it wasn't all that similar at all—but there was an undercurrent to it that linked both places together. Something about the scent, something primal, that connected them.

Meat. That was all they were, he supposed, in the end.

"Donald Sloane?"

Sloane raised the cleaver, brought it down again.

THACK!

"Yes?"

"I was hoping you might answer a few questions."

The cleaver came up.

The cleaver came down.

THACK!

"About?"

Sloane twirled the cleaver around in his hand, then set it down on the stainless steel worktop and pulled the paper mask down so it was below his chin. As his face was revealed, Logan's stomach tightened, ejecting an involuntary grunt of surprise.

He'd seen Sloane's mugshot on the case report, and while the lad had lost a lot of weight since then, there was no mistaking it was him.

But that wasn't the only place Logan had seen his face. How could he not have realised? How could he not have put them together?

"You're the hippie," he said aloud. "You're the hippie in Esme Miller's photo."

Sloane lunged for a heavy wooden chopping block. Grabbed it. Tossed it. Logan ducked too late, heard the *thonk* as the edge of the board clipped his head, felt the pain jar through him, rattling his teeth in their sockets.

"Bastard!" he hissed, stumbling blindly back through the curtain. He landed in the refrigerated counter, arse-deep in black pudding.

"Watch it!" protested the butcher. Across the glass, a woman and a toddler both watched the DCI in stunned silence as he hauled himself up out of the meat and went charging through the curtain, a rivulet of red running down his forehead.

Logan skidded into the back shop, fists raised, ready for anything. To his relief, nothing came flying at him. No blades came *whumming* towards his skull.

Instead, a breeze blew in through the open fire exit in the

corner of the room. Another curtain of beads *chinked* and *clacked* as it wafted in and out on the wind.

"Aw, *shite,*" Logan spat.

And with that, he ran.

CHAPTER NINETEEN

THE BACK DOOR OF THE BUTCHER'S OPENED ON TO A little courtyard barely wide enough to swing a cat in. A tall gate led out to an alleyway. It was wedged half-open by a broken brick. Logan shot a look through the gap but saw no sign of Sloane.

Another door stood open in the wall opposite. Two stunned-looking older women stood beside it, smoke curling from the cigarettes they held clutched between their lips.

"Where did he go?" Logan demanded, and both women jabbed their thumbs in the direction of the open door.

Logan barrelled in past them, his feet slapping on the cracked tile flooring as he emerged between two of the shops in Inverness's Victorian Market. He'd only been in the place a couple of times before and couldn't remember the layout.

He remembered that the path he was on meandered around the covered market's shops and cafés but had no clue which direction led to the closest exit. A quick scan left and right brought up no trace of Sloane, but a few heads in the thin crowd were turned along the path on his right, like they'd just seen something interesting.

That way.

"Move. Polis. Out of the road!" Logan barked, scattering shoppers as he set off in the direction he reckoned Sloane had gone.

"Hey, watch it!" complained a woman around a corner up ahead. Logan powered towards it, coat swishing, heart thumping, lungs demanding to know what the bloody hell he thought he was playing at.

Skidding around a corner, Logan tripped, stumbled, and kicked his way through a display of fruit that had been scattered all over the floor. An orange exploded beneath his boot. His other foot found a banana which, fortunately, turned out to be nowhere near as slippery as he'd always been led to believe.

He hurled himself past it all, barged out through the glass doors, and stopped in the middle of the pavement. He loomed there, chest heaving, eyes scanning the street around him. The traffic was mostly stationary, and a couple of dirty great buses blocked much of his view of the surrounding area.

"You alright there, pal?" asked a male voice, the tone *just* condescending enough that Logan already knew what he'd see before he turned.

He flashed his warrant card in the faces of the two uniformed officers. "DCI Logan. MIT. There's a bastard running around in a butcher's apron. Potentially armed, definitely dangerous. I want him found!"

The Uniforms hesitated, swapping uncertain glances.

"Move!"

Both officers jumped and quickly darted off in opposite directions, their high-vis vests zig-zagging through the busy streets. One of them thumbed the radio on his shoulder, calling for back-up, but Logan had a sinking feeling that it was pointless. There was no saying which direction Sloane had gone. The only hope was that he'd been picked up on CCTV, but that was out of his hands.

"You know your head's bleeding, son?"

Logan looked down to find a concerned-looking old woman peering up at him.

"I know," he said. It came out harsher than he'd intended. He tried to make up for it by smiling, but it was thin and unconvincing. "Thanks."

"Well, you look after yourself, son," the woman said, shuffling off. "We're none of us as young as we used to be."

Logan drew in a breath that made pain flare through his lungs. "Aye," he muttered. "You can say that again."

THE BUTCHER EMERGED through the bead curtains just as Logan strode back in through the front door of the shop. The side of the DCI's face was a pattern of crimson shades, and an egg-sized bump was forming right below his hairline. He also had a pound of black pudding stuck to the back of his coat, but that was lower on his list of concerns.

"What the hell was all that about?" the butcher demanded.

"I was hoping you could tell me."

"Me? He's nothing to do with me. He just works here, that's all! If he's in trouble, that's his business, not mine."

Logan grunted. "Aye. Well. You'll have his address and phone number."

"Oh. Yes. But not here. My wife handles all that stuff. She'll be at home. I'll have to give her a ring."

"You do that," Logan said.

"Right. Aye. I will. No bother," the butcher said. "I'll give her a ring now and get you the information. Oh, and..."

He slapped a neatly wrapped parcel of sausages on the counter and flashed the detective a smile.

"That'll be four pound fifty."

CHAPTER TWENTY

"I'M STARTING TO THINK WE SHOULD BE WRAPPING YOU IN cotton wool, Jack," said Ben. He dabbed at the wound on Logan's head, eliciting a sharp intake of breath. "Sorry. Brace yourself. This might sting."

"Bit late for that," Logan said through gritted teeth. "What the hell are you putting on it? Acid?"

"No, it's..." Ben looked down at the tube of cream in his hand, then held it at arm's length and squinted to try to make out the lettering. "What is that, actually? Is that the right stuff?"

"What do you mean 'is that the right stuff?'" Logan barked, snatching the tube from the DI's hand. "Maybe check it's the right stuff before you..."

He read the label, tutted, then handed it back to Ben. "Aye. It's the right stuff. Just go canny with it, eh?"

He plucked it back out of Ben's grasp again. "In fact, why are you even doing it? I'll do it myself."

Squeezing a slug of disinfectant cream onto the tip of a finger, Logan poked gingerly at the site of his wound.

"At least this one won't need stitches," Ben said, peering at the injury. "Want me to stick a plaster on it, or would you prefer to do that yourself, too?"

"Maybe if you're a bit more careful and don't just slap it on," Logan bit back. He dabbed the injury site with the back of his hand, then studied it. Besides the creamy residue, it came away dry. "Anyway, it's fine. It's stopped bleeding."

The events of the afternoon had meant Logan had come storming back into the Incident Room like a bear with a sore head. The fact that he literally did have a sore head wasn't helping matters, either.

"So, what does this mean, then?" Ben asked, as Logan got up from the chair he'd been sitting on and stalked over to the Big Board. "Sloane's our main suspect?"

"Well, put it this way, I'm certainly keen to have a word with the bastard," Logan said. He stared at the city centre map pinned to the board, like he might see Sloane darting down some lane or side alley somewhere on it. "CCTV pick him up?"

"No, sir. Nothing," said DS McQuarrie, joining the DCI at the board. "City centre, too. Lot of cameras around, but not a sniff of him. Not sure how he pulled that off."

"Did you no' say there were buses around, boss?" Tyler volunteered from his desk. "Maybe he jumped on one of them."

Logan exhaled slowly through his nose. "Aye. Maybe." He looked back over his shoulder in the direction of DC Khaled. Hamza was hunched over his computer screen, scowling at the screen. "You got me those recordings from when he was last interviewed?"

"Not yet, sir. I can probably get you the transcripts, but

HOLMES is still all over the place," Hamza replied. "Bloody update."

Logan cursed below his breath. "What about his house, did we check there?"

"He's no' there, Jack. Not that that comes as a surprise," Ben said.

"What about—"

"He left his mobile in his jacket pocket. Can't trace him through that, either," said Ben, correctly anticipating the DCI's next question. "It's just a waiting game for now. He'll turn up. We'll get him."

Logan rubbed the tips of his forefinger and thumb together, rolling up the dried antiseptic paste. "We'd better."

"What was it you said to him anyway, boss?" asked Tyler. "To set him off like that?"

"Nothing really," Logan said, his gaze still fixed on the map, and the area around the Victorian Market. "It was out of me before I knew it. I recognised him as the hippie in that photo I sent."

"From Esme Miller's house?" asked Ben. "He knew Esme Miller?"

"He did," Logan confirmed. "Used to work together at the hospital. As soon as I mentioned her name, he horsed a chopping block at me and fucked off out of there."

Ben whistled through his teeth. His eyes darted left and right as he contemplated the implications of Logan's revelation. "That's... That could be huge."

"It could. Which is why we need to find him, sharpish," the DCI said.

"We've got a heavy presence in the area, sir," Caitlyn informed him. "He has to be hiding somewhere nearby. We might still catch sight of him yet, with a bit of luck."

Logan wasn't getting his hopes up. "We've never exactly had luck to spare, have we?" he asked, then he gave a dismissive wave that made it clear he wasn't expecting an answer. "What else do we have? That Forensics report come in on the victim's clothes yet?"

"It did, but it's a bit of an anti-climax," Ben reported. "Multiple DNA samples taken from it, but apparently that's par for the course with nurses and other medical professionals. They interact with a lot of people in a day and deal with their fair share of bodily fluids.

"They're getting samples from the patients she's likely to have dealt with that day, as well as her colleagues, but it's going to be a long process. There isn't any one sample that screams 'murderer,' unfortunately, so even once they've all been identified, they're unlikely to be a big help."

This was not the news Logan had been hoping to hear.

"And no sign of the gag or the murder weapon either, I'm assuming?"

"Nothing," Ben confirmed.

From behind his monitor, Hamza let out a short sharp cry of frustration, and repeatedly hammered the space bar on his keyboard. Logan knew exactly how he felt.

"Stupid bloody thing!" Hamza spat. "Why run an update if it's only going to make things worse?"

"Still having problems?" Tyler asked.

"No, I just shouted all that for a laugh. *Yes.* Still having problems."

Logan pinched the bridge of his nose and squeezed, trying to push back against his headache. It had started as a sharp sting where the board had hit him, gradually faded into a dull background throb, but was now in the process of getting its second wind.

Turning back to the board, he studied the map for a while, then drew a circle around the Victorian Market with a fingertip. "What's the camera situation around here?"

"More than ample, sir," said Caitlyn. "The exit you took, there are four within sixty feet of the door, then one at each corner of the street."

"And none of them picked Sloane up?"

"No, sir. Like I say, Uniform is still on the scene. We might pick him up yet."

Logan sucked in his top lip and poked absent-mindedly at the cut on his head. His fingers came away sticky, pinkened by the white of the cream and the red of...

Blood.

"Wait. Hold on, hold on," said Logan, stiffening. "Shite. Gloves. He had gloves on. He'd been chopping meat. He was bloody."

Ben Forde's brow furrowed. "Aye. You said. So what?"

"Argh! Jesus Christ, what an idiot!" Logan snapped, spinning on his heels.

"Here, steady on..."

"No' you. Me. How could I have been so bloody stupid?" Logan groaned. "It's a glass door."

"And?" Ben asked.

"Glass door, blood-soaked gloves. Where was the handprint?"

Ben glanced around at the others. "Is that a rhetorical question or...?"

"There wasn't one. Because he didn't go out through the doors!" Logan announced. He jabbed a finger in Tyler's direction. "Get onto Uniform. Get them to lock the whole place down," he instructed. "The bastard's still in the building!"

CHAPTER TWENTY-ONE

CONSTABLE PENNY WILLOW OPENED THE DOOR OF THE Victorian Market's fruit and veg shop, chiming the bell that was fixed to the frame above it.

The shop was dim and cramped, and lined on all sides with racks of organic produce that reeked to high heaven. It wasn't an unpleasant smell, exactly, just an overwhelming one. The fruit and vegetables all smelled fresh enough, but there was a suggestion of dampness from the fabric of the shop that added a sour note to the overall aroma of the place.

The front part of the shop was deserted, and while there was a curtained-off door leading through to what was presumably a storage area at the back, the bell hadn't drawn anyone out.

"Knock knock," PC Willow announced. "Hello? Police."

For a moment, there was nothing to indicate anyone was through there, but then the curtains were half-pulled aside and a man in his mid-fifties sidled through, smiling broadly at the uniformed officer as he dried his hands on a thin, slightly grimy-looking towel.

"Sorry. I was in the toilet," he announced.

"You leave the shop open when you go to the toilet? Bit risky, that."

"Yes. I only intended to be quick, but it took longer than expected to..." the shopkeeper began. His face took on a slightly desperate expression as he searched for an appropriate ending to the sentence. He settled on, "...get the job done," and then visibly flinched at his choice of words.

"Right," said PC Willow, not quite sure how to respond to that. She rapped her knuckles on a rock-hard Swede. "You should get more fibre in your diet."

"Ha! Yes!" he replied. "Can't beat a bit of roughage for getting the old bowels moving."

He instantly regretted that one too, judging by the way his face crumpled and he became intensely focused on finishing drying his hands.

Once done, he folded the towel and set it down on the counter, then gestured to the racks of produce lining the walls.

"Looking for anything in particular?"

"Not anything, exactly. Any*one*," PC Willow replied. "Have you seen anyone acting suspicious in the last half hour or so?"

The shopkeeper gestured to the window. "Someone knocked over the display out front. Made a right bloody mess, they did. Is that the sort of thing you mean?"

"It may be connected," PC Willow said. "Someone came through here recently after assaulting one of our officers. We believe they may be hiding on the premises."

"These premises? Here?" the shopkeeper asked, pointing to the floor.

"Not necessarily in this shop, sir, no. Somewhere in the

market. We're doing a sweep at the moment, checking if anyone has seen anything."

"Right. Yes. Of course. Well, other than my display being trashed, there's not a lot I can tell you, I'm afraid."

The constable's gaze flicked to the curtain behind the shopkeeper. "You've checked through the back?"

"There's not a lot of it to check!" the man laughed. He caught the edge of the curtain. "You're welcome to have a look yourself, if you like? Just mind the mess."

PC Willow hesitated, then shook her head. "That won't be necessary. Thank you," she said. The smell in the shop was getting to her, and she didn't really want to spend any more time than necessary breathing it in. "If you see anything unusual, please just flag someone down. We'll be here for a while yet."

"Will do," said the shopkeeper.

The constable pulled open the door, sending the bell into another chiming frenzy.

"Oh, and if you do catch him, tell him he owes me for all that fruit he stomped on!"

PC Willow stopped. Turned.

"Sorry?"

The shopkeeper's smile widened just a little too far. "The... my fruit. If you catch him."

"I didn't say anything about it being a man, sir."

The bell went again as the constable let the door swing closed.

"Didn't you? Oh. I just... I must've just..."

"On second thoughts, sir, maybe I will have a look through the back."

The shopkeeper's smile remained fixed in place, but the

rest of his face and his body language all conspired to tell a different story. He swallowed.

"I thought you said you didn't need to?"

"I did, sir. But I've changed my mind," said the constable, approaching the open hatch at the side of the counter. "Woman's prerogative, and all that."

"You're wasting your time. Honestly. It's a mess back there," the shopkeeper said, the words coming as a breathless sort of laugh. Sweat glistened on his brow. His cheeks, which looked to be in a permanent state of rosiness, blazed red.

He was a little taller than the officer, but seemed to be shrinking fast. His eyes flitted to the curtain, then back to PC Willow. Wide. Staring.

Pleading.

"Help me," he whispered.

Then, the curtain erupted beside them and a man in a bloodied apron exploded through it.

A hand wrapped around PC Willow's throat. Another caught her by the hair, fingers twisting until her scalp burned in pain.

"Fucking pigs!" a voice snarled in her ear. "Why won't you leave me alone?"

LOGAN PACED BACK and forth in the Incident Room, his hands folded behind his back, his tongue clicking against the roof of his mouth.

The others were all sitting at their desks, reading, or writing, or —in Hamza's case—muttering obscenities at the computer screen.

Every once in a while, one of them would glance up at the

phone on DI Forde's desk, willing it to ring. It remained steadfastly silent.

"Come on. What's bloody taking so long?" Logan asked of nobody in particular. "It's no' like it's a big place. I mean, how many shops are even in there?"

Tyler looked up from the paperwork he was reading through. "Want me to find out, boss?"

"Well, obviously not. I don't actually care," Logan snapped.

"Oh," said Tyler. "Right. Sorry, boss."

Logan continued to pace. Back and forth. Back and forth. It had been forty minutes since the market had been cordoned off. If he'd known it was going to take this long, he'd have gone down there and found the bastard himself.

"Any word on... I don't know. Anything?" Logan asked.

"No updates, Jack," said Ben.

Logan tutted his annoyance. "Hamza? What's HOLMES doing?"

"Being a pain in the arse, sir," DC Khaled replied. "I've logged an issue with the help desk, but it's getting worse, if anything. Just grinding to a halt."

"Great. Well, keep on at support. If you need me to give them a bollocking, I'm more than happy to."

"It might come to that, sir," Hamza said. "I'll keep you posted."

It was Logan's turn to shoot Ben's phone a look. It was a threatening look, at that, but the bloody thing still didn't take the hint.

"Thirty-three, boss," Tyler announced.

Logan stopped pacing and stared at DC Neish. "What?"

"The number of shops in the market. I looked it up. Thirty-three. That's counting cafés and—"

"I don't give a shite," Logan told him. He made an abrupt

gesture at the paperwork spread out in front of the younger detective. "Do something useful."

"Right, boss. Sorry, boss," said Tyler, turning his attention back to the paperwork.

He looked up again a moment later when the phone on Ben's desk rang.

"Well, bloody answer it, then," Logan urged, before it had even reached the second ring.

"Jesus, I'm no' spring-loaded," Ben grumbled. He reached across the desk, picked up the handset, and cradled it to his ear. "DI Forde."

Everyone watched. Waited. Held their breath.

"Uh-huh," said Ben.

"Oh," said Ben.

"Right," said Ben. "And is she...?"

His eyes darted across the faces of the rest of the team. "I see. Thanks."

The handset was barely half an inch from Ben's ear when Logan spoke.

"Well?"

Ben returned the phone to the cradle. "A female constable discovered him hiding in the greengrocers. He attacked her."

The atmosphere in the room became heavier, more oppressive.

"Bastard," Logan hissed. "And? How is she?"

"Hmm? Oh, she's fine," said Ben. A smile tugged at the corners of his mouth. "Leathered the living shite out of him. They're bringing him in now."

Logan thrust both hands in the air and looked to the ceiling, giving thanks to a god he didn't believe in. "YES!"

He spun on the spot, brought up an arm, and pointed at DS McQuarrie. "Caitlyn, get us an interview room prepped.

Make sure we get our guest the most uncomfortable chair we've got. Put a pin in the seat, if you have to. Let's make it as unpleasant an experience as we can for him."

Caitlyn got up from her desk. "I like your thinking, sir. On it."

"Tyler, I want access to his house. We might not be able to tie him to Esme Miller yet, but that's two officers he's assaulted, so the bastard's hiding something. Get onto the PF, get a search warrant, and get Forensics in there to give the place a bloody good going over."

"I'll see what I can do, boss," Tyler said, reaching for his phone.

"You'll do better than that. Get it done," Logan told him. "And get the shop where he works shut down, too. I don't want anyone else in or out. They've got a lot of knives there, one of them could be the murder weapon."

Tyler nodded, his finger already stabbing at the numbers on the phone's handset.

"And Hamza?" Logan continued. He turned just in time to see DC Khaled banging his computer keyboard against the desk, then biting down on his fist.

"You get that bloody thing working, ASAP," the DCI instructed. "We can't have it slowing us down on this."

Hamza sighed. "Yes, sir. I'm working on it."

"Good lad."

Logan turned. He breathed out for what felt like the first time since he'd chased Sloane through the market. Ben met his gaze from across the Incident Room.

"You're going to have your work cut out for you, Jack. If it's anything like last time, he'll be combative."

"Aye, well," said Logan. He cracked his knuckles. "We can but hope."

CHAPTER TWENTY-TWO

It was well after six by the time everything was set up for the interview. Sloane's solicitor had been a nightmare to get hold of, and even once they had, he'd insisted on finishing his dinner before coming in.

Sloane himself had been intent on making himself as big a pain in the arse as he possibly could. With some difficulty, he'd been stripped of his clothes and given a pair of shapeless grey joggies and a t-shirt to wear. He'd refused to put them on at first, and had instead ranted and cursed and gone parading around the cell stark bollock naked.

Eventually, he'd been coaxed into getting dressed by one of the older female officers, who had made some earnest-sounding yet deeply sarcastic remarks about the size of his manhood. He hadn't quite known how to respond to that, and had begrudgingly agreed to put some clothes on as long as she agreed to stop talking and go away.

"Christ, he's a changed man," Ben remarked, watching on a monitor as Sloane prowled around inside his cell. "He was a skinny wee runt of a thing last time I saw him. Look at him now."

In some ways, Sloane was still skinny, but a runt he was not. There wasn't an ounce of fat on him, and everything else had been honed and sculpted to such an extent that he actually looked ill. He'd clearly been obsessively hitting the gym, but whereas some guys bulked out, everything about Sloane had just sort of sharpened.

He looked strong and fast, and had it not been for the female constable having the presence of mind to crack him across the knee with her baton and then drive one of her own knees into his groin, Logan dreaded to think what might have happened.

"His solicitor's here, sir," said Caitlyn, appearing in the doorway behind Logan and Ben. "We're about ready to go."

"Finally. Who is it?"

"Clive Copeland, sir. From Copeland and Fraser Legal."

Logan gave a little shake of his head, indicating he'd never heard of them.

"Either of you dealt with him before?"

"Aye," Ben confirmed. "Arsehole."

Logan appreciated the succinctness of the older detective's review, unsurprising as it was. It was rare to encounter a defence lawyer who didn't accurately fit that description.

"Who wants to go in there with me?" Logan asked.

"I have to admit, I wouldn't say no to another crack at him," Ben said. "But the fact we have history might be a problem."

Logan considered this. On-screen, two uniformed officers came to take Sloane through to the interview room.

"No. I want you in there," the DCI decided. "If he's fixated on you, he'll be paying less attention to me. Besides, Caitlyn, I want you to go round to pre-warn Danni Gillespie. Sloane didn't exactly come quietly, so it's bound to be hitting social media. I'd rather she heard from us that we've brought him in."

"Right, sir," Caitlyn said. "What about the victim's family? Are we saying anything to them at this point?"

"Not yet. Let's see what we get out of him first." He turned to look at both of them. "Everyone alright with that decision?"

"Fine by me, Jack."

"Yes, sir."

Logan nodded. "Good, then let's get to it," he said, taking a final look at Sloane as he was led out of the cell in shackles. "I want this bastard broken before the chippie shuts."

LOGAN HAD BEEN CONCERNED that getting Sloane to talk would be difficult. He needn't have been. Getting him to shut up was proving to be the problem.

He'd started ranting even before DI Forde had made the introductions for the benefit of the recording, and his solicitor had spent a few minutes trying to calm him down enough for things to proceed.

Logan hadn't needed Ben's review of Clive Copeland in the end. He'd disliked the man on sight. He had an expensive, if tight-fitting suit that suggested a high net worth and an even higher calorie intake. On the flip side, he was sorely lacking in hair. And, presumably, moral integrity, given how he'd made the money to pay for that suit.

His attempts to soothe his client were decidedly half-arsed. He sounded almost as impatient as Logan felt, evidently furious about having been called away from dinner before the dessert course had arrived.

"What the fuck's he here for?" Sloane demanded, shooting

the dirtiest of looks across the table at DI Forde. "He shouldn't be here. I fucking complained about him. I fucking complained about you."

"Aye, I remember," said Ben, deflecting Sloane's anger with a well-aimed smile. "Nothing came of that, by the way. No fault found. They even apologised for wasting my time, in fact." His smile widened. "In case you were wondering."

"Fuck you," Sloane spat. He made a lunging motion, but the cuffs that fastened him to the table stopped him moving more than a few inches. Neither of the two detectives so much as blinked.

"You quite finished?" Logan asked.

Sloane sneered at him, his nostrils flaring in disgust. He looked Logan up and down, as if only now seeing him for the first time.

"How's your head, pal?" he asked, sniggering.

"Sore, actually. Feels like it took a right pounding," Logan replied. He clasped his hands in front of him and leaned in. "Which, coincidentally, is more or less word-for-word what you'll be saying about your arsehole in a few months, after we sling you in the jail."

Sloane kept his grin fixed in place, but some of the defiance faded behind his eyes. "I'm not going to jail."

"Aye, you are," Logan told him.

Sloane leaned forward as far as the cuffs would allow, mirroring Logan's own position.

"Naw, I'm fucking *not*."

Logan raised an index finger. "Hang on. Allow me to consult with my fellow officer here," he said, then he turned to Ben. "Detective Inspector Forde?"

"Yes, Detective Chief Inspector? How can I help?"

"He's going to the jail, isn't he?"

"Oh God, aye," Ben confirmed. "He's going to the jail, alright."

Logan nodded, then turned back to Sloane. "Thanks for waiting there. Aye. I just checked. You are."

Clive Copeland opened his mouth to speak. Logan jumped in before he could say a word. "Assaulting a police officer. Twice. Assault with the intent to resist arrest."

He glanced over at the solicitor. "Could we push for perverting the course of justice? What do you think? You're the expert."

"Don't forget the hostage-taking and property damage," Ben said.

"Oh, I'd hardly call it 'hostage-taking,'" Copeland protested, but the detectives both ignored him.

"Christ, aye," said Logan. "That poor shopkeeper. He'd actually slipped my mind. How is he, by the way?"

"Oh, he's shaken," said Ben. "He's badly shaken. He'll be pressing charges, alright. Criminal and civil, I'd have thought. Taking it all the way."

Logan puffed out his cheeks. "And then there's breach of the peace, after you screamed the place down when we were taking you into custody."

"Frightened the weans," Ben added.

"Frightened a *lot* of weans, aye," Logan said. He sucked air in through his teeth. "No, I'll be honest, things aren't looking good for you, Donnie. Can I call you Donnie, by the way?"

"Can you fuck."

"I'm going to go ahead and call you Donnie," Logan said, flashing a smile. "Things are no' looking good for you, Donnie. But maybe we can come to some sort of arrangement. Maybe DI Forde and I, maybe we'll go easy on all that stuff if you help us out with another matter."

"How did you know Esme Miller?" Ben asked.

Sloane squirmed in his seat. "Who?"

Logan opened a paper folder on the table and presented a printout of the photograph he'd taken at the Millers' house.

"Cut the shite, Donnie. That's you," he said, tapping the image. "And that's Esme Miller. You worked together, did you not?"

"I worked at a lot of places," Sloane grunted.

"Aye. You have that. We were looking you up," Logan said. "Why is that? All the career changes? How come you never settle in one place?"

Sloane shrugged. A petulant child. "Get bored, don't I?"

"Right. I see. Well, we phoned around and asked a few of your former employers, and that's not what they said, is it, Detective Inspector?"

"No," Ben confirmed. "That's not what they said."

"And remind me what it was they said," Logan pressed.

"They said he was an unpopular bastard," said Ben. "No' well liked at all. Bit weird, in fact."

"And wasn't there something about personal hygiene?"

"There was," Ben confirmed. "Came up a couple of times, actually. The main thrust of it was the unpopular bastard bit, though."

Logan drew Sloane a very deliberate up and down look before continuing. "But, that's by the by." He tapped the photograph. "Esme Miller. You knew her. We know you knew her, so stop pissing us about."

Sloane shot his solicitor a sideways look, but Copeland was studying the photograph and failed to pick up on it.

"I only knew her vaguely. I saw her around. That was all."

"And when did you last see her around?" Ben asked.

"Well, I don't know, do I?"

"Last night, maybe?" Logan suggested. "Say, nine-ish?"

"I knew this was going to happen. I fucking knew it!" Sloane spat, becoming agitated again. He rattled his restraints. "Soon as I heard about the writing on her. Soon as that prick messaged me to tell me, I fucking knew this was going to happen."

Logan's brow furrowed. "What prick?"

Sloane's mouth closed, his teeth snapping together with a *clack*. He breathed slowly through his nose, eyes darting between the two detectives. He'd made a mistake, said too much.

"No comment."

"Who messaged you? What did they tell you?" Logan pressed.

"No comment."

"We've got your phone, Donnie. We can find out," Logan said.

Sloane tutted. "Fine. Shaun. Alright?"

"Gillespie?" said Logan.

"No, Connery. Aye, Gillespie. He messaged me to say he knew it was me, but it fucking wasn't, alright?" Sloane said, rattling the cuffs. "It fucking wasn't!"

"Alright, calm down, son," Ben told him. "Acting up's no' going to get you anywhere."

"Don't fucking 'son' me, you crooked piece of shit," Sloane spat. "You made my life hell. All you people. You think I killed Esme, like you think I raped that stuck-up bitch. Well, I didn't, alright? I didn't do it."

"Which one didn't you do?" Logan asked. "The rape or the murder."

"Either. Both! You know what I fucking mean!"

"Then why run, Donnie? That's what I keep coming back

to. Why chuck a dirty great lump of wood at me and leg it? Why hide out? Why attack one of my officers?"

"Because I knew this would fucking happen! I knew you'd find some bullshit excuse to drag me back in here."

Logan looked offended. "I was just in to buy sausages, son. Thought I'd take the opportunity to ask you a couple of quick questions. You weren't a suspect until you flew off the handle and started throwing your weight around."

Sloane said nothing, just ground his teeth together and stared straight ahead.

"As far as I was concerned, you had an alibi for the sexual assault. Far as I was concerned, it wasn't you."

"Yeah, well, it wasn't me," Sloane spat, coming alive again.

Logan's chair creaked as he leaned forward a little further. "Now, though, I've got good reason to go back over that case with a fine-tooth comb, Donnie, paying very close attention to your whereabouts on the night of the attack."

He sat back, keeping eye contact. "To think, I went in there for some sausages and came out with a new line of enquiry and a prime suspect. Talk about my lucky day."

The detectives left him stewing in that for a bit.

"Whose idea was the Irn Bru sausages, by the way?" Logan asked.

Ben did a double-take, his nose crinkling in disgust. "The what?"

"They do Irn Bru sausages now," Logan said. He still hadn't taken his eyes off Sloane. "Whose idea was that?"

"I don't know. Mine."

"Irn bloody Bru sausages?" Ben said, scowling. "We should lock him up for that alone."

Clive Copeland quickly jumped in. "You can't lock—"

"We know, Mr Copeland," Logan sighed. "Fucking up a

perfectly good sausage is not currently a crime. Besides..." He returned his gaze to Sloane. "We've got more than enough to be going on with."

Logan steepled his fingers in front of him. Beside him, Ben Forde flicked to a blank page in an A4 notepad, and popped the lid off a brand new pen.

"Now, let's try this again, Mr Sloane," Logan said. "Tell me what you know about Esme Miller."

CHAPTER TWENTY-THREE

Depending on which way you looked at it, the interview had gone reasonably well.

After some more cajoling, a few thinly veiled threats, and a quiet word from his solicitor, Sloane had started to open up. He'd told them most of what they wanted to know, in the end. The problem was, it was currently difficult to verify much of it.

Sloane confirmed that he had worked at the hospital for a few months, doing general cleaning duties. He'd worked behind the scenes in the staff canteen for most of his time there, but had started out on the same ward that Esme Miller worked on. He insisted they didn't really know each other though, and even on the night out where he and Esme had both been pictured, he didn't recall speaking to her once.

Checking up on how long he'd worked at the hospital wouldn't be a problem, although it was too late to get it done tonight. A quick call in the morning would be able to confirm or deny that part of his story, at least, although it would be unlikely to shine any light on his relationship with Esme, or his lack of one.

Fortunately, Logan had an idea about that.

"Kel Conlyn," he said, after a slurp of tea.

He and Ben were the only two left in the Incident Room, and had taken up residence on either side of the DCI's desk. The world beyond the window was dark, the night having drawn all the way in over the course of the interview.

Whoever had been last to leave had turned off all the lights, and neither detective had bothered to turn them back on again. The only illumination came from an angled lamp on Logan's desk, which cast a puddle of light, pushing aside the shadows in the otherwise darkened room.

Ben took a sip of his own drink, then frowned. "Who's that now?"

"Friend of Esme's. We went round to see him earlier. He's in the photo of the night out," Logan explained. "He should be able to tell us what sort of relationship Esme and Sloane had."

"Good. That'll help," Ben said. There was a *buzz* from his pocket. He groaned. "Shite."

"Alice?" Logan asked.

"Oh, no doubt. Her sister's visiting us from Stornoway. Arrives tonight. She'll be there now."

"Well, what are you sitting around here for?" Logan asked him. He motioned to the door. "Go."

"You sure?"

"Aye, I'm sure. I'm not having Alice hold me responsible for you not being there."

God knew, the woman held enough against him as it was, from the destruction of her favourite ceramic hedgehog onwards. He didn't need something else added to what was already a fairly sizeable list.

Logan held up the Post-It note Tyler had left for him to let him know that he wouldn't hear back on the search warrant until the following morning. "Not a lot we can do tonight, anyway."

"Suppose," Ben said. He drained the rest of his tea, then set the mug on Logan's desk as he grunted up onto his feet. "I'll get that in the morning."

"It's fine. I'll get it," Logan told him. "I was going to hang on for a bit, anyway."

"Why?" Ben asked, reaching for his coat. It wasn't currently raining outside, but it was never far away.

Logan realised he had no response. Why *was* he planning on sticking around? What could he possibly do tonight, now that everywhere was shut, and everyone else had gone home?

"I won't be long," Logan said. "Just want to, you know."

Ben did know. Given the chance, he'd be sitting here with the DCI, sharing his current lack of purpose. How many nights had they done just that over the years? How many hours spent just thinking in the dark?

"Aye. Get home soon, though. Man your age needs your rest," Ben told him, heading for the door.

"You're a fine one to talk," Logan called after him. "You using your bus pass to get home, aye?"

"Thought I might cadge a lift with Meals on Wheels," Ben replied.

He stopped in the doorway, silhouetted against the light spilling in from the corridor beyond.

"You think we've got him, Jack?"

Logan rolled the response around in his mouth a few times, shaping it. Smoothing it. Sloane was a definite fit. He also had no alibi for last night. None that could be verified, at least.

And yet...

"I hope so, Ben," was all the DCI would commit to. "I really hope so."

"Aye, you and me both," Ben agreed. "But what's your gut instinct?"

"My gut instinct?" Logan exhaled. "My gut instinct doesn't matter. The evidence is leading us towards it being him. That's what matters."

Ben opened his mouth to say something, then changed his mind. "Goodnight, Jack," he said.

And with that, he slipped out into the corridor and closed the door, and the Incident Room was swallowed by the darkness once more.

THE MAIN ENTRANCE to Logan's block of flats was supposed to lock, but the condition of the door suggested it hadn't done for quite a number of years.

Logan shoved it open, plodded through the close, and was about to start up the stairs when he heard the sob. It was soft and muffled, like it was deliberately being stifled.

He found her around the other side of the stone staircase, tucked in between it and the close's back wall. She was sitting on the floor, her back jammed against the side of the steps, her face buried in her knees. The lassie from the flat on the floor below Logan's own. Damn it. What was her name again?

"Tanya?" Logan said, the name coming to him in a flash of inspiration. "You alright?"

She was a young woman, but hunched up there she looked like a child. The crack in her voice made her sound like it, too.

"Fine," she sniffed, not looking up. "Just leave me alone."

A part of Logan wanted to oblige. Quite a big part, actually. He'd much rather be putting his feet up in his flat than dealing with whatever he was about to be dealing with.

But that wasn't going to happen.

"Has something happened, Tanya? You can tell me," he said. His knees *cracked* as he dropped down onto his haunches in front of the crying woman.

He gave her a couple of moments to answer him, then pressed on with the obvious.

"Has he hurt you?"

Her voice was a squeak. A whisper. "It was my fault."

"I find that hard to believe," Logan said. "Look at me, Tanya. Let me see."

At first, it didn't look as if she'd heard him. Then, she sniffed a couple of times, pulling herself together, and slowly raised her head.

The first thing Logan saw was the blood. It had flowed freely from both nostrils, over her mouth, down her chin, and started to form rivulets on her neck. Evidently, that had been a little while ago, as it had all mostly dried into shades of dark crimson.

Her right eye had taken a clout. A hard one too, judging by the colour and size of the area around it. The eyes themselves were wide and worried. They darted anxiously across Logan's face, unable to settle on any one part.

"Jesus Christ," Logan muttered. "Listen to me, Tanya. This wasn't your fault, alright?"

"It was," she insisted, although there wasn't a lot of conviction behind it. "I could see he was angry. I shouldn't have kept on at him."

"I'm guessing he told you that," Logan said. "Listen to me, Tanya, I've seen this a lot of times before, and it's always the same story. This wasn't your fault, alright? This..." He glanced over her injuries. "...is *never* your fault."

"How... How have you seen it before?" she ventured.

Logan reached into his coat pocket and produced his warrant card. "Detective Chief Inspector Logan. Jack. I can get the bastard picked up within the next five minutes."

At the sight of the ID, Tanya's expression had become one of panic. "No. Shit. I don't want him lifted."

"He hit you, Tanya. More than once, by the looks of it. You can't go back in there," Logan insisted.

Tanya shook her head. "I don't want him lifted. I don't want to have to deal with all that. I just..."

She leaned her head back and looked up through the gap in the stairwell above. "I just want him out," she said, whispering it like she was terrified he might hear.

"I strongly suggest that I call this in, Tanya. We can get him taken away. If you give evidence, he'll do time for this. We can help make sure he never hurts you again."

Tanya didn't even waste a second considering it. She shook her head. "He'll go mental if he knows I spoke to the police. I don't want to go through all that. I just want him out."

Logan sighed. He'd seen this too many times before. He knew how it ended.

"You sure you don't want me to call it in?"

Tanya nodded. "Aye," she said. "I'm sure."

"Right. Your call. Do you have keys?" Logan asked.

"I left them in the flat."

"OK. What's his name?"

"Bud."

Logan frowned. "Bud? What's that short for?"

"Nothing. Just Bud."

Logan pulled a face that suggested he didn't approve. Then, he stood up, took off his coat, and draped it over her. "Here. Hang onto this for now. It's cold."

She watched him as he headed for the stairs and climbed the first few steps.

"What are you going to do?" she asked.

Logan stopped. "I'm going to get him out."

Tanya squeezed herself into the corner between the stairs and the wall. "I don't want him to see me."

Logan hesitated, then clicked his tongue against the roof of his mouth. "I'll see what I can do."

CHAPTER TWENTY-FOUR

THE DOOR OPENED AFTER THE FOURTH ROUND OF hammering. Bud pulled it wide with a sudden yank, his scowl appearing in the space the door had previously occupied.

"What the fuck do you—" he began, then he stumbled back as Logan pushed past him into the hallway.

The place reeked of old rubbish and cannabis. An overflowing bin and a couple of loosely tied black bags met Logan as he diverted off the hallway and into the kitchen. The layout was the same as his own flat, albeit flipped around, so he had the advantage of knowing where everything was.

The stench of the rubbish was cloying in the kitchen. It got in about Logan's nostrils and reached down into his throat, almost triggering his gag reflex.

"The fuck do you think you're doing?" demanded the scrote from out in the hall.

"Bud, isn't it?" Logan asked, pulling open the door to the cupboard under the sink. There were a few cleaning products that he suspected had never been used, but not what he was after.

"I can fucking do you in for being in here," Bud snapped. "It's legal for me to do you right in."

"Is that a fact?" Logan asked him, pulling open another couple of cupboards. Pots and pans. Tinned food.

Not in those, either.

"Aye! Fucking right it is! So get out, or I'll—"

Logan spun, eyes blazing. "Or you'll what, son? Eh? Or you'll what?"

Bud's expression briefly changed to one of panic, but the sneer quickly returned. The step back he took was telling, though. Quick with his fists when he was up against a woman smaller than he was. Not so handy when a big burly bastard was staring him down.

"Aye, I thought so," Logan grunted. He turned back and was about to open another cupboard when he spotted a sausage of fabric hanging from a hook on the wall. A blue Co-op Bag For Life poked out of a hole at the bottom of it. "Aha! Here we are."

Logan took the crumpled bag from the dispenser. He straightened it out very slowly and very deliberately, maintaining eye contact with the scrote in the hall.

"I've been speaking to Tanya, Bud. She's in a real mess."

Bud shifted his weight from foot to foot. "Oh aye? And what shite has she been spilling, eh? She been talking shite about me again? Is that what she's—"

Logan put a finger to his lips. "Shh."

"Fucking *shh* me, ya old bastard!" Bud spat, finding some of his earlier venom. This pleased Logan immensely. He didn't want the man doubting himself. Much better to have him at his biggest and boldest for what was to follow, chest all puffed up, shoulders back like the cock of the walk.

"She wants you out of here, Bud. Tonight. Now."

"Oh, she does, does she? Is that so? Well she can suck—"

"*I* want you out, too. We chatted about it. Came to a wee agreement between ourselves," Logan continued.

Bud snorted and looked the detective up and down. "What? So, you're here to chuck me out, are you?"

"Hmm? Oh, no. I'm here to ask you to leave. Nicely, like," Logan said. He took a step closer.

"And what if I tell you to go an' get fucked?" Bud asked.

The plastic bag *creaked* faintly as Logan stretched its corners out, returning it to its original shape.

"*Then* I chuck you out," Logan said. He smiled. There were a lot of teeth in that smile. "So, son, what's it to be? Your choice. You going to go quietly, or am I going to have to show you the door?"

Bud's breath became faster. Shorter. More urgent. His face twisted up in rage and he launched himself into the kitchen, one hand grabbing for the detective, the other drawing back as a fist.

Logan sidestepped the attack, turned, and caught Bud by the back of the head. There was a particularly solid-sounding *crunch* as the bridge of Bud's nose was introduced to the edge of the worktop.

There then followed a moment of silence while Bud tried to work out what had just happened.

And then, the screaming started.

"Ma nobe! Ma fuckin' nobe!" he wailed, blood choking him, slurring his words. "Ye boke ma fuckin' nobe!"

It was at this point that Logan pulled the bag over Bud's head, and clamped it in place around his neck with one hand.

"Right then, Buddy, my boy. Just remember, this could've gone a lot easier for you," Logan said. Beneath the bag, Bud had stopped screaming, and was now just rasping and wheezing in ever-increasing panic.

Logan leaned in closer and lowered his voice. "Although, personally? Between you and me? I'm glad you went for option two," he said. "You're going to leave Tanya alone, alright? If I hear you've come back here, or get the vaguest inkling that you've hurt her again, it'll no' just be your head in a bag, it'll be your whole body. That clear?"

The muffled noises from inside the bag were a little too non-committal for Logan's liking.

"Is that *clear*?" he demanded, giving Bud a shake.

"Aye! Aye, I get it!"

"Good," said Logan. "Right. Out we go."

"I've got no shoes on," Bud pointed out.

Logan looked down. Sure enough, Bud stood in a pair of socks that were actually nothing of the sort. One was a dirty grey, the other navy blue with a hole at the big toe.

"Oh. Neither you do," Logan said. He shoved Bud out of the kitchen, banging him into the wall across from the door. "That's unfortunate."

Bud tried to resist as Logan huckled him along the corridor and out the door, but Logan had twenty years experience of dealing with jumped-up wee arseholes just like him and had no difficulty keeping him in line.

"Haw! Assault! This is fucking assault!" Bud wailed. Logan half-guided, half-shoved him down the stone steps leading down into the close. "I'll have you in the fucking jail for this," the scrote protested.

"Good luck with that," Logan told him, pushing him down the last couple of steps.

Tanya was peeking out from around the side of the stairs when Bud stumbled onto solid ground. He reached for the bag over his head, but Logan's hand clamped around his neck, pinning the bag in place.

"Oh no, you don't," Logan told him, manhandling him towards the door. He hauled it open with his free hand, and a swirl of cold night air blew in around both men.

"Look, I'm fucking sorry, alright?" Bud wailed. "I'm sorry."

"That's good. I'll be sure to pass that on," Logan told him. With a final shove, he sent him sprawling down the two steps that led to the block's front door.

Bud yelped in fright as, still blinded, he lost his balance and clattered onto the rough surface of the pavement.

"Ah! Fuck! Jesus!" he howled, tucking a skinned hand in under his armpit. Wrestling free of the bag, he tossed it aside and got to his feet, his eyes locked on Logan. "You can't do this. You can't just chuck me out of my own fucking—"

"Littering," Logan intoned.

That stopped Bud in his tracks. He blinked his eyes, which were already turning a shade of purple-black. Blood was smeared across his face, and dripped from the end of his chin.

"What?"

Logan pointed to the bag. "Littering," he said again. "Pick it up."

"I'm no' picking it—"

Logan stepped onto the first of the stone stairs.

"Alright. Fuck's sake. There," Bud said, snatching up the bag.

"Good." Logan pointed past him, along the street. "Now, off you go. You can phone Tanya tomorrow to arrange picking up your stuff at a time that's mutually convenient for all three of us."

Bud looked around him. Several of the streetlights were out along the road, and the place was in half-darkness. The sky was a void of black, cloud cover blocking out the moon and stars.

"Where am I meant to go?" Bud asked.

"Hmm. That is a poser," Logan said. He stroked his chin for a moment, then clicked his fingers. "Wait!" he said. He smiled. "I couldn't care less."

His smile fell away, his face becoming sombre, his eyes blazing anger. "But wherever you're going, I'd make it quick, son, before I lose my temper."

Bud bounced from sock to sock. The fingers of his free hand—the one that wasn't currently holding a Co-op Bag For Life—curled into a fist.

"You've no' heard the end of this," he warned.

Logan advanced to the next step down. Bud darted back like a startled animal, eyes wide and panicking.

"You've no' heard the fucking end of this!" he called again, then he turned and hobbled off along the street, only glancing back when the front door of the flats closed with a final, definitive *clunk.*

Tanya was standing at the foot of the stairs when Logan returned to the close. She held his coat out to him with her head down. Her eyes flitted to his for a second or two at a time, before looking away again.

"Thanks," Logan said, taking the coat.

"You know you've got a packet of sausages in your pocket?" Tanya asked.

"Aye. Want them?" Logan asked.

Tanya shook her head. "No."

"No. Can't say I'm overly enamoured with the idea of them myself," Logan said. He noticed the anxious look she shot at the door. "You'll be fine. He won't be back tonight. Keep the door locked though, and if he does come back I'll hear him."

"You knew, didn't you?" Tanya asked. "That he was..."

"An arsehole? Oh aye. Clocked that right away," Logan said.

Tanya smiled, showing the blood on her teeth. "You've got good instincts."

Logan hesitated, just for a moment. "Aye. I suppose I do," he said, then he ushered her up the stairs. "Come on. We'll get you cleaned up."

"It's... I'll be fine," Tanya said, as they made their way up the stairs together. "It just washes off."

Just washes off. Not the first time it had happened, then.

"Are you sure?" Logan asked. "I don't mind helping. I've cleaned up a few injuries in my time."

Tanya glanced at the swollen cut on Logan's forehead. "So I see."

Logan dabbed at the site of his injury. "One of the perks of the job," he said.

They stopped outside the door to Tanya's flat, which still stood open. "Right, well... Thanks," she said. "And sorry I dragged you—"

"Not your fault," Logan said, shutting the apology down. He nodded up the next flight of steps. "I'm just upstairs, alright? In fact..."

He fished in his pocket until he found a business card. "Mobile's on there."

Tanya looked at the card like it might explode in her hand, then carefully took it from him. She turned it over a couple of times, looking at the words but not necessarily reading them. "Thanks. Mr...?"

"Logan. It's on the card."

Tanya gave a dry little laugh. "Oh. Yeah. DCI Logan. Thanks."

"No bother," said Logan. He made it to the next step before stopping. "And please, call me Jack," he told her. "We're neighbours, after all."

LOGAN FLOPPED down onto the couch, his coat still hooked over his arm. He breathed out properly for what felt like the first time that day.

It hadn't been as productive a day as he'd been hoping for. Aye, they had a suspect in custody, but they had nothing concrete on him, nothing that connected him to Esme Miller's murder beyond an over-developed 'fight or flight' response and an attitude that was likely to earn him a slap in the not too distant future.

Maybe a search of Sloane's house would turn up something in the morning. Or maybe a night in the cells would soften him up a bit and make him confess to the whole thing.

"Aye," Logan mumbled into the darkness. "Maybe."

He fished in the pocket of his coat and pulled out a neatly wrapped, but slightly battered, bundle of sausages. Opening the pack, he gave them a tentative sniff. You could smell the Irn Bru, right enough. He prodded one warily, like it might spring into life at any moment and go for his throat.

"*You've got good instincts,*" he mumbled.

Then, he snorted, wrapped the paper around the bangers, and lobbed the whole thing into the waste paper basket on the other side of the room.

CHAPTER TWENTY-FIVE

"Did you see what they did?" asked Tyler. He unwrapped the bag of chips, and the smell expanded to fill the whole of the bus stop.

Big fat drops of rain *plunked* against the clear Perspex roof, and an insistent October wind swirled in through the gap at the bottom of the walls, rolling an empty Coke can back and forth across the uneven concrete base.

Sinead plucked a chip from the pile and blew on it. "No," she said. "What did they do?"

"Salt, then vinegar," Tyler said. He held up a little wooden trident. "Want a fork?"

Sinead shook her head. "No, you're fine," she said. "And what's the problem? You asked for salt and vinegar."

"Aye, but not in that order," Tyler told her. "You don't go salt then vinegar, you go vinegar then salt."

Sinead popped the chip in her mouth, spent a few seconds inhaling to try to cool it down a bit, then replied.

"Why?"

"What do you mean 'why?' Because if you go salt then vinegar, the vinegar washes the salt off, doesn't it?"

"Does it?" Sinead asked, helping herself to another chip.

"Yes! Obviously! Why wouldn't it? It's just, I don't know, physics," Tyler told her. "You go vinegar first, *then* salt. That way, the salt sticks to the vinegar."

Sinead nodded slowly, contemplating this while she chewed. "You should go back in and mansplain that to her. I'm sure she'd thank you for pointing out how she's doing it wrong."

"Good thinking," said Tyler. He took a step towards the opening in the side of the bus stop. Sinead laughed and caught him by the arm. He looked at her, wide-eyed and innocent. "What? You said I should go and tell her."

"Just shut up and give us another chip," Sinead grinned.

"You said you didn't want any!" Tyler protested, but he held the tray out to her, anyway.

"I said I didn't want my own bag. Totally eating yours, though."

"I noticed."

They stood in silence for a while, shoulder to shoulder, eating chips and gazing out at the rain. The bus stop was just a dozen or so yards from Sinead's front gate, on the other side of the street. The curtains were drawn, but there was a light on in the living room and in one of the rooms upstairs.

"Looks like your brother's in bed," Tyler ventured. "That's his room, right?"

"What gave it away?" Sinead asked.

"What can I say? I've got the detective skills," Tyler said. He gestured to the upstairs curtains with a nod. "Also, I didn't have you down as an Iron Man fan."

"Well, you'd be wrong," Sinead said.

Tyler side-eyed her. "What? That's your bedroom?"

"No, you're right about that. That's Harris's room," Sinead said. "But I *am* an Iron Man fan."

"Ah. Gotcha."

"Don't feel inferior, though," Sinead teased.

Tyler shook his head. "I wasn't."

"I mean, he is a billionaire genius superhero..."

"He didn't buy you chips, though, did he?" Tyler pointed out.

Sinead laughed. He had her there.

"True."

She helped herself to another. They were cooling down a bit now, so she didn't have to spend so long blowing on them before she could eat them.

"He didn't used to sleep with the light on," she announced, almost absentmindedly. "It's just since..."

"Your mum and dad?"

Sinead nodded, but said nothing.

"Hardly surprising, really, is it?" Tyler said. "It must've been a shock. For both of you, I mean."

Sinead continued to nod, staring straight ahead. It had been just over a year since the accident that had claimed the lives of her parents. The call had come in while she'd been down Glencoe direction with the speed gun: *Road traffic accident. Assistance required.*

She'd fired up the sirens. Rushed to the scene. She recognised the car as soon as it came into view. The make and model, anyway. Same colour, too.

Her heart had immediately plunged into the swirling morass that her stomach had become. Her legs were heavy, leaden, as she got out of the car and made her way past the line of stationary traffic.

And yet, she didn't believe it was them. Not then. Not at first.

It was only when she spotted the *Dogs Trust* sticker in the back window that the reality of it started to creep in.

And then, when she saw her dad's glasses on the ground, one lens smashed, one leg missing, the horrible, unavoidable truth of it had hit her.

She'd wanted to cry, to scream, to drop to her knees.

But she was polis. And she'd had a job to do.

"You alright?" Tyler asked.

Sinead smiled a little too brightly. "Fine. Aye. Fine."

She took another chip and bit the end off, but she'd lost the taste for them now.

"I should head in. The babysitter needs to get off."

Tyler glanced down at the still mostly full bag of chips. "Oh. Right. Aye," he said. He took a quick breath, then went for broke. "I could... I could come in with you. If you like."

He could tell right away that she wasn't keen on the idea.

"Not to... I don't mean... Just... the chips," he added, abandoning a selection of different statements, then finishing by pointing at the bag in his hand. "There's loads left."

"I'm not sure it's a good idea," Sinead told him.

It was her turn to note the change in his expression.

"I want to. I want you to," she said. "It's just Harris. He's still settling in. I'm not sure... I don't want him getting to know you and getting attached if this isn't... In case we aren't..."

She smiled weakly. "You know?"

Tyler folded the paper around the tray of chips. "I mean, he would get attached, obviously. Because I'm awesome."

Sinead laughed, then wrinkled her nose up. "At best, I think he'd tolerate you."

"*Tolerate me*?"

"Barely."

Tyler smiled. It wasn't really a smile of amusement, but one that said he understood. He didn't like it, but he understood.

"Well. We'll just have to put it to the test one day."

"One day," Sinead confirmed. "And you'll be at the birthday party. You'll get to meet him then."

"Is it weird that I'm actually nervous?" Tyler asked, then he stepped back in surprise when Sinead stepped in close and kissed him on the lips.

They stood like that for a moment, together, lips locked, the rain pummelling the Perspex above them.

And then, Sinead stepped back, blushing slightly as she pulled her jacket around herself.

"You squashed my chips," Tyler told her.

Sinead flashed him a smile. "I'll make it up to you," she said.

Then, she pulled up her hood, stepped out of the bus stop, and hurried across the road.

"Goodnight!" Tyler called after her. She waved as she threw open the front gate, and then she was up the path and inside the house.

Tyler leaned out of the bus stop just enough to be able to look in both directions along the road.

"Right, then," he said to himself. He fished a squashed chip from the bag and popped it in his mouth. "Where the hell did I park the car?"

CHAPTER TWENTY-SIX

Detective Superintendent Bob Hoon peered at Logan and Ben Forde from behind his clasped hands. Logan was well aware of the trick. Keep your fingers locked together and you were more able to resist the urge to throttle whatever daft bastard had positioned themselves within grabbing distance. It was an age-old technique, and Logan found himself doing the same thing these days whenever DC Neish walked into the room.

"You're aware I've got the high heid yins breathing down my neck on this case, gentlemen, yes?" Hoon asked. "You understand the position I'm in?"

Ben waited for Logan to answer. When the DCI didn't, he jumped in himself.

"We do, sir," Ben confirmed.

"Then maybe you'll explain to me why we haven't fucking charged this Sloane character," Hoon barked. He squeezed his fingers together as he eyeballed both detectives.

"We don't have enough to charge him yet," Ben ventured.

"Oh, I know. I know that all too fucking well, Benjamin. I

looked at the interview report once I'd finally got HOLMES to stop being a pain in the arse, and it looks like you've got a whole lot of fuck all on him at the moment, besides the fact he clouted this useless bastard, and gave a Uniform a run for her money."

Ben glanced at Logan, expecting to see the DCI swallowing back his anger, but there was a slightly distant look on Logan's face, like his mind was elsewhere.

"We're working on it, sir," Ben said. "We've got Forensics going into his house this morning, and we've already seized the knives from the butcher's where he works. Pathology is going to compare them with the victim's injuries and see if we get a match. We plan on continuing the interview today. We're hopeful of a confession."

"He won't confess."

All eyes went to Logan.

"And why the fuck not?" Hoon demanded.

"Because he didn't do it."

Ben, who had been looking sideways at Logan, now turned to face him. "Eh?"

"I don't think he did it," Logan said.

"What, the rape or the murder?" Ben asked.

"Either. I don't think it was him."

Hoon and Ben both opened their mouths.

"I can't say why. I don't know, exactly. It's just... my instinct," Logan told them. "Just a hunch."

"A hunch? A fucking hunch?" Hoon scoffed. "You know what you can do with your fucking hunch?" He pointed to Ben. "Shove it up his arse and call him Quasimodo."

Ben looked taken aback, not quite sure why he'd been dragged into this.

Hoon shook his head in disbelief. "A fucking *hunch*, he fucking says."

Until he'd met Bob Hoon, Logan had thought of himself as someone for whom swearing played a large part of his daily vocabulary. Two minutes with Hoon though, had made him realise that his language was positively genteel by comparison.

He listened to a prolonged outburst of profanity while he waited for the DSup to stop ranting. Surprisingly, it didn't take too long.

All three men in the room had moved through the ranks of Police Scotland precisely because they had good instincts and knew when to trust them. A hunch could be mocked. A hunch could be derided, even. But all three of them knew from experience that a hunch should never be completely ignored.

"And does this hunch of yours happen to tell you who *did* do it?" asked Hoon, his voice gruff like he was grudging every word.

"Unfortunately, it does not, no."

"Oh. Well, surprise sur-fucking-prise," Hoon muttered.

He flexed his fingers for a few seconds, then went right back to squashing them together until the knuckles turned white.

"Well, let's not rule out Sloane yet. Keep on him. Follow through with the search. Drag him through the fucking bushes and see if you can get him to talk. Hunch or no fucking hunch. He ran for a reason. I want to fucking know what that fucking reason was. Got it?"

"Got it, sir," Ben confirmed.

Logan nodded. "Aye."

"And if it isn't him?" Ben asked.

"Then fuck me, you'd better find another fucking suspect quick smart, or a whole lot of shite is going to land on me from on high," Hoon said. He leaned closer, his eyes bulging with barely contained rage. "And gravity will not be kind to those below me, gentlemen. Is that clear? Gravity will not be fucking kind."

BEN WAITED until they were back in the Incident Room before saying anything.

"Jack. Can I get a wee word in your office?" he said.

Around the room, DS McQuarrie glanced over from the Big Board, and DCs Neish and Khaled both raised their eyes from their respective screens. When they saw Logan clocking this, they all quickly got back to what they'd been doing.

"After you," Logan said.

Inside the office, Ben closed the door. His face was creased in confusion, and Logan knew what he was going to say before he'd opened his mouth.

"I can't explain it, exactly," Logan said. "Like I said, it's just a feeling."

"A feeling? The man attacked you, Jack. And that lassie from Uniform. He has no alibi. We can connect him to the victims in both cases. He's clearly an unpleasant bastard..."

"I'm not arguing with any of that, Ben," Logan replied. He half-sat on the edge of the desk, crossed his arms, and looked down at his shoes. "Logically, he's our best bet, and we'll stay on him for now. It's just... I don't feel it. Talking to him last night... I don't feel it. My instincts are usually pretty sound, and they're telling me we're barking up the wrong tree with Sloane."

Ben sighed sharply. "I don't agree," he said. "I think your instincts are wrong on this one, Jack. I think he did it."

"I hope you're right. I really do. We've got bugger all else to go on," Logan said. He shot his old friend a smile. It was thin and weary, and barely qualified as a smile at all. "Maybe I am wrong. Maybe we'll find something in the house."

"A written confession would be nice."

"That'd be lovely, aye," Logan agreed. He stood. "Forensics in yet?"

"They were headed in about twenty minutes ago. Be a few hours, then we can go in," Ben said.

"Good. I'm going to swing round and see Kel Conlyn. Why don't you take Caitlyn in to interview Sloane? See how he responds to a woman's touch," Logan suggested. He glanced out through the office window at the Incident Room beyond. "What's Hamza working on?"

"HOLMES is back up and running this morning. He's loading everything up."

"Right. Looks like I'm taking Tyler with me to visit Conlyn, then."

Ben patted the DCI on the shoulder. "You have my condolences."

"I appreciate that," Logan said. He pulled open the door and raised his voice to a shout. "Detective Constable Neish!"

Tyler's head popped up from behind his computer monitor, looking worried. "Yes, boss?"

"Get your jacket," Logan told him. "We're making a house call."

"I MEAN, I get it, boss. I do. It makes total sense. It's early days, and everything. You know, relationship-wise. It's just, I can't help but feel like she's shutting me out, you know what I mean? Don't get me wrong—"

Logan put a finger to his lips as he and DC Neish approached Kel Conlyn's front door. "*Shh*," he said, with some urgency.

Tyler's eyes went to the building ahead of them. His voice dropped to a whisper.

"What is it?"

"Nothing," Logan told him. "I just wanted you to stop talking."

"Oh. Right," Tyler said. He blinked, which seemed to erase the last couple of seconds from his memory. "It's just, I like her. You know? And I think she likes me. And I *totally* get what she means about not wanting to mess her wee brother around, but—"

Logan stopped. His heels crunched on the pavement as he pulled a crisp about-turn. "What is it you want me to say, son?"

Tyler's mouth flapped open and closed. "Um, I don't know. Just, like... What do you think I should do?"

"I think you should do whatever she tells you to do," Logan said. "You're punching way above your weight with Sinead. Way above your weight. You want my advice? Keep your mouth shut, do as you're told, and try no' to make an arse of it."

He turned to move on, then stopped.

"And that goes for any woman, by the way. That's across the board advice. Mouth shut, do as you're told, thank your lucky stars, and try no' to fuck it up. Alright?"

Tyler swallowed. "Right."

"Good. Now, if you don't mind, I was about to investigate a murder. Are you going to join me, or are you going to stand here whinging about your love life?"

There was a moment's pause while Tyler cleared his throat.

"Lead the way, boss."

"Thank you," Logan said.

He led the junior officer up the path that led to Kel Conlyn's front door, waited for him to catch up, then rang the doorbell.

They waited. Tyler clicked his fingers and hummed quietly beneath his breath.

After twenty seconds or so, the DC reached for the doorbell again.

"Be patient," Logan told him. He waited for Tyler to step back into line beside him before continuing. "You can't rush some things. They take time. Aye, it's a pain in the arse, but that's just the way it is. You wait. You be patient."

Tyler looked from Logan to the bell and back again. He was about to repeat this process when the penny dropped. "Wait, you're not talking about the doorbell, are you, boss?" he asked.

Before Logan could confirm or deny that, the front door opened. Kel Conlyn appeared in the gap, bleary-eyed and half asleep. "Yes?" he asked, then recognition flitted across his face. "Sorry."

He wedged the heel of his hand into his eye socket and rubbed, then yawned. "Sorry," he said again. "Late night. Um..."

Kel pointed a finger at the older detective. "Jack?"

"Aye, that's me. This is DC Tyler Neish."

"Alright?" said Tyler.

Kel gave the DC a quick once-over, then straightened, suddenly a little more awake.

"Hi there," he said, pulling together a smile.

"We're sorry to disturb you, Mr Conlyn, but we were hoping we could ask you a few quick questions," Logan said.

A couple of faint creases formed on Kel's otherwise smooth forehead as he tore his eyes from Tyler. "Is it about Dr Fletcher? Did you talk to him?" He put a hand on his chest. "It wasn't him, was it? God, did he do it? Did he kill Esme?"

"No, it's not about Dr Fletcher," Logan said. "It's about someone else you worked with. A while back. A Donald Sloane."

Something changed in the lines of Kel's face. "Oh. Him," he said. He looked past them at the street beyond, glancing surreptitiously this way and that, like he was afraid someone might see.

Finally, he held open the front door.

"In that case, you'd best come in."

The detectives' shoes *clunked* on the bare floorboards as they stepped inside. Tyler squeezed in behind Logan, knocking over a small pile of unopened letters just by the door, scattering them.

"Shite, sorry," he said, bending to pick them up.

"It's fine," Kel said, waving a hand. "I think they must be for the last person who lived here. I keep meaning to hand them in at the post office."

Tyler finished restacking the letters, tucked them in next to the wall, then followed the other two men down the hall and into the not-yet-a-living-room. Logan had seen it before, of course, but Tyler spent a few seconds taking in the absence of... well, anything, before commenting.

"Nice place," he said. "You been watching that woman on Netflix?"

"What woman?" Kel asked.

"The tidying woman. Always on about decluttering and sparking joy, or whatever."

Kel's mouth became a lop-sided smile that suggested he had absolutely no idea what the DC was on about. "I don't have Netflix," he pointed out. "Or a telly."

Tyler looked around again, confirming this. "Right."

"Yet!" Kel said. "It's on the list. Maybe in a month or two."

"Well, you should check that show out," Tyler said. "I mean, it's all about getting rid of stuff, so I suppose you'd kind of be coming at it from the opposite direction." He shrugged. "It's good, though."

"Thanks for the hot tip," Kel said, just a little salaciously. He turned to Logan. "So, what is it you want to know about Donald?"

Logan shot Tyler a look. The DC reached into his pocket and produced a notebook.

"Anything you can tell us, Mr Conlyn," Logan said. "Anything at all."

CHAPTER TWENTY-SEVEN

LOGAN STOOD IN THE GARDEN OF DONALD SLOANE'S rented house, watching the white paper suits come filing out, and waiting for the all-clear to be given for him to go in.

Technically, he could've gone in any time he liked, but if there was evidence to be found in there he didn't want to be the one to jeopardise it. Better to let the experts handle it.

Besides, he wasn't expecting them to find much, if anything, so the usual driving urge to stick his nose in wasn't there.

A cordon had been set up around the house to keep the press and the Nosy Parkers at bay. There hadn't been a big media response to the murder, which Logan was pleased about. The last thing he needed was half of Fleet Street coming up here and making the place look untidy.

Still, there was a small knot of the bastards gathered just on the other side of the cordon tape. Logan had been asked for a statement on his way past but had managed to resist giving them the two-word one that had immediately sprung to mind.

While he waited for Forensics to finish clearing the scene, he went over the conversation he and Tyler had with Kel Conlyn. It had been enlightening in some ways, but disappointing in others. Despite his misgivings about Sloane's guilt, or lack thereof, Logan had been hoping for Conlyn to drop some big bombshell.

Oh aye, he hated Esme's guts, would've been nice.

Always said he was going to kill her someday, would have been nicer still.

But no. Conlyn could offer very little about Sloane that they didn't already know, aside from one detail that had taken both detectives by surprise.

Logan had phoned it in when they'd left Conlyn's house. He'd spoken to Ben directly, in case the information could turn out to be useful.

"Sleeping together?" Ben had said, lowering his voice to a whisper like he was worried about offending someone. "Sloane and Esme?"

"No, ye div," Logan had replied. "Sloane and Conlyn. It was a fling, by all accounts, on-off. Only lasted a couple of weeks, if that. But aye. They were at it."

The line had gone silent for a few moments while Ben contemplated this. "What does that change? Does it change anything?" he'd asked.

"I'm not sure. Doesn't count him out for the rape. That's about power, it's not necessarily even a sexual thing," Logan replied. "But... I don't know. Worth bringing up with him, anyway."

Ben had agreed on that and promised to keep Logan updated of anything that came out of the interview. Sloane's solicitor had finally graced them with his presence, so Ben and DS McQuarrie were about to head in to give Sloane another grilling.

"I'll feed through on anything we find here," Logan told him, and then both men had hung up without bothering to say any goodbyes.

Logan checked his watch. Almost noon. They wouldn't be able to hold Sloane much longer without charging him. Fortunately, they had a couple of counts of assault they could hold him on, which would buy them a bit more time.

He watched the door as another guy in a paper suit emerged, carrying a cardboard box full of computer equipment. Even with the mask over his mouth and the elasticated hood pulled over his head, Logan recognised Geoff Palmer.

"Any news?" Logan asked, intercepting Palmer halfway up the path.

"Nothing obvious. If you're looking for a blood-stained dagger or a written confession then I'm afraid you're out of luck."

He gave the box a shake, juddering the contents. "Found a few computer hard drives, though. We'll go through those. We've also taken prints and swabs, but I doubt anything will come out of them."

Palmer tilted his head back in the direction of the door. "He's got a lot of swords and stuff in there, but they're all ornamental. Nothing that could've been used in the attack, from what I hear of the body."

"Great," said Logan, drawing a hand down his face. "Well, do what you can."

"Why wouldn't I?"

Logan's eyes narrowed. "Eh?"

"Why wouldn't I do what I can? What, you think I was just going to go back to the office and put my feet up? I do know how to do my job, you know."

Logan was reminded again why he disliked the man so much.

"Aye. Fine. Whatever you say, Geoff."

Palmer gave a self-satisfied little nod, like he'd just won the engagement, then continued on past Logan up the path.

Now that the Scene of Crime team had done their sweep, it was Logan's turn. Anything of any potential forensic value would've been bagged up and removed, but he squashed his hands into a pair of vinyl gloves, just in case.

A poster of a wolf greeted him as he entered the hallway. It was pinned to the wall across from the door, its silver-blue eyes fixed hungrily on anyone who dared enter its lair. On the floor below it was a black metal rack filled with DVDs. Arnold Schwarzenegger featured heavily in at least half a dozen of them, and they were all coated with a layer of dust that suggested Sloane had either lost his appetite for 80s action movies or had long-since made the switch to digital.

The door to the left of the poster led into a small, drably decorated living room. Another poster adorned the breast of a chimney, the hearth of which had been bricked up and plastered over. This one showed a blue-green dragon blasting a jet of fire from its cavernous throat. It was well done. Logan wouldn't have given it house room himself, obviously, but from a technical point of view, it was an accomplished piece of art.

There were a few bits and pieces on the other walls. A framed film cell from *Die Hard With a Vengeance*. A black and white poster of a topless Bruce Lee. A signed photograph of *Star Wars* actress, Carrie Fisher, forever preserved behind a sheet of glass.

That sort of thing.

The main attraction was saved for the wall across from the old chimney. It had been adorned with a dozen or more

Samurai swords in sheaths, as well as a couple of battle axes, a claymore, and something so ludicrously spiky and multi-bladed that it could only have come from *Star Trek* or some other sci-fi nonsense.

Logan checked the blades on a few of the weapons. Just as Palmer had said, they were blunt. Far too blunt. The only way they were being used to kill someone was as a bludgeon.

The rest of the living room offered very little of interest, so Logan returned to the hall. He had just opened a door into the kitchen when his phone rang.

He fished it from his pocket and checked the screen. Ben Forde. He felt his heart skip a beat. A breakthrough, maybe? A confession?

Tapping the screen, Logan brought the phone to his ear.

"Ben. What have we—"

The phone continued to ring. Muttering, Logan pulled off one of the gloves, tapped the green phone icon, and tried again.

"Hello? Ben?"

"Jack," Ben said. Logan knew immediately that there had been a development. It was there in just that one word. Something had happened.

And nothing good.

"Aye. What's the news?"

"There's been another one," Ben told him. "There's been another murder."

CHAPTER TWENTY-EIGHT

LOGAN STOPPED AT THE EDGE OF THE CORDON AND FLASHED his warrant card at one of the Uniforms standing guard. With a nod, the officer stepped aside, and the DCI ducked under the tape.

"Ben. What have we got?" Logan asked, slightly breathless after the hike up the ramp of the multi-storey car park. No tent had been set up yet, but then, as far as Logan could tell there was no body to be seen.

Ben's face was grey and drawn. Logan knew then that there most definitely was a body, and could hazard a guess as to its condition.

"Call came in from a member of the public," Ben intoned.

"Where's the victim?" Logan asked, glancing around.

Ben indicated two parked cars—a big Range Rover and a smaller Kia. "Between those two," he said. "Palmer's team is on the way. They had to drop everything from Sloane's at base. Can't risk cross-contamination."

Logan nodded slowly. "You've had a look," he said. It wasn't a question.

"I did," Ben confirmed.

"And?"

"It's him, alright," Ben said. "Same M.O. 'Fake' carved right into her. Across the belly this time."

"Recent?" Logan asked.

"Recent enough that it couldn't have been Sloane," Ben said. He puffed out his cheeks. "Looks like I was wrong and your instincts were right, Jack."

"Aye. Looks like it," said Logan, although there was no victory in it. "Palmer say how long it'd be until he got here?"

"He said he'd be about twenty minutes. That was ten minutes ago, maybe."

Logan shifted his weight from foot to foot and scratched thoughtfully at his chin. "Right. We got any shoe covers? I'm going to take a look."

Ben looked sceptical. "You think that's a good idea?"

"I'm not going to touch anything," Logan assured him. "I just want a look."

That was far from the truth, in fact. The last thing he wanted to do was look.

But he was going to. He had to. And that was that.

"Here. But don't say you got them from me," Ben told him, handing over the blue slip-on covers.

Logan pulled them on, took another pair of gloves from his pocket, then nodded in the direction of the two parked cars. "You coming?"

"Once is quite enough for me, thanks," Ben told him.

Logan pulled on the gloves as he approached the cars. The smell of death started to creep in while he was still ten yards away. Clawing. Pungent. Metallic.

When he was five yards away, he knelt down and looked

beneath the Range Rover. A face stared back at him through the gap, eyes wide, mouth taped, life extinguished.

Logan glanced along the underside of the car, searching for anything of interest but finding nothing. Standing, he made his way around the big four-by-four, keeping a calculated distance from it and anything else that might harbour evidence.

The victim lay on her back in a state of semi-undress. Her blouse had been torn open, one side of her bra pushed up to reveal a pale breast. There was a patina of dried blood across her stomach, the letters F A K E standing out on her skin like she'd been branded with them.

Her skirt had been pushed up. Her underwear pulled down.

Pinpricks, like little jolts of electricity, crawled across Logan's scalp. His gloves *creaked* as his fingers curled into fists.

He wanted to look away, turn away, *run* away. But he forced himself to keep looking. Forced his brain to fight the impulse to block out the horror and concentrate—*fucking concentrate*—on what had happened here.

The wounds on her stomach weren't deep, but there was a lot of blood on her clothing and pooled on the concrete floor. It flooded under the cars, mostly the smaller one on Logan's right. A set of keys lay in the pool, a Kia badge emblazoned across one of the two keyrings.

The other keyring was a square of clear plastic containing a photograph—a woman, a man, two children, all sipping milkshakes in some café somewhere. Abroad, probably. Relatively recently too, judging by the age of her in the photo. Late forties. Maybe a year or two either way.

Most of the blood seemed to have come from a neck wound. There was some arterial spray on the cars, but only low down. She'd been on the ground, then, when it had happened.

Presumably, after the assault, although part of him hoped she'd been killed first, for her sake.

The tape was thick and black. Were he to pull it off, Logan guessed he'd find a rag stuffed in her mouth, too. That was a job for someone else though, and he'd rarely been more grateful of anything in his life.

He was no expert when it came to time of death, and would leave that to Shona Maguire to determine. Six to eight hours, he guessed, judging by the signs of rigor mortis on the top half of the body. That would make it... what? Between 3am and 5am? Odd time for a single woman to be returning to her car.

"What's the opening hours of this place?" Logan called back to Ben.

"Twenty-four-seven," Ben replied from closer behind him than Logan had been expecting.

He turned to find the DI standing a few feet away, but using the bonnet of the Range Rover to block his view of the victim.

"Clarissa McDade," Ben continued. "Husband reported her missing in the early hours of this morning. She was on a night out with friends. He waited up but fell asleep on the couch. When he woke up and found out she wasn't home, he called it in."

The muscles in Logan's jaws flexed as he clenched and unclenched them. "Have we told him?"

"Not yet. We're waiting to see if we can pull any ID off the body first. Car registration matches, though. The Kia's hers," Ben said. "A team from Uniform's tracking down the friends she was out with to see if they can shed any light on her movements."

Logan raised an index finger and made a little circle motion, indicating the car park around them. "Cameras?"

"Forty-nine, according to the security guard."

A glimmer of hope. A spark.

"That's something."

"Afraid not," Ben sighed.

Logan tore his eyes away from the body of Clarissa McDade. "Eh?"

"They all went down at just after midnight last night. Whole system crashed. It's been displaying gibberish all night."

"Shite!" Logan spat. "That can't be coincidence, can it?"

Ben shrugged. "That's one for the tech boys to figure out. But if it's not—if some bastard somehow brought the cameras down so he could do... this, then..." He shrugged for a second time. "I don't know what we're dealing with. It was all computer numbers, apparently."

Logan raised a questioning eyebrow. "Computer numbers?"

"Aye."

"What are computer numbers?"

Ben shifted awkwardly, like he'd been hoping the DCI wasn't going to pursue this particular line of questioning. "Oh, I don't know. One of the staff here told me. Ones and zeroes."

"You mean binary?"

"Aye. That's it," Ben confirmed. "Computer numbers."

Logan glanced around until he spotted a camera, briefly contemplated the significance of them all going down at the same time, then turned his attention back to the body.

He offered up the same silent promise he'd made to all those countless other victims he'd found himself looking down on over the years, then turned and headed back for the cordon, and the growing knot of people there.

Palmer and his team were just ducking under the tape when Logan reached it.

"I hope you weren't poking around over there, Jack," Palmer scolded. "You know the procedure."

Logan's already clenched fists became tighter. A clearing of Ben's throat behind him made him see sense before he could say or do anything stupid.

"She's all yours," Logan said.

"Oh, well, *thank you*," said Palmer, giving a little bow. "It's very kind of you to—"

"Just get it done, Geoff," Logan hissed. He stabbed a finger past Palmer's head, his hand coming so close that Palmer flinched. "Go do what you need to do so we can cover that woman up and give her some dignity. No smart-arse comments, no snidey remarks, just get on with it. Alright?"

Judging by his body language, Palmer briefly considered arguing, but the look on Logan's face was a thunderstorm waiting to break and he rapidly thought better of it.

"Feel better for that?" Ben asked, as they both watched Palmer scuttle off to join the rest of his team.

"Well, I'm not sure I could feel any worse," Logan said. "So, the only way is up, eh?"

"Fingers crossed," Ben said. He had his notebook out and was flipping to a page he'd marked with the pad's elastic strap. "Couple of things that might be of interest with regards our victim."

"Go on."

"First up, I mentioned she was on a night out."

"Right."

"I didn't say where. Osmosis. The nightclub owned by—"

"Shaun Gillespie," said Logan.

"Brother of Danni, the first victim," Ben confirmed. "A

substantial stake in which was recently acquired on behalf of one Bosco Maximuke."

Logan's head snapped around. His eyes widened, then narrowed in one smooth movement. "Bosco co-owns the club?"

"Well, technically it's one of his guys who co-owns it, but it doesn't take a genius to see through that."

"No," Logan agreed. "Interesting. What else?"

"OK. Number two. Brace yourself," Ben said.

Over by the cordon tape, a couple of eager-looking members of the press were straining to see past a growing line of uniformed officers. Logan opened his mouth to bark at them to clear off, but a Uniform sergeant wasted no time in doing it for him.

"Sorry, you were saying?" Logan asked, turning his attention back to Ben.

"I was about to say that Clarissa McDade worked in HR. You know, recruitment?"

"I know what HR is," Logan said. He pulled a disappointed face. "I'll be honest, Ben, the first one was more interesting."

"That's because I've no' reached the interesting part yet," Ben told him. He closed his notepad and rocked back on his heels. "Clarissa McDade worked at the HR department..."

He lowered his voice, partly so the press didn't hear, and partly—he hated to admit—for impact.

"...at Raigmore Hospital."

CHAPTER TWENTY-NINE

THINGS PROGRESSED THE WAY THESE THINGS DID. SLOWLY. Methodically. A shroud of sorrow draped over everyone and everything.

Orders were given. Officers were dispatched. Doors were knocked. The Rose Street area was mostly commercial though, so almost all of those doors belonged to businesses which had been shut at the time of the attack.

Logan himself went down and hammered on the door of Osmosis, which was right below the car park. As expected, nobody answered, so he put in a call back to the office and gave Caitlyn the task of tracking Shaun Gillespie down and getting any CCTV footage from the club's cameras.

"Will do, sir," Caitlyn said. "Hamza wants a quick word."

There was some rustling on the other end of the line. Logan stood outside the nightclub, his phone pressed to his ear. He watched a family of four come trotting out of the big toy shop across the road, both kids eagerly clutching carrier bags to their chests like they were the most precious things in the world.

"Hi, sir, it's Hamza," his unmistakeable Aberdonian accent completely negating the need for him to identify himself.

"Aye. Hello. What's up?" Logan asked.

"It was just to let you know, HOLMES is... Well, it's fucked, sir."

"It's always fucked," Logan pointed out. "There's rarely a day when it's unfucked."

"Not like this, sir," Hamza said. "The server team think it's a DoS attack."

"A what?"

"Denial of Service, sir. Looks like someone is deliberately trying to bring it down."

Logan grunted. This wasn't a first, either. He remembered a couple of other occasions when hackers or spammers or whatever the hell they called themselves had tried something similar. He didn't really understand the details or have any interest in finding out.

"I'm sure they're working on it," Logan said. He watched the toy shop family get into their car, then turned towards the car park entrance. "Now, Hamza, if there's nothing—"

"They are working on it, sir. But, well, I was thinking. The cameras at the car park."

Logan stopped. "What about them?"

"I spoke to the security team there on the phone about twenty minutes ago. The cameras are all on a LAN—Local Area Network. It's accessible from the web, but well-protected."

The impatience in Logan's voice was obvious. "Meaning what, Hamza?"

"Meaning someone hacked the system from outside the local area network, sir. Someone who knew what they were doing."

The penny dropped.

"And what, you think it's the same person who's attacking HOLMES?"

"Maybe, sir. Aye," Hamza said. "I mean, I don't know. It just seems like a coincidence. And it might be. It's just—"

"Find out what you can," Logan told him. "Talk to the HOLMES team. See if they can tell you anything."

"I think they've got their hands full at the minute, sir, but I'll see what I can do," Hamza said. "I just thought you should know."

"Good. Thanks. Is that all?"

Hamza confirmed that it was, and after some brief good-byes, Logan hung up. His phone rang again almost immediately.

"Ben?" Logan said, after a quick glance at the screen. "I'm on my way up."

"I wouldn't bother. There's not a lot to be doing here. I'm going to head down soon and leave them to it," Ben said. "They're going to move the body in the next half hour or so, once they've got some more photos, and done all the other bits and bobs."

Bits and bobs. Only Ben Forde could refer to the cataloguing of a murder scene as *bits and bobs*.

If he were honest, Logan couldn't help but be relieved at not having to go back up there. The car park was dark and oppressive and had done nothing to help his current state of mind. He felt helpless up there, just standing around watching while the SOC team did their thing.

Those ramps were a bloody killer, too.

"Right. I'll swing by the office, then head to the hospital," he said.

"You might want to make a detour first," Ben told him.

"We've run the plates on the Range Rover that was parked next to the victim's car and got a match. Are you sitting comfortably?"

"Bosco Maximuke," Logan said. A guess, albeit an educated one. Logan had seen similar cars parked at the yard of the Russian's building company, and it was just that flash bastard's style.

"How did you know that?" asked Ben, clearly disappointed at having his thunder stolen.

"I didn't get this badge in a box of cornflakes," Logan told him. "I'll go pay him a visit."

"Want company?"

Logan counted to three in his head, making it appear as if he was considering the offer.

"No," he said, at last. "You're fine. You go back to the office and start running things from there."

He watched the toy shop family drive past him, the kids excitedly opening boxes in the back seat. He glanced up at the car park, where a mother lay who would never be going home.

"I'll deal with Bosco myself."

LOGAN WAS MET with the usual resistance when he strolled into Bosco's building yard, demanding to speak to the boss. The faces of the men who blocked his path were new, yet familiar all the same. Same shaved heads. Same angular features. Both sported neck tattoos, and both were dressed in identical black bomber jackets that didn't really fit with any 'construction worker' theme.

But then, these guys didn't work in construction. On paper,

maybe. In reality, though, they helped with the business behind the business.

Various CID officers across Scotland had been investigating Bosco Maximuke for years. Everyone knew the construction company was a front for his drug empire. There were fairly solid suspicions he was involved in people trafficking, too. The problem was, no one had ever been able to prove it.

Several raids had found nothing and had instead, led to a harassment lawsuit that the bastard had won. He was loud and brash, and revelled in his notoriety, but he was a slippery bugger too, and nothing seemed to stick to him for long.

"He not here," one of the guards said. Eastern European. No surprises there.

"Right." Logan glanced past the men to the portable office that stood at the far end of the yard, right beside a pristine JCB that looked like its bucket had never touched soil. "So, he's not in there, then?"

"He not here," the guard reiterated. The guy beside him was a little taller and heavier set, his brow furrowed into so deep a scowl he resembled an ogre of some sort. There was something vague and uncomprehending behind his eyes though, and Logan guessed he didn't speak a word of English.

"Well, when will he be back?" Logan asked.

"I do not know. I am not his wife."

The other man laughed. It was a sudden ejection, sharp and loud, like a machine-gun. "Wife!"

OK, so maybe he spoke a little English.

The first guard shot the second a disparaging look, which cut his laughter short. Both men returned to scowling at their unwelcome guest.

"Well, I'll just wait for him," Logan told them. "Maybe one of you boys could get me a cup of tea while I'm hanging about."

He smacked his lips together a couple of times. "I am parched."

"You do not wait," the first guard retorted. He sounded a little uncertain, like he wasn't sure he'd translated the sentence properly in his head.

Logan sighed, then shrugged. "Fine. Fine," he said. "You two can come down to the station instead."

The first guard side-eyed the second. He was still fully fixated on scowling though, and didn't notice.

"What?" the first asked, shifting his gaze back to the DCI.

"I need to ask Bosco some questions in regards to the rape and murder of a woman in Inverness city centre in the early hours of this morning," Logan informed the men. "If he's not around, you two can come with me, instead."

"I do not... We are not..."

"You can come quietly, or I can get a fleet of flat-footed angry bastards down here to drag you in," Logan continued. His eyes went very deliberately to both men's jackets. "They'll check you for concealed weapons, of course. Probably get immigration involved, although I'm sure that won't be a problem. I'm sure two smart lads like yourselves wouldn't be so stupid as to be in the country illegally."

He gave that a few moments to bed in, then nodded in the direction of the office. "Or, you could get out of my way, and I can go talk to Mr Maximuke."

Both men tensed when Logan reached into his inside coat pocket, their hands mirroring the movement as they instinctively thrust their hands into their own jackets.

They relaxed when he produced a phone and started dialling, but not by much.

"Hello, DI Forde?" Logan said into the handset. "I might need you to send a few officers to assist me here. One sec..."

Logan took the phone from his ear and cupped a hand over the mouthpiece. "Well, lads?" he asked, looking from one to the other. "What's it to be?"

CHAPTER THIRTY

Bosco Maximuke shook his head in mock reproach. "They told you I was out? Why would they think this? I do not know. They are new. Still to be broken in."

He wagged a finger at the detective looming in the doorway. "I tell them, 'If my policeman friend, Jack Logan, comes around here, then you let him in.' I tell them this, time and again, but..." He sighed and made a shrugging gesture. "What can you do?"

Maximuke was sitting behind his desk, hands clasped on the paunch of a belly that had been growing steadily since Logan had first met him and showed no signs of slowing down.

His taste for junk food was matched only by his taste for bad clothing. He was currently rocking an electric blue nylon tracksuit with the sleeves rolled up to the elbows. His thinning hair had been permed so recently that Logan could practically still smell the lotion. If the man were a fashion statement, that statement would be: 'Wid ye look at the fucking state o' that?'

Still, at least he'd made one cosmetic change for the better.

"You've got rid of the moustache, I see," Logan observed.

Bosco ran a finger and thumb across his top lip. "Gone, yes," he said, a note of regret colouring the edges of his Russian accent. "My wife, she not approve. My daughter, she not approve. Me? I approve, but..."

"What can you do?" Logan said, finishing the sentence for him.

Bosco slapped the edge of his desk. "Ha! Yes! What can you do when the women turn against you?"

He settled back into his chair and smiled, showing his yellowing teeth. "Now, my old friend, what can I do for you?"

Logan started to reply, but Bosco jumped in and cut him off before he could get a word out.

"By the way, it is good to see you looking so well. After accident, you not look so good. I worry. Bosco worries. Yes?" He gestured to Logan. "But now, you look good. Strong."

He leaned forward, face suddenly serious. "They ever find out who is responsible for accident?"

Logan knew full well who was responsible for his 'accident'. They both did.

"Still working on it," he said. "But when we find out, they'll be facing a murder charge."

Bosco's brow furrowed unconvincingly. "Murder? Oh! You had passenger at time, right?" He sucked air in through his teeth. "Terrible. Just terrible. Perhaps I could offer help? I have connections, yes? Business. Maybe I could help you find who is responsible. For you, my friend."

"You're fine," Logan said. "It's being dealt with."

Bosco held his hands out, palms up, fingers splayed. "The offer, it is there." His smile spread across his face again. "Now, what was it you said you wanted?"

"It's about your car," Logan said.

"Which one?" Bosco asked, his smile not shifting. "I have many cars."

"Range Rover. KT19 XOH. It's currently parked at the multi-storey on Rose Street."

"OK. And? Is ticket overdue? Is that what they sent you to tell me?" Bosco asked, practically sniggering.

"A woman was murdered. Her body was found right beside it."

The laughter died in the Russian's throat. The smile faded. "Oh. I see," he said. He contemplated this for a moment. "Any damage?"

Logan blinked. "I'm sorry?"

"It is expensive car," Bosco said. "Any damage?"

The bastard was deliberately trying to goad him. Logan wasn't rising to it.

"No. No damage," he said, adding the, "not yet," silently in his head.

"Good. This is good," Bosco said, his smile returning. "And the woman?"

"Plenty of damage there, aye," Logan told him.

"Who is she, I mean?"

"She's still to be formally identified," Logan told him. "My concern right now is why she was found right next to your car, Bosco. And not because I'm worried she might've scratched the paintwork."

He leaned forward, putting both clenched fists on the desk. A gorilla, staring down a rival. "Why was your car there?"

"I do not know this."

"What do you mean you don't know? It's your car."

"Like I said, I have many cars. My employees, they use. This one you say... Car park on Rose Street?"

Logan nodded his confirmation.

"Then all I know is it was not me driving."

"Who, then?"

Bosco gave a little shrug and a chuckle. "I do not know. It is… what is word? Pool car? Is this right? Free to use by my employees. Perk of job."

"I want to know who was using it last night. I want to know why they were parked in that spot, in that car park, and why a woman turned up dead right beside it."

"You want to know a lot of things," Bosco replied. He drummed his fingers on his belly. "I will ask around. Maybe someone will know. Maybe they won't. I ask."

"Maybe it was your man, Valdis," Logan suggested. "He's got a stake in the club downstairs, hasn't he?"

"Does he? I do not keep track," Bosco said, his face a picture of innocence.

"You must be helluva generous with the bonuses for him to be able to afford an investment like that."

Bosco ran a hand down the front of his tracksuit, smoothing the bumps on the zip. "Perhaps he has other money. I do not know. It is not my business."

Logan leaned closer still, anger creasing the lines of his face. "I want to know who was using that car," he said. "You have until four o'clock this afternoon."

Bosco continued to smile. Logan straightened, glanced around the little office, then headed for the door.

"Or?"

Logan stopped.

Logan turned.

"What?"

"I have until four this afternoon… or what?" Bosco asked. That bloody smirk was still there, pinned in place. "You cannot make threat without consequences. I have until four, you say.

And so, I ask you, 'or what?'"

Logan narrowed his eyes and sucked in his bottom lip, considering the question.

"I'm sure I'll think of something," he said. He tapped his watch. "Clock's ticking, Bosco. If I were you, I'd get asking around."

CHAPTER THIRTY-ONE

Logan was just pulling the Volvo into the station car park when his phone rang through the car's speakers. He tapped the handbrake lever, waited for it to engage, then cut the engine.

There was a brief lull in the ringing while the phone tried to figure out what the hell had just happened, then it returned, this time chiming out from his inside pocket.

"Hamza. What's up?" Logan asked, closing the car door and setting off towards the station's front door. He glanced up at the front of the building, roughly where the Incident Room they were using was. "Aye, I'm here now. I'm on my way up. Why, what's...?"

He pushed through the front door, frowning at Hamza's garbled reply. "Slow down. I'm not... Just, hang on. I'll be up in a second."

Logan headed for the lift, returning the phone to his pocket. There was an odd atmosphere in the station's reception. A few Uniforms were gathered around the receptionist's monitor, all looking concerned. He thought about stopping to ask them what was going on, but Hamza had sounded worried. Something was wrong. Seriously wrong, judging by the way the DC had stumbled over his words.

When he reached the Incident Room, Logan's suspicions were confirmed. The rest of the team were there, including Ben, who still had his jacket on. They were gathered around Hamza's desk, all but Hamza standing with their arms folded and grave expressions fixed on their faces.

"What's happened?" Logan asked, wasting no time on pleasantries. "What's wrong now?"

"It's HOLMES," Ben said.

Logan exhaled. "Jesus. Is that all? I thought there'd been another murder or something."

The faces of the others remained stoic, and Logan knew there was something more going on than a computer error or cyber attack.

"What?" he asked. "What is it?"

Ben gestured to the screen. "It's... You'd best come and see. Hamza, can you play it again?"

"Yes, sir," Hamza said. He dragged the mouse across the screen and clicked. It seemed to take a lot more effort than it should've.

He waited until Logan had walked around the desk to join them before hovering the mouse over the *play* icon on a web video. It was embedded into the HOLMES login page, directly above the username and password boxes.

"What the hell is this?" Logan asked.

"Play it, Hamza," Ben said. He caught Logan's eye, and there was something in that look that made Logan's stomach bunch into a knot. "Just watch, Jack."

Hamza clicked the mouse button. The black rectangle of the video flashed briefly white, then a man was standing there against a dark background. Or a figure, at least—it was difficult to determine the gender thanks to the featureless white mask they wore. He or she was dressed in dark clothing, too, which made it hard to judge the build.

The voice, when it came, was male. Heavily disguised and distorted, but male. It rumbled from the computer's speakers, booming like the voice of God.

"To whomever it may concern," it began. "I am the one who attacked Danni Gillespie. I am the one who killed Esme Miller. I am the one who is about to rape and murder Clarissa McDade. By the time you see this, it will have already happened. Maybe you'll have found her. Maybe you won't. Regardless, she will already be dead."

Something seemed to dance in the dark hollows of the mask's eyes.

"She will not be the last."

"Jesus..." Logan hissed.

"You will have questions, I'm sure. Who am I? Why am I doing this? But those are the wrong questions. Those are not the questions you should be asking," the man on the screen continued. "The question you should be asking is why are *you* doing this? Why are you investigating? Why are you wasting what little time you have on something so pointless and insignificant?"

He took a step closer, his voice dropping a few decibels until it was a loud whisper. "Because those women weren't real. They were fake. Lies. All lies. Like me. Like you. Like all of this."

He gestured around at the darkness. "Fake. It's all fake. We make up these rules we're supposed to follow—that you're supposed to enforce—and for what? Why? This isn't real. This world of ours? It doesn't exist. You. Me. Those women. None of it exists."

His voice was rising again, becoming excited. "And when you realise that—when you realise that nothing is real, then nothing matters. Nothing we do matters. How can I kill someone who has never existed? How can I hurt them if they're nothing but... but... *numbers*. Code. Because that's all we are. That's all we've ever been. Not flesh and bone. Numbers and code. Digits, floating in the void."

He looked straight up, and for a moment Logan caught a glimpse of a neck. Thin, cleanly shaven he automatically noted.

"Maybe they're up there. Out there. Watching this. Maybe they're taking note. Maybe, if I do this enough, I'll attract their attention."

The mask lowered until it was facing front again. "Or maybe they'll turn us off. *Bing!* Hard reset. Game over. Reload from Last Checkpoint."

He giggled—a series of low, sinister hisses that were made to sound even worse by the audio distortion. "Or maybe they don't care. Maybe they set it all running, and just walked away. Maybe we have absentee landlords. It doesn't matter. Nothing matters."

The laughter had given a touch of lightness to his voice. It fell away then, his tone becoming sombre and serious. "Nothing ever has. We have been living in a lie. All of us. Stressing, worrying, concerning ourselves with all the petty little details they've added to keep us distracted. To keep us from seeing the truth."

He took another step closer, until the mask was almost filling the screen. The eyes remained dark, impenetrable hollows, and Logan felt like they were staring straight at him. Not at some camera somewhere, but at him in particular.

"I see the truth now. I see through the lies. And now, I'm going to help everyone open their eyes. Watch this."

The video cut to black almost immediately. Logan was about to start firing out questions and orders, but DS McQuarrie stopped him.

"There's... There's more," she said, her voice a dry croak at the back of her throat.

The black rectangle came alive with shaky movement, like the camera was now being handheld. It swept across the ground for a moment, showing a pair of black trainers, a patch of grey concrete, then a white painted line.

Finally, it settled on two cars. A Range Rover. A Kia.

From somewhere off-screen, Logan heard the sound of footsteps approaching. Heels. A woman.

"No," he mumbled. "Don't tell me..."

The camera peeked out from behind a pillar. The focus swam for a few seconds, then pulled tight on a woman in a blouse and skirt. She was approaching the Kia, her keys in her hand, a spring in her step, despite the late hour.

"Don't feel sorry for her," the distorted voice whispered. A hand came up, waving a scalpel for the benefit of the camera. "She isn't real, remember? None of what you are about to see is real. Nobody will *actually* get hurt."

Then, he crept out of his hiding place, scurried over to where Clarissa McDade was closing in on her car, and Logan and the others could do nothing but watch as the attack began.

"Stop," Logan said.

Hamza immediately clicked the mouse, like he'd been hanging on tenterhooks, waiting for the command.

Silence filled the Incident Room. On-screen, a gloved hand

had caught Clarissa McDade by the hair and was yanking her head back. Only part of her face was visible, but it was twisted up in pain and fear.

Logan knew he'd have to watch the rest of it. He had no choice. But not here. Not now. He didn't have to subject the others to it any more than they already had been.

He massaged his temples with his fingertips. He had questions. Probably a lot of questions. Right now, though, none of them were forming themselves enough for him to speak them out loud.

"Is this…? This is on HOLMES?"

"Aye, sir," Hamza confirmed. "Appeared about twenty minutes ago. All over the country. It's on the login page, so non-users can access it via the internet."

"What? Shite," Logan spat. "Get it taken down then. Get them to shut down the bloody server. We can't have people watching this."

Hamza shot the others an anxious look. It was DC Neish who answered for him.

"Bit late for that, boss," he said. "Same time as it went live on HOLMES, it went up on 8Chan."

Logan's brow furrowed. "Am I supposed to know what that is?"

"It's a forum. Completely anonymous. Full of the worst kind of arsehole," Tyler explained. "It's spreading like wildfire. All over social media, Reddit… Everywhere, basically."

Logan felt something uncoiling in his stomach, like a serpent waking on the ocean floor. "People are watching that? Through choice? Fucking *sharing* it for other people to watch?"

Tyler cleared his throat. "Afraid so, boss."

"Sick bastards," Caitlyn spat.

"I want anyone sharing this arrested," Logan barked, pointing to the screen. "Get that out there now. Anyone who shares that footage is going to fucking jail, and I will personally be the one throwing them in. Get that message out. Put out a statement. Do whatever needs to be done."

"Yes, boss," Tyler said.

"And then, find a way to get it taken down. Get onto Facebook, Twitter, and whoever fucking else is helping to spread it and get it..." He shook his head, agitated. "In fact, no. I'll get Hoon on that. May as well make himself useful. We're catching this bastard. Caitlyn."

DS McQuarrie straightened her shoulders. "Sir."

"That mask. Find me a match. Where did he get it? Was it local? We need to know."

"Yes, sir," Caitlyn said. She hurried over to her desk, dropped into her chair, then spun to face her own computer screen. Logan watched her take a deep breath before she began typing out the web address for the HOLMES login screen.

"What was he on about with all that 'not real' shite?" Ben wondered.

"Simulation Theory, sir," Hamza said, in a tone that suggested he thought everyone had already figured that out.

Logan saved Ben the job of asking.

"What's Simulation Theory?"

"You know, like...?" Hamza caught the looks from the two older detectives. "You've never heard of it?"

"No, Hamza, we've never heard of it. What is it?" Logan snapped.

Hamza turned his chair all the way around to face them. "Right. Well, you know video games, sir?"

"Like Space Invaders?" Ben asked.

Hamza tilted his head from side to side. "Bit more modern

than that, sir. Say, like, *The Sims*. It's a game where you control all these little people. They live in a house, have jobs, make dinner, go on dates, all that stuff."

Ben looked non-plussed. "How is that a game? Sounds like bloody drudgery."

"It's actually really popular," Hamza told him. "Anyway, all the characters in it, they have their own AI. Artificial intelligence. They get tired, can go in bad moods, fall in love, whatever. Everything we can do, really."

"What's this got to do with our guy?" Ben asked. Logan remained silent, the cogs in his brain quietly whirring as he pieced it together.

"He thinks we're in that game?" he said.

"Well, aye. Kind of. Maybe not that game specifically, sir," Hamza said. "See, the theory goes like this: If we can create a simulation, and the people in that simulation *think* their world is real, then it's statistically improbable that we're not also in a simulation of our own."

Ben blinked.

Then, he blinked again.

"You what?"

Hamza grabbed a piece of paper and a pen from his desk and began to scribble. "OK, let's say that we make some amazing computer simulation of a world. Like... *The Sims Version Fifty*."

He drew a circle on the page.

"That's it there. Now, in the game, one of the jobs your Sim can do is be a games designer. So, you have an AI character—meaning that within the confines of the game he *thinks* he's real—making games of his own. Games that he's coming up with himself, because he's artificially intelligent. With me?"

Ben and Logan exchanged glances.

"So far so good," Logan said, although Ben looked a little less confident.

"Right. Good. OK. So, let's say one of those games is a simulation like *The Sims*," Hamza said. He drew a smaller circle inside the first one. "So, now we've got a simulated world inside a simulated world. And within that new simulation, another simulation could be created, then another, then another, and on and on it goes. A chain of virtual universes, where everyone in them thinks they're real, and is unaware of the one before. They go about their business, living, working, dying, completely unaware that they're in a simulation."

"But that's not going to happen, is it?" asked Ben. "That's bloody *Star Trek* stuff."

"It's already happening, sir," Hamza said. "We're a few years off it being quite at the level we're talking about, but we're most of the way there. It's a matter of when, not if."

He pointed with his pen to the page. "So, if we assume that there will be a point in the not too distant future when this chain of simulated universes exists, then the chances of us being the Prime Universe—the original and real one—are infinitesimally small. Meaning..."

He drew a third circle, bigger than the others and surrounding them both. "This is us. And everything we see, including ourselves, is a simulation. Computer code, created by some other simulation, which was in turn created by... Well. You get the point."

Ben grunted. "Like I said, all sounds a bit *Star Trek* to me."

"There's actually growing scientific interest in the theory," Hamza said. "It's pretty interesting."

"You don't believe that shite, do you?" Ben scoffed.

Hamza considered his answer. "Doesn't really matter if we believe it or not, sir. Whether it's true or not, it doesn't change anything. Whether everything's real, or it's all inside a computer somewhere, the rules are the same. Gravity works. People get sick, fall in love."

"Get stabbed repeatedly in the back," Tyler volunteered.

Hamza gave him the finger, then continued. "Saying 'none of it is real' doesn't change the fact that, from our point of view, it *is* real. Whatever we do, we're still bound by the rules of the simulation. There are still consequences."

Logan shrugged off his coat. "Too bloody right there are consequences," he intoned. "There's us."

"What's the plan, boss?" Tyler asked.

"Same plan as always," Logan replied, his voice bordering on a snarl. "We catch this mad bastard and we put him away."

He turned away from the others, headed for the office he so rarely used, bracing himself for the video he knew he had to watch.

"And, if anyone happens to kick the living shite out of him between those two points in time, then so much the bloody better."

CHAPTER THIRTY-TWO

Logan sat alone in his office, his eyes fixed on the mercifully blank video player that now filled half of his computer screen. His fingers were clasped together as if in prayer, knuckles white. Whiter even than his face, which had lost almost all of its colour over the course of the last fifteen minutes.

He cleared his throat, like he was about to say something. In truth, he just wanted to hear something normal. Something familiar. He wanted to be somewhere else, surrounded by friends and family, a million miles from this office and that screen and everything he had just seen. Another outlook. Another life.

Much more than that though, he wanted to find this guy. He wanted to stop him.

There was a soft, enquiring knock at the door. Logan ran a hand down his face, cleared his throat again, then sat up straight.

"In you come."

The door opened, and Ben Forde's head appeared around the frame. "You alright?"

"Fine," Logan said. "I mean... You know."

"Aye," Ben confirmed, stepping into the office and closing the door. "I know. It's rough. I mean, I haven't watched all of it. We put it off." He drew himself up to his full height. "But I will. If it'll help. I will."

Logan shook his head. "You're fine. One of the specialist teams can go over it in more..." His eyes flicked to the screen. "...detail. From what I saw, there's not a lot that can help us figure out who he is. He's edited chunks of it out. Maybe there was something in those parts, but now..."

He sighed and sat back in his chair. "Who was it who told me to come to Inverness again?" he asked. "*Nice quiet life*, they said. Can you remember who that was?"

Ben chuckled dryly. "Not a clue, Jack. But I'd have words with them, if I were you."

"Aye. I may just do that," Logan replied.

DI Forde took an exaggerated backward step towards the door, and both men shared a half-hearted smile.

"Couple of updates," Ben said, getting down to business. "Donald Sloane. We need to charge him or let him go. It's unlikely he's involved in the murder cases, but I can't stand the horrible bastard, so I thought we could get him on assaulting you and that lassie from Uniform."

"Aye, fine. Go with that," Logan said. "Anything on those hard drives they took from his place?"

"Movies. Pirated copies, we think."

"Charge him on that, too."

Ben gave a satisfied nod. "Great. We've also just had a report from the tech team about the cameras at the car park."

Logan stiffened. "Tell me it's something we can use."

A shake of Ben's head made the DCI's shoulders sag back into their original position.

"No. They've translated the code, though. You know, the computer numbers?"

"Binary."

"Aye, that. Apparently, it's a language? Did you know that?"

Logan confirmed that he was aware of that fact, albeit only vaguely.

"Well, they translated it. Turns out, it's just the same word over and over. 'Fake.' Should have guessed, really."

Logan gave a non-committal sort of grunt. He couldn't say he was particularly surprised by the information, but it was worrying, all the same. If this guy could deface HOLMES *and* get access to a secure camera network, he knew what he was doing. Logan hated the ones who knew what they were doing. Give him a drunken half-wit with a temper problem, any day.

"They're trying to find out... Oh, I don't know," Ben said. "Some technical shite. See if they can find out how he got into the system, and then try to trace him."

"I doubt they'll get anywhere," Logan said. "He'll have covered his tracks."

"For someone who says there's no consequences, he's certainly going out of his way to avoid them," Ben pointed out. "The mask, disguising his voice, and all that stuff."

"He knows full bloody well there are consequences," Logan said. "And I for one can't wait to inflict them on the bastard."

Ben nodded his agreement. "You can say that again. Oh, and the mask? Caitlyn reckons she's found a match."

"Already? That was bloody quick," Logan said, his eyebrows rising in surprise.

"Not a lot of places locally to get something like that," Ben said. "She checked the Hobbycraft website, and there's one that looks identical to the one in the video. We've sent a car over to pick one up so we can compare in person. If we do have a match, then we'll work with the shop to see if we can find out who bought one recently."

"No saying it's recent," Jack said. "Danni Gillespie's attacker was wearing one. Could well be the same mask."

Ben's glum expression suggested he'd already considered this. "Aye. Could be another dead end, but worth pursuing."

"No arguments there," Logan said. He clapped his hands together and stood up. "Right, what else? What's next? Where do we go from here?"

"Scene of Crime are finished at the car park. They're cataloguing everything and are going to send over a preliminary report later today," Ben said, flipping open his notebook. "Your doctor friend has got the body. We've got a positive ID on the victim already, and the husband doesn't want to come in and see her for himself."

Shite. The husband.

"What about the video? Has he seen that video?"

"He's aware of it, apparently, and has an idea what the contents are. If he's got any sense, he'll steer clear. A couple of folks from Victim Support are with him and the kids now, and we've got a liaison standing by. They're all in a pretty bad way, as you'd expect."

"Aye. I can imagine," said Logan, although he knew that he couldn't. Not really. Not enough.

"I went through and spoke to Hoon, while you were..." Ben gestured to the computer screen. "...busy. He'd heard about the video, obviously, and he's escalating it right up the chain. The higher-ups are going to work with the social media platforms to try to get it taken down."

"Good," said Logan.

Both men knew the truth, though. It was too late. The horse had already bolted. A million arseholes would already have downloaded that video all over the world. It was out there now, in the wild, and no matter how cooperative the social media sites might be, Clarissa McDade's degradation and dying minutes would forever be just a couple of link clicks away.

"You ever dealt with one like this, Jack?" Ben asked, his voice lowering, like he was afraid the others might overhear.

"Aye. We both have," Logan said. "He's just a nutter. We've dealt with plenty like him."

"True. But his motive..."

"The simulation shite is not his motive," Logan said. "It's his excuse. He likes the power, that's all. Funny how, if nobody's real, it's always women he goes after. No, he's not special, or different. He's the same as all the rest, and we'll catch him the same way we've caught them—solid polis work."

He checked his watch. "Right, what are we on? Jesus. OK. I'll get over to the mortuary, see what Shona's got. I want you here but send the rest of the team to the hospital. It's no coincidence that both recent victims worked there."

"The doctor, you think?" Ben said. "What was his name? Fletcher?"

"Aye, we definitely need to talk to him again. We need to find out what sort of relationship he had with Clarissa, but we need to keep an open mind. She was in HR. Had she disciplined anyone recently? Was there anyone she'd got on the wrong side of?"

"Got it," Ben said. He turned to leave, then stopped. "Oh,

and you'll be pleased to know that Hoon has suggested he handle the press on this. He said, and I quote: 'I'm not having that useless big bastard knocking a journalist's teeth down their throat in front of the fucking cameras.'"

"That was a decent impression, actually," Logan said. "Well done."

"You should hear my Sean Connery," Ben said. "Itsh exshepshional."

"Nah, that was shite," Logan told him. He rapped his knuckles on the desk. "Right, we know what we're doing?"

"We do."

"Good."

Logan jabbed the power button on his computer and the screen went dark. It made an electronic whine, as if sighing with relief after everything it had just been forced to display.

"Then, let's get out there and nail this bastard."

CHAPTER THIRTY-THREE

THERE WAS NONE OF THE USUAL BANTER WHEN LOGAN turned up to speak to the pathologist. Shona's voice crackled through an intercom in the outer office, calling Logan through to what she'd once referred to as 'the business end' of the mortuary.

After helping himself to gloves and a mask, he pushed open the heavy double doors, and shuddered in the sudden blast of refrigerated air. It rolled out of air conditioning units above, as if trying to push down the rising stench of death.

Shona looked up from the body on the slab before her. There was no smile or wave, no salute of acknowledgement. There was just a sadness in her eyes, and a heaviness to the way she moved.

"You alright?" Logan asked her.

"No," she said, matter-of-factly.

Logan stopped across from her, the uncovered naked body of Clarissa McDade between them. Logan had managed to grow largely indifferent to the sight of a corpse over the years, although he could never decide if this was to his credit or to his detriment.

This one, though, he found difficult to look at. It was because of the video, he thought. He was so used to seeing victims after death, but witnessing their final, horrifying moments made it harder for him to detach himself. The body was no longer just a body. It was a person. A woman. A wife, a mother, a daughter, a friend.

And he'd had to watch her suffer. He'd had to watch the wounds he was about to discuss be inflicted upon her in leering, lingering close-up.

"She was... Not a friend. Not exactly," Shona said, her eyes downcast. "But we'd chat sometimes. In the canteen, or whatever. She was nice."

Shona puffed out her cheeks. Her voice quaked. "I fucking hate this job," she whispered. She said it so quietly that Logan didn't know if he was supposed to have heard it. He decided to pretend that he hadn't.

Shona gave herself a shake, pushed back her shoulders, then launched into what felt like a rehearsed speech.

"Cause of death, as you probably already know, was a single cut to the jugular vein. Scalpel. Same one he used to carve the letters into her stomach before he killed her. Skillfully done—small nick, but just in the right position. He knows his stuff. Medical training, I'd guess, but then again, you can find a tutorial for anything on YouTube these days."

She indicated the victim's face. "He gagged her with a rag and tape—again, I'm sure you know this. I've sent it off for analysis. You'll hear back on that before I do."

Logan glanced awkwardly down the victim's body, his eyes alighting for the briefest fraction of a second on her crotch. "What about...? From the sexual assault?"

"No obvious DNA left. I think he raped her with an implement of some kind, rather than... the usual," Shona said. Her face prickled red and she placed a hand on her stomach, like she was fighting back against a rising wave of nausea. "There's some laceration," she managed to continue. "Like it had some sharp edges."

"Like a knife?" Logan asked. The video footage had remained fixed mostly on the victim's upper body during the footage of the assault, aside from a minute or so at the start. It was one of the small mercies the footage afforded.

Shona shook her head. "No. More like... I don't know. A stick, maybe?"

"A stick?"

"With one or two little twigs coming off it. But not long. Broken down so they just stick out. It could even be some kind of sex toy."

"A lacerating sex toy?" Logan said.

"Some people are into some right weird shit," Shona pointed out.

Logan conceded this point with a nod. God knew, he'd met enough people to appreciate just how true that statement was.

"Anyway. There's a video of it all, I hear," Shona said. Her eyes met Logan's. They were pleading, desperately hoping that he'd tell her she'd heard wrong.

"I'm afraid so," he said.

Shona's throat tightened as she stifled a sob. "Bastard," she whispered. "How could someone...? I mean, I see it all the time. We see it, I mean. But..."

She looked down at the body, or maybe through it to the floor beyond. "What makes them do these things? How can they?"

Logan heaved out a sigh. "I wish I knew," he told her. "This one says it's because we don't exist. On the video, I mean. Simulation Theory, or some bollocks. Says it's all fake, and none of it is real. Says he's going to do it again, too."

Shona looked up sharply. "And do you believe him?"

Logan wished he had another answer for her. He really did.

"Aye," he said. "I believe him."

They stood in silence for several seconds, the weight of Logan's words slowly settling in.

"Why her?" Shona eventually asked. "Why Clarissa? First Esme, now her. Is it the hospital? Is that the connection? I mean, it has to be, doesn't it?"

"We don't know yet," Logan admitted. "Ben and the others are questioning people now. I'm going to head up and join them, see if we can find some more direct connection. But aye, it looks like the hospital's a factor in it, although we're currently pursuing some other lines of—"

"Don't give me the official line, Jack," Shona replied, her voice clipped around the edges by anger. "I don't want a sound-bite. Do you have any idea who did this? Honestly?"

Logan hesitated. Then, he gave a single shake of his head.

"Jesus. So... what? All the other women here, we're all in danger?"

"We've got no evidence to suggest that," Logan said.

"You've got no evidence that we aren't!" Shona spat back. "You've got no evidence, full stop!"

She appeared momentarily surprised by her outburst and looked down at the body of Clarissa McDade again. "Sorry," she said, her eyes briefly flicking back to Logan. "I didn't mean that."

"No, you're absolutely right," Logan admitted. "We don't know what he's planning next, or who might be in danger. But we're working on it. In the meantime, I can have someone from Uniform keep an eye on you, make sure you're—"

"Me? I'm not worried about me. I'm worried about everyone else. Have you got enough officers to keep an eye on everyone? There's something like eighteen-hundred women working here. Can you give them all escorts?"

"No," Jack admitted. "We can't."

"Then I don't want one," Shona told him.

"We don't know that anyone at the hospital is in danger, but we'll recommend staff travel to and from work in groups or pairs," Logan said. "Just until we know more. We've got the tech bods analysing the video and trying to trace his hack. We're hopeful they might..."

His voice trailed away into an uncomfortable silence. That wasn't the truth. He wasn't hopeful about any of it. Aye, there was always a chance they might get lucky, but his instincts told him the killer would be too smart to leave any clues that might point to who or where he was.

"You'd better get back," Shona told him, her voice losing its earlier anger. "I'll type all this up. The report, I mean, not me being hyper-critical and panicky. I'll leave that bit out."

They shared a smile, but it was small, and it was fleeting, and it barely qualified as a real smile at all.

"Thanks. And we're doing all we can," Logan said. He wanted her to know that. To believe it, and hopefully take comfort from it.

But the words sounded empty and hollow as they tumbled from his mouth. He was giving her the official line again. *We're doing all we can. We're working hard to apprehend the perpetrator of these heinous crimes. We're pulling out all the stops.*

She deserved more than that. Much more.

"I'm going to catch him, Shona," he told her, and the

sincerity of it made her stand up straight and pay attention. "I promise you that."

She nodded, then the faintest suggestion of a smile tugged at the corners of her mouth. "I'd say you always keep your promises, but I'm still waiting on that lunch you owe me..."

The smile stuttered and died as quickly as it had started. "Keep this one, Jack," she urged, her eyes pleading. "Keep this one."

CHAPTER THIRTY-FOUR

The atmosphere in the hospital was noticeably different to the last time Logan had walked through the corridors. After the attack on Esme, the place had been awash with shock, anger, and sadness. Now though, there was something else in there, flavouring the mix.

Fear.

Guilt, too. Logan saw it on the faces of several of the nurses he passed. The way they looked at him, then quickly glanced away, casting their eyes down towards the floor. He could practically pick out those who had watched at least some of the video from those who hadn't.

He hoped, for their sakes, that they hadn't watched it all.

Logan had called into the Incident Room and got Ben to contact the hospital chiefs to suggest that staff pair up going to and from work.

"Safety in numbers, makes sense," Ben had agreed, before hanging up to make the call.

Logan was passing through one of the wards, trying to get

his bearings, when he heard the clatter of footsteps running up behind him.

He turned in time to see Kel Conlyn running the last few steps towards him, one hand clutching his side. He winced, and gestured to his chest as he tried to get his breath back.

"Stitch," he explained, his hand massaging the side of his stomach. "Sorry."

"Take your time, Mr Conlyn," Logan said, as patiently as possible. "Was there something you wanted to tell me?"

"What? No. Sorry," Kel said. "I just... I heard about the video. People are saying that the guy who killed Esme killed that woman from HR. Is that true?"

"He's certainly claiming to have committed both attacks, yes," Logan confirmed. He looked the younger man up and down. "You haven't watched it, then?"

"No!" Kel spluttered, visibly recoiling. "Why would I watch...? Why would anyone watch something like that?"

"Beats me, son," Logan said.

The orderly shook his head, his face still screwed up in distaste. "Some people are just..." He sighed, and forced a smile that didn't amount to much. "If there's anything I can do to help, just let me know."

"Just keep your eyes peeled," Logan told him. "If you see anyone acting suspicious, report it, but don't approach. And we're suggesting anyone walking to and from work, particularly late at night, travel in pairs or groups. You can help spread the word on that."

Kel seemed to grow a couple of inches in height, like he was growing into the responsibility before Logan's eyes. "OK. I'll do that. You can count on me," he said. "I'll go start telling people now."

"Thank you," Logan said.

"Happy to help," said Kel. Then, he pulled off an almost military-grade about-turn and set off back in the direction he'd come from.

"Oh, and Mr Conlyn!" Logan called after him.

The orderly stopped and turned. "Yes?"

"I don't suppose you can point me in the direction of the HR department?"

THE DEPARTMENT WAS TECHNICALLY CLOSED by the time Logan finally found his way there, but his team had set up inside, and all the lights were blazing. Darkness had descended outside, and the office lights had turned the windows into mirrors, each one a reminder to Logan of just how rough he currently looked.

DCs Khaled and Neish were already hard at work when Logan turned up. Under normal circumstances, Logan would've expected to find Tyler spinning in one of the big office chairs, or commenting on the photo of the attractive twenty-something—someone's wife or daughter, presumably—that was sitting on one of the three desks.

But the same atmosphere that had hung heavily over the rest of the hospital had permeated this place, too, and both detectives just briefly glanced up in acknowledgement when Logan arrived, then got right back to it. Logan was glad to see that Tyler's early excitement about the prospect of working a serial case had abandoned him once he'd realised he was now doing exactly that.

There was hope for the bugger yet.

Logan took off his coat and hung it on a hook by the door. Might as well make himself comfortable. He was likely to be here for the long haul.

"Right, where are we?" he asked. "What have we got?"

DC Khaled turned in his chair to face the DCI. Tyler, who had been searching through a desk drawer paused, mid-rummage.

Hamza indicated the computer he had been tapping away at. "I'm going through her calendar and work emails, sir. Her boss gave us the login information. Caitlyn's interviewing her and some of the victim's colleagues now. A few of them were with her at the club last night, so we're hoping they might have noticed anyone acting weirdly."

Logan clicked his tongue against the back of his teeth. "Right. Good. Anything in the emails?"

"No, sir. Nothing interesting yet."

"Keep looking. Check for recent disciplinaries, too. Has she had to give anyone a bollocking in the last couple of weeks? If so, I want to know who, and what for."

Hamza turned back to the screen. "On it, sir. Oh!" He turned back again. "Caitlyn asked around about Colin Fletcher. The doctor?"

"What about him?"

"He's called in sick, sir. We sent Uniform around, but no answer at his house."

"Shite. OK. That's potentially significant. Get him found."

"We're on it, sir."

Logan directed his attention to DC Neish. "Tyler? What about you?"

"I'm looking for her notepad, boss," Tyler said. He pulled the drawer all the way out of its housing and set it on top of the desk.

"Her notepad?"

"Aye, boss. There are three people working in HR.

According to the boss, they all make notes during interviews—you know, like appraisals, disciplinaries, whatever—and then type everything up later."

"I think we're already pretty familiar with that concept, Detective Constable," Logan pointed out. "What about it?"

"I can find the notepads for the other two members of the team, but not Clarissa's," Tyler said. "It's not on her desk. I've been through every drawer and cupboard apart from this one, and it's nowhere to be found."

"Could she have taken it home?" Logan asked.

"Doubt it, boss. Data protection. They're not allowed to take them out of the office."

Logan turned on the spot, looking around. The office was about a third of the size of the Incident Room back at the station, and filled with furniture that probably hadn't been updated in a decade. The desks and chairs were mismatched, suggesting they'd all been bought at different times, and a row of filing cabinets were all different heights, widths, and colours.

"You check in those cabinets?"

"Not yet, boss," Tyler admitted. "Everyone else keeps theirs in their desk drawer. Not sure why she'd file hers, but I'll go through."

Logan crossed to the first of the filing cabinets and pulled it open. The metal drawer squealed in protest, stuck an inch or two open, then finally relented when the DCI gave it a sharp tug.

The drawer was filled with dozens of suspended cardboard file holders, each one bulging with the weight of the paperwork stuffed inside. Going through this lot was going to take hours.

"I think I need coffee for this," he grunted, shunting the drawer closed again. "Tyler. You see a machine anywhere nearby?"

DC Neish stopped rummaging in the drawer and gave an almost imperceptible sigh. "Aye, boss. There's one a couple of corridors along in a waiting room. What are you after?"

"I'll get it," Logan said.

Tyler's face took on a blank expression, like he didn't know how to respond to this. "What?"

"I said I'll get it," Logan told him. "No need to stare at me like I've grown an extra bloody head, Detective Constable. I do occasionally get the tea and coffee in."

"Do you, boss?" Tyler asked, his tone one of genuine surprise. He cleared his throat. "I mean, yeah. Right. Cool."

"What do you both take?" Logan asked.

"Milk and two, boss," Tyler replied.

"I'll have a tea, if it's going," Hamza said. "Nothing in it."

"You'll have a coffee," Logan told him, striding for the door. "Trust me, we're all going to need it."

THE NEXT FEW hours passed slowly, time grinding by, minute by excruciating minute. Developments were few and far between. Breakthroughs, non-existent.

Ben called in with an update on the Range Rover at the car park. CCTV footage from earlier in the day showed Bosco's man, Valdis Petronis, arriving in it, along with Shaun Gillespie. Neither man had returned to the car in the hours leading up to the camera network being hacked, and even with the audio distortion, there was no way the killer in the video shared the same accent as Valdis. Valdis also had a neck like a bulldog that had been force-fed steroids from birth, which ruled him out physically, too.

It wasn't so easy to rule out Shaun Gillespie, and he tied

into the series of attacks in a few different ways. His sister being the main one, obviously, but the latest attack had taken place in the car park above his nightclub, shortly after the victim had left said club, heading for home.

If you considered that he'd attacked Donald Sloane a few years back, and that Sloane was pictured alongside Esme Miller, then you could tie him to the second victim too, albeit tenuously.

He had computer skills, too. Some kind of teen genius, by all accounts. His app business had netted him a fortune, and while Logan was far from being an expert, he had to assume the guy had the know-how to hack the car park cameras and stick that video on HOLMES.

Logan instructed Ben to have someone keep an eye on Gillespie. They could bring him in for a chat in the morning, if nothing else jumped out at them tonight.

Colin Fletcher remained a man of mystery. He wasn't at home, and his mobile was off. Logan had instructed a couple of Uniforms to head to Elgin to have a chat with the wife, but they hadn't fed back yet.

Caitlyn's interviews hadn't turned up much. Work-wise, Clarissa had been in the office herself for most of the previous week, with one of her colleagues on holiday, and another only working part-time. Neither of them had been able to shine any light on who'd been in and out of the department over the past few days, and while they both agreed that Clarissa could be fierce in a disciplinary when she had to, everyone they knew had always spoken highly of her. If someone was carrying a grudge, they hid it well.

Logan had texted DS McQuarrie to get her to ask about the victim's notebook. Both women who shared the office had insisted it would be in the tray on her desk, and the department head had confirmed this was standard procedure.

It still hadn't turned up, even after Logan and Tyler had gone through the filing cabinets and shifted some of the most likely pieces of furniture so they could check down the back. So, it looked like someone had taken it, which opened up a whole raft of questions.

Logan sat behind a desk, sipping his fourth coffee of the night, and marvelling that it somehow managed to taste even less palatable than the previous three. There was a harsh, *ashy* taste to it, like someone had previously used the cup as an ashtray before returning it to the machine.

The moment the image popped into his head, he set the cup down, slid it a little way along the desk, and silently vowed not to drink any more of it again.

The desk had been clear when he'd set up shop at it, but now it was covered in printouts and files, none of which had proved to be all that useful. Logan had managed to build up a pretty good picture of the victim's work life and had gained some insight into her personality and who she was, but none of it was pointing anywhere yet. Nowhere useful, at least.

"This is interesting, sir," said Hamza, and Logan was on his feet at once.

DC Khaled indicated the screen as Logan joined him at the victim's desk. The DCI bent down and found himself looking at a calendar screen, with each working day broken up into varyingly sized, differently coloured blocks of time. Most days were a rainbow of activities–meetings, admin time, breaks, conference calls, and more. Clarissa had accounted for everything, scheduling her tasks with a level of discipline Logan could only dream of.

Or, more likely, have recurring nightmares about.

"What am I looking at?" Logan asked.

"It's the victim's calendar, sir," Hamza replied.

Logan tutted. "No, I know that. What's the interesting bit?"

"Oh. Right. Aye, sorry, sir," Hamza said, blushing slightly and shifting in the seat. He pointed with the end of a well-chewed pen at two solid blocks of blue on the screen, one above the other. "Three days ago. Check this out."

"Admin time," Logan said, reading the text on the top block.

"And again below," Hamza said. "Admin time twice in a row."

Logan's eyes flicked back at the previous days. The colours were always alternating, always different. Occasionally, a whole afternoon would be blocked off for something, but it would be one solid mass of colour, not two.

"I've looked back, sir, and she does admin three times a week, religiously. Always the same time, and she marks it the same colour."

He scrolled past to previous weeks. Logan saw all the blocks of light blue. They were the one constant in a sea of ever-changing hues.

"See? Always the same. Three times a week, always the same day and time, and always blocked off for two hours each time. Except three days ago," Hamza said, scrolling back to the current week. "She's got admin down twice, one after the other."

"Busy time, maybe?" Logan guessed. "If someone was off on holiday..."

"I thought of that sir, and cross-referenced with previous holiday periods. Admin time stays the same. No change," Hamza said. "Also, why not just make it one block? Why two?"

Logan wasn't ready to let go of the holiday cover idea yet. "If she was doing someone else's work, she might have split it up to differentiate."

Hamza conceded the point with a nod. "Aye, suppose so, sir," he said. "Except..."

He clicked into the top block. There was a paragraph of text in there, detailing what Clarissa had done.

"See that? List of stuff she had to do. Create a new job ad, collate applications for another job, sort out a presentation for a school careers fair..."

He backed out of the calendar event, then clicked on the one below. "And now..."

Logan read the notes in silence.

"They're the same," he said.

"Identical, sir," Hamza confirmed. "It's a copy and paste job. She copied the top event and pasted it below."

"Or someone did," Logan said.

Hamza glanced from the screen to the DCI. "My thoughts, exactly. I can't say for sure, obviously, but my guess is that someone deleted what *was* in that spot, then filled it by copying the event above. They could do it remotely if they could hack her password."

Logan shook his head. "They did it from here," he said.

Hamza looked down at the keys. The keys his fingertips had been touching for the past couple of hours. "How do you know that, sir?" he asked.

"Because they also took her notebook," Logan pointed out. "If she had a meeting with someone, she'd have made notes."

Tyler sidled over to join them. Unlike Logan, he hadn't yet given up on his latest cup of coffee, although couldn't quite bring himself to drink any more of it. He clutched it between finger and thumb, wary of squeezing the fragile plastic too firmly and sending the lukewarm contents cascading over the rim.

"So, we find out who changed the calendar and took the notebook, and we've got him?"

"It's rarely that easy, but maybe," Logan said.

"Should Hamza have been using that keyboard, then?" Tyler asked. "Should I have been rifling through the drawers? Shouldn't we get this place checked over for forensic evidence, boss?"

"Bit late for that," Logan said. "Besides, shared office, lots of coming and going—and our man is smart, he hasn't left us anything forensics-wise until now. I highly doubt anything would've come up. We've made good progress here. Now, I want—"

His phone rang, the ringtone *brrrringing* as the smartphone vibrated across the desk he'd been sitting at a few minutes before.

Picking it up, he checked the screen. *Unknown Caller*.

"DCI Logan," he said, tapping the green icon and pressing the phone to his ear.

There was silence. Not the silence of a line that hadn't yet connected, but a hollow, rasping sort of silence that suggested someone on the other end. Logan got the impression of a small room, although he couldn't even begin to explain why. Something about the colour of the silence, the way it seemed to echo off a set of closed-in walls.

"Hello?" Logan said. He heard his voice tumble off into the void. "Who is this?" he asked. "What do you want?"

A voice replied. At least, he thought so. In truth, it was so soft and faint that he might have imagined it.

"You, Jack," it whispered, and then the phone *bleeped* in

his ear, and the display returned to the icons of the home screen.

"Everything alright, boss?" asked Tyler.

Logan realised he was standing motionless, staring at the phone. How long had he been like that? A few seconds, at least, maybe more.

"Hm? Oh. Aye. Aye," he said, setting the phone down on the desk. He continued to stare at it, like it might be about to do something amazing he didn't want to miss.

"Who was that?" Tyler asked.

"I don't know," Logan admitted, still not lifting his gaze from the handset on the table. The screen darkened, then went black. The spell was broken then, and Logan finally tore his eyes away. "I'll find out. But, for now, we've got a job to do. Find me who Clarissa McDade met with that afternoon, and point me in the bastard's direction."

He shot the phone another look, then picked up the coffee he had sworn to himself he wouldn't touch again.

It was going to be a long, long night.

CHAPTER THIRTY-FIVE

IT HAD BEEN A LONG, LONG DAY.

Laura Elder's muscles fired stabbing pains of complaint up her back and across her shoulders as she slipped off her navy blue NHS tunic and reached for the shirt she'd left hanging in her locker. She caught a whiff of herself as she lifted her arm to pull the shirt on, and her mind leapt to a hot bath full of soapy bubbles.

She'd texted her mum earlier, asking her to stick the immerser on. It was just about possible to get a bath without it, but she'd been dreaming of a good soaking all day, and if she didn't emerge from it a shade of lobster-red, then she was going to be disappointed.

Before then, of course, she had to get home. It was easy walking distance—ten minutes on average, less if she power-walked—but the police were recommending everyone travel in pairs or groups. Given what had happened to Esme, and now the woman from HR, it made sense, even if it did suddenly bring into focus just how much danger any one of them could be in.

She could take a taxi, she supposed. They were expensive, though, for all the distance she was going. She and Craig had been doing so well saving up for the wedding, too. She'd even stopped going to Costa, and started making her own lunch. It would be a shame to chuck it away for the sake of half a mile, even if there was a murderer on the loose.

The words struck her as she thought them, *dinging* around inside her head like a bullet ricocheting in an enclosed space.

Murderer on the loose.

Bloody hell. When you thought of it like that...

"Better safe than sorry," she sighed, as she finished buttoning up her shirt.

She had just taken out her phone and was about to call the taxi company when the door opened. A head appeared around the frame, one hand over his eyes so as not to see anything he shouldn't.

"Hey. Laura, you still here?" he asked.

"Yeah. And it's fine. I'm changed."

The man in the doorway removed his hand and smiled at her. "Better safe than sorry, I thought," he said.

Laura smiled back. "Funny, I was thinking the same thing. Was just about to phone a taxi to take me home."

"Ah, yes. Glad I caught you, then," the man replied. "I'm knocking off now, too. Want me to walk you? Police are advising—"

Laura closed her locker door, picked her coat up off the bench beside her, then shoved her phone into the pocket of her jeans. "That," she said, practically skipping towards the door, "would be brilliant!"

LOGAN WAS PACING. This was rarely a good sign.

Hamza had scoured Clarissa McDade's inbox, searching for anything that might reasonably be considered a clue. So far, he'd drawn a complete blank.

Tyler, meanwhile, was still ploughing his way through an apparently never-ending stack of paperwork. No one had any idea what he was looking for—least of all himself—but the hope was that he'd know it when he saw it.

So far, he'd seen nothing, aside from a report on a disciplinary hearing with Dr Colin Fletcher, after a nurse had accused him of using inappropriately sexual language. It had been six months ago, though, and the meeting had seemed amicable enough.

Logan was just about to ask if there had been any update on Fletcher when one came through. Uniform had found him. Or, at least, they knew where he was.

"A fucking tennis tournament?" Logan spat. "I thought he was sick?"

"Pulled a sickie, boss," Tyler said, hanging up the phone he'd taken the call on. "Been playing tennis in Aberdeen all day. Left last night, according to his ex-wife. He asked her along, but she told him to ram it up his arse."

"Did you—"

"Check? Aye. Hotel confirms he arrived just after ten last night. He's due to check out tomorrow."

Logan cursed below his breath. Another door closed.

"I think we're barking up the wrong tree with all this stuff, boss," Tyler said, opening another cardboard folder and pulling out yet another bundle of paperwork. "It feels like a dead end."

"They all feel like dead ends until you find an opening," Logan said. "That's the reality of polis work, son. Keep checking."

Tyler glanced at his watch, sighed, then turned the next page.

"I'm guessing I won't be able to get that time off tomorrow now, eh boss?" he said, his eyes scanning the neatly-spaced print.

Logan stopped pacing. "Time off? What time off?"

"Harris's birthday," Tyler said, still not looking up. Either this was the most fascinating report he'd come across so far, or he couldn't quite bring himself to meet the DCI's eye. "I'd said to Sinead that I'd come along."

"Aye," Logan said. He tutted. "I'm sorry, son, but I doubt it."

Tyler nodded. "Yeah. Fair enough, boss," he said, putting up far less of a fight than Logan had been bracing himself for. "Perks of the job, innit?"

"Afraid so."

He turned away from one DC and addressed the other. "Still nothing, Hamza?"

"Only a growing realisation that working in HR is bloody tedious, sir," DC Khaled said. "I mean, there are a lot of emails here all saying pretty much nothing. Can't find anything that could relate to any meeting she had on the day the calendar was changed."

"You check the deleted items folder?" Tyler asked.

"*Of course* I checked the deleted items folder," Hamza replied. "I'm not nine. There's nothing in there. It's been cleared out."

"What about the mail server?" Tyler asked.

Logan's head tick-tocked between both DCs, like a spectator at a tennis match.

"It's IMAP," Hamza said. "So whatever was deleted here will be deleted there, too."

"Could be back-ups, though," Tyler suggested.

"Aye, I've put a request in with the server team to see if they can dig something out, but I'm not holding out much hope. These systems are pretty ancient, and it doesn't look like they've been well set-up. I'll be very surprised if they're regularly backing up the email servers."

Logan raised his hands, interrupting. "Right, long story short. What does that mean?"

Hamza turned from the screen. "It means that someone potentially deleted any emails referencing their meeting with the victim to cover their tracks. There's a slim possibility we might be able to pull copies of the deleted emails from the server, but I doubt it, and we'd probably need to get a warrant. The HR boss's authorisation won't be enough."

"Shite. We won't get that tonight," Logan said.

"Doubt anyone from the server team would be around at this time anyway, sir," Hamza pointed out.

"They'll be around if I bloody tell them to be around," Logan snapped. He pinched the bridge of his nose and sighed. "But we won't get the warrant until tomorrow, so no point dragging them down."

The door to the office opened, and DS McQuarrie entered. She looked almost as tired as Logan felt. They all did, he realised. Time to send them home. This was getting them nowhere, anyway.

"Caitlyn. Anything?" he asked, grasping for one last lifeline.

"Nothing really, sir, no," DS McQuarrie replied. "The usual. Everyone shocked and saddened, she was always so friendly, she'll be sadly missed. That sort of thing."

Logan could only offer a disappointed grunt in reply.

"How's it going in here?" Caitlyn asked.

Logan grunted, then gestured vaguely in Hamza's direction. DC Khaled picked up on his cue and launched into a recap of what they'd found so far. This did not take long.

"So... Someone deleted references to themselves, we reckon?" Caitlyn asked, once Hamza's all-too-brief report was over. "From her email, I mean?"

"Looks like it, yeah," Hamza said.

Caitlyn ran her tongue across the front of her top teeth, her eyes narrowing.

"What?" Logan asked. "What are you thinking?"

"I don't even know if it's possible, sir," DS McQuarrie began.

"I'll try anything. What is it?" Logan pressed.

Caitlyn crossed to where Hamza was sitting. He turned to face the screen, and she rested a hand on the back of his chair. "So, she's HR. She'll have emails coming in all the time about the staff here, right?"

"She does," Hamza confirmed. "Loads of it."

"Search Esme Miller."

Hamza typed the name in the search box and clicked 'Go'. The mouse icon became a whirring egg-timer for a few seconds, then a list of emails appeared.

"Twelve results," he said. "Want me to look through them?"

Caitlyn shook her head. "No. Try Colin Fletcher."

"We've already found some stuff on him," Tyler interjected. "Here's a shocker for you, turns out he's a bit of a perv."

"Not surprising," Caitlyn said, still fixed on the screen. "Search him."

Logan joined her standing behind Hamza's chair as the DC typed in the name.

Click. Whirr.

"Nineteen results," Hamza announced.

"Right. Good," Caitlyn said.

"Why is that good?" Logan asked. "What does that tell us?"

"These search results? Nothing, sir," the DS replied. She continued before Logan could start shouting. "But, I was thinking, if we can search for what's there, can we search for what's not there?"

Hamza craned his neck to look up at her. "Eh?"

Logan was quicker to catch on. "Search for all the staff names. See if there's someone who doesn't bring up any results," he said. His eyes widened. "Christ. That could work."

"Worth a shot, sir," Caitlyn said.

"Why have I been stuck in here with this pair of clowns all night? Why weren't you here? We could've had this wrapped up hours ago," Logan said. He turned to Hamza. "Can you get us a list of all staff?"

Tyler piped up from the other desk. "I've got one here, boss," he said, kneeling down and rifling through a stack of folders that teetered beside the desk. "Somewhere. Hang on."

Logan rolled up his shirt sleeves and pointed to one of the other computers. "Can we get into her email from this?"

"Should be able to, sir. Even if her account isn't set up in Outlook, we can access the webmail to—"

"I'm no' wanting a dissertation on it, son. A simple yes or no will do."

"Yes, sir. Shouldn't be a problem," Hamza said.

"Good. Caitlyn, get set up on that one," Logan instructed, pointing to the third computer. "Tyler, find that list, then see if you can get us some laptops and a few Uniforms. We'll divide the list up and all take a section. It shouldn't take more than a few hours to work our way through—"

"Got it, sir," Hamza said.

Logan stopped midway through rolling up his second sleeve. "What?"

"I found a list and just ran an OR search in the inbox," Hamza replied. "Just copied and pasted."

Across the room, the stack of folders Tyler had been looking through toppled over and spilled across the floor. There was a *thump* and a 'Fuck' as he tried to straighten up and bumped his head on the underside of the desk.

"Oh. Right," Logan said. He rolled his sleeves down again. "And?"

"One sec, sir. Just working on the filters..."

"How long will that take?"

"Done," Hamza announced. He studied the results on-screen. "Huh. Looks like every member of staff gets mentioned at some point. Except one. No reference to him anywhere."

Logan bent at Hamza's shoulder, the glare of the monitor picking out the weathered lines of his face. "Who?"

"Some guy named... Conlyn, sir," Hamza said. "Kel Conlyn."

CHAPTER THIRTY-SIX

Laura Elder pulled her coat around her and side-eyed two men standing outside The Fluke pub, cigarettes tucked at the corners of their mouths. Music blared out from within as the door was opened, and a third man—older than the others—shuffled out to join them, lighter already in hand.

She relaxed a little once she and her companion were safely past the place, and gave herself a silent ticking off. She'd walked this way... what? Two hundred times? Four hundred? She'd long-since lost count. She'd never given it a second thought, either. She'd never felt afraid, or like she was in danger.

Until tonight.

"It's really good of you to do this," she said, shooting the man beside her a grateful smile. "I should've just got a taxi."

Kel Conlyn shook his head emphatically. "The price those robbing bastards charge? I don't blame you," he said, returning the smile with interest. "It's no bother. I can get my bus from just along the road from yours, anyway. Makes no odds to me."

He glanced both ways along the street and let out a little

giggle. "Can you imagine if someone does jump out on us, though? I'm not sure who'll scream the loudest."

Laura chewed a fingernail. "Shit. Good point. Maybe I should've asked Dr Fletcher for a lift home. He's always offering one."

Kel erupted into laughter. "I'll bet he is! Christ, can you imagine?" He adopted a deeper voice and gestured to his crotch. "What this? No, nurse, I always drive with my cock out, I assure you. There's nothing untoward about it whatsoever."

Laura joined in with the laughter. "Spot on."

"You'd have his fingers up you before you'd even got your seatbelt on," Kel said.

Laura pulled a shocked face, then slapped him on the arm. "Aye, in his bloody dreams. Anyway, I think he's off sick, or something. Didn't see him around."

They walked on in silence for a while, taking it in turns to shoot a quick look around them to make sure they weren't being followed by any knife-wielding maniacs, or sex-starved former surgeons. The golf course lay on either side of the road around them, the flags fluttering in the darkness beyond the reach of the streetlights.

"Did you watch it?" Laura asked. She turned to Kel, her eyes shimmering, her face alive with uncertainty, like she wasn't sure what reaction she was going to get. "The video, I mean. Of the HR woman. Did you watch it?"

"God, no," Kel said, shaking his head. "Not for me, that. I have a hard enough time getting to sleep as it is."

They went another dozen or so steps before he asked the obvious.

"You?"

Laura searched his face for a moment, then nodded. The movement was quick and mouse-like. "Some of it. I didn't know what it was going to be… I didn't watch it all. It was horrible."

"I'd imagine it would be," Kel said. He shuddered at the thought of it.

"He said some weird stuff at the start. The guy, I mean," Laura continued. "Kept saying it wasn't real, that she didn't exist, so he wasn't doing anything wrong, or whatever."

She shot Kel a sideways look. "Bit mental that, isn't it?"

Kel said nothing.

"I mean, why wouldn't she exist? And not just her. He said that none of us existed. Him, too. Kept saying we weren't real."

"Maybe we aren't."

Laura snorted. "What?" She jabbed him on the arm. "You feel pretty real to me."

A flicker of annoyance darted briefly across Kel's face, then he smiled. "I mean, obviously he's mental, but if it was true–if he was right, and this was all, say, a dream, or… I don't know, a computer simulation–then would anything matter?"

"I don't follow," Laura said.

"What's not to follow? It's not difficult," Kel replied, the tone of his voice hardening. "If we were in a computer simulation–if we were characters in a game created by someone else for their entertainment–then why not kill someone? Why not just do whatever you want?"

"Well, because…"

"Because what?" Kel asked, stopping. "If it's not real, then the consequences aren't real. If it's all just a dream, then why care?"

Laura smiled again, but Kel didn't join in. She shifted uneasily from foot to foot, suddenly aware of the darkness pressing in from just beyond the glow of the streetlights.

"Well, I mean, it's still real to us, isn't it?"

Kel eyeballed her for a few long, drawn-out moments, then relaxed. "Exactly," he said, setting off again. "We get that. Even if everything's fake, the rules we've created for ourselves still apply. Kill someone, you still go to jail. Their family still grieves. But, my point is, to someone who doesn't get that part, the idea that there are no consequences to *anything* must make it pretty tempting to just go out and do—"

He stopped again, suddenly alert. Turning, he scanned the shadows of the golf course.

"What?" Laura asked.

"Shh," he urged, holding up a finger. He squinted into the gloom, eyes darting left and right, head cocked a fraction. "Did you hear that?"

Laura followed his gaze. Her voice, when it came, was a whisper. "Hear what?"

"I don't know," Kel admitted. "For a second, I thought I heard..."

He shook his head, then took Laura by the hand. "Come on," he said, hurrying her along the street. "Let's get you home."

Glancing both ways to make sure the coast was clear, he led her across the road, towards the other half of the golf course across the street.

"This is the wrong way," Laura protested, scampering along behind him.

"Don't worry," Kel said. He looked back at her, then past to the wall of darkness at their backs. "I know a short cut."

CHAPTER THIRTY-SEVEN

DCI Logan stormed through the corridors of Raigmore hospital, backtracking to where he'd met Kel Conlyn earlier in the evening.

Caitlyn had remained back in the HR Department, checking shift rotas to see if she could figure out which ward he had been based in that day, while Hamza and Tyler had set off in opposite directions to try to track Conlyn down.

A nurse jumped in fright as she emerged from a side door to find Logan storming towards her. "Kel Conlyn. He's a porter. You seen him?"

"Sorry. I... I am new," she replied in a lilting Indian accent. "I do not know."

"Who's in charge?" the DCI demanded.

The nurse looked up at him, uncomprehending.

"The boss. Where's your boss?" Logan asked, lowering his voice. "Who's your boss?"

"Oh. She is this way," the nurse replied, pulling the door open and gesturing for Logan to go through. "Maybe... um... Yes. She help you?"

Logan stormed through and found himself face-to-face with a mural of *Winnie the Pooh.* Other characters had been painted onto the otherwise dull cream walls. A sign hung from the ceiling, informing those who hadn't already figured it out that this was the way to the children's ward.

The nurse led him through a brightly-painted door, and onto a corridor with a number of doors and large windows along one wall. He could see a bed through the closest window, a boy of around eight or nine sleeping soundly in it, apparently oblivious to the wires and tubes connected to various parts of his anatomy.

"Esha? Is everything alright?" asked an older nurse who sat behind a desk close to the first of the doors. She had a hawk-like appearance and gave off a distinct 'do not mess with me' vibe that Logan approved of.

The younger nurse gestured to Logan with both hands, as if presenting a gameshow prize. "This man. He looks for you."

"Does he now? And who might—"

Logan held up his warrant card. "You the charge nurse?"

She took the card from him and scrutinised it. Only once she was happy with it, did she reply.

"Yes," she said, handing the card back. She pumped a couple of squirts of disinfectant gel onto her hands and rubbed it in. "Esha, you can go for your break now. Thank you."

Esha practically bowed as she backed out of the corridor.

"What can I do for you?" the charge nurse asked.

"Kel Conlyn."

"What about him?"

"You know him, then?"

The nurse nodded. "I do. Why?"

"Where is he? Is he on this ward?"

"No," the nurse said. "But he was. Why?"

"Was?" Logan asked. "What, is he finished?"

"He's gone home, yes," the nurse confirmed. "Again, why?"

"Shite. When?" Logan demanded. "When did he leave?"

His phone rang before the nurse could answer. Snatching it from his pocket, he caught a glimpse of Caitlyn's name on-screen, then tapped the icon to answer it.

"You're not supposed to use those in here," the nurse scolded, but Logan had his back to her now, and ignored the comment completely.

"Caitlyn. What have we got?"

"We've found Conlyn, sir," Caitlyn replied. There was something about the way she said it that made Logan pause. "He's in A&E."

Logan glanced back over his shoulder at the charge nurse. "I've just been told he'd gone home."

"He had, sir. I don't mean he's on shift," Caitlyn said. "I mean he's been admitted. He's been attacked."

"Conlyn has?"

"Not just him, sir," Caitlyn said. "There was a woman with him."

Logan's breath caught somewhere in his throat. He felt his lungs burn almost at once. "And?"

"She's dead, sir," Caitlyn replied. "It's happened again."

KEL CONLYN HAD BEEN PATCHED up by the time Logan was allowed to see him. He'd taken a knife to the right shoulder, and his forearms were crisscrossed with defensive wounds. A passer-by had found him after he'd crawled out of Walker Park and onto the pavement, bleeding and semi-conscious.

Uniform had found Laura Elder twenty minutes later, hidden beneath a crop of trees in the park. Dead. Mutilated.

Fake.

Kel was sitting propped upright in bed when Logan and DC Neish entered, his gaze fixed on the window of the private room he'd been given. He had a mobile phone in one hand, but clutched it limply, like he wasn't really aware it was there.

There was a vase on the table by the bed, a bunch of tired-looking flowers drooping over the sides. They complemented Conlyn's expression perfectly.

It was only when the door closed with a *thunk* that he blinked away a blurring of tears, ran the back of a bandaged arm across his cheek, then summoned the energy to sit up straighter.

"Hello. God. Hi," he said. His voice was scarcely a whisper, lost amongst the *bleeping* and *pinging* and all the other noises of the hospital. "How is Laura? They won't tell me. Is she...?"

Logan gave a single nod. "She is. I'm sorry."

Kel's face crumpled. He sobbed for a full minute—big, silent heaves that racked his body and made Tyler visibly awkward. The DC looked around the room, then consulted the chart at the end of the bed in an effort to hide his embarrassment.

Logan, meanwhile, didn't flinch. He stood by the bed, watching Kel cry, his eye locked on the man like a targeting missile.

"Sorry. Sorry, I'm sorry," Kel said, hastily wiping his eyes again. He winced at the pain the movement brought, and Logan's gaze went to the bandage on the man's bare shoulder.

"It's fine, Mr Conlyn. We understand," Logan said. He indicated the bandage. "Is it bad?"

"Hmm? Oh, yeah. Bad enough, I think. Didn't hit anything major, though, thankfully."

"Really? That's lucky," Logan said. "Given how accurate the attacker has been thus far."

Kel smiled weakly. "Yes. Yes, I suppose so." His expression soured. "I'll be honest, though, none of it feels very lucky right now."

He bit his bottom lip so hard the skin around it turned white, then red. "Oh, God. Laura. I was supposed to be looking after her. I told her I'd get her home safe."

Tyler tried to head off another outburst of tears. "It's not your fault. There's nothing anyone could have done."

Kel sniffed, met Tyler's gaze, then managed another small smile. "Thank you. I'm not sure it's true, but... thanks."

He held a hand out. Tyler side-eyed Logan for a moment, then reached out with his own hand. Kel took it, squeezed it, then let it go again. "That means a lot," he said. "Really."

"Uh, aye. No bother," Tyler said, stepping back and vowing to keep his mouth shut from now on.

"We hate to do this so soon after what you've just been through, Mr Conlyn, but we need to ask you a few questions about the attack. Is that OK?"

Kel shuffled himself more upright in the bed, then nodded. "Of course. Anything. I want this fucker caught just as much as you do. What do you need to know?"

Logan motioned for Tyler to take a seat in the visitor chair set up by the bed. The DC took his phone from his pocket and held it up to Conlyn. "Mind if I record this?"

"Please. Anything. Whatever helps."

Tyler sat, activated the voice recorder app on his phone, then set it on the trolley table by the bed with the microphone pointed in the patient's direction.

"Talk us through what happened, Mr Conlyn," Logan intoned.

"Right. Well, he came out of nowhere, really—"

"From the start, if you don't mind," Logan interjected. "What time did you leave the hospital?"

Kel's eyelids fluttered for a moment like his brain was recalibrating, then he replied.

"Just after ten. We had both been on a bit later, and I know she doesn't live too far away—just past the park where we... Where it happened. I thought I'd offer to walk her," Kel said. "You know, after our conversation?"

"Aye. Good. So, you left the hospital together just after ten o'clock tonight. Then what?"

"We just, I don't know, walked and chatted, really," Kel said. "We passed The Fluke. You know, the pub along the road?"

Logan glanced at Tyler, and got a nod in return.

"It's pretty well-known locally," Kel said, picking up on the non-verbal communication. "There were a few people standing outside having a fag. They'll have seen us, if you want to check."

"I'm sure that won't be necessary," Logan said. "Go on."

Kel took a breath, as if bracing himself for an uphill struggle. "We kept walking. She was talking about the HR woman. What was her name?"

"Clarissa."

"Yes. Shit. Of course it was. Clarissa. She was talking about Clarissa—she'd watched some of the video that's doing the rounds, apparently. Seemed pretty cut-up about it."

"About the death or watching the video?" Logan asked.

This caught Kel off guard. He gave it due consideration before replying. "Both, I suppose. I think she felt guilty about watching it. You know, a bit ashamed? I think it was, like, a confession. Like she wanted to tell someone she'd done it, but that she regretted it."

"Understandable," Logan said. "What then?"

"Then..." Kel's brow furrowed, recalling the details. "I heard someone. Or... I don't know. I thought I heard someone, anyway. On the golf course over on our left."

He looked to DC Neish. "It's split across both sides of the road."

"I know it, aye," Tyler replied, earning himself a grateful smile from the man in the bed.

"I was sure I heard something in the dark bit over on the left."

"Something like what?" Logan pressed.

Kel's forehead was ridged with lines now, like he was wrestling against the memory, trying to pin it in place. "Movement, I think. Or... I don't know. Maybe I didn't even hear it. Maybe I just *sensed* it. I just know I had this strong feeling that someone was there. Watching us. And that we had to get the fuck out of there."

His eyes went to the polystyrene ceiling tiles as he fought to hold himself together.

"So, we did," he said, his voice barely a squeak through his narrowing throat. "We crossed the road and decided to cut across the park."

"Why the park?" Tyler asked.

"It's quicker."

"No lights, though," Tyler pointed out. "Bit risky."

The hurt registered on Kel's face like he'd been physically wounded. "Obviously, I know that now," he said, his voice going up a couple of octaves. "But we thought he was behind us somewhere. We thought it would just get us back to..."

He shook his head. Closed his eyes.

"No."

Logan glanced from Kel to Tyler and back again. "No?"

"Not 'we.' We didn't decide to go across the park," Kel admitted. He rolled his tongue around in his mouth until he could force the next two words out. "I did."

He cleared his throat. Once. Twice. His fingers flexed in and out. It looked like he was battling to keep control of his body. Battling to keep talking. Battling to keep himself from curling up into a ball and sobbing until there was nothing of him left.

"The shortcut was my idea. It was all mine," he said. His voice had become a dull monotone, like maybe if he didn't think too much about their meaning, he'd be able to say them. "It's my fault this happened. It's my fault Laura's dead."

Tyler looked up at Logan, waiting for the DCI to impart some words of comfort. When none came, he realised it was being left to him.

"You can't blame yourself, Mr Conlyn," Tyler told him. "You couldn't possibly have known."

"Thank you," Kel said, managing another of those not-quite-smiles. He placed a hand on Tyler's arm. "And call me Kel."

"Uh, OK. Cool," said Tyler. "Will do."

Logan took the reins again, and Kel removed his hand from DC Neish's arm.

"Now, I need you to think very carefully about the order of events that followed," the DCI said.

Kel immediately shook his head. "No."

Logan's eyebrows knotted so tightly together they practically became singular. "*No*?"

"I don't need to think carefully," Kel continued.

His gaze went to the wall directly across from his bed, eyes darting left and right like a kid at the cinema. One hand—the one that hadn't been on Tyler's arm—twisted the edge of his blanket into knots.

"I can still see it," he whispered. "I can still see it all. I can still see *him*. That mask."

He looked up at Logan, eyes brimming with tears.

"I can still see what he did."

CHAPTER THIRTY-EIGHT

Ben Forde sidled up to Logan at the cordon tape and pressed a steaming hot paper cup into his hand. The DCI nodded his appreciation, then clutched the cup to his stomach, absorbing some of its heat.

"Christ, Jack, when did you last get some sleep?" Ben asked, looking his old friend up and down. He had an umbrella up to protect himself from the rain. The droplets rattled against it like a frenzied percussionist. "You look awful."

"No' that long ago," Logan said. "This morning."

Ben did a double-take. "Seriously?"

"Aye. Ye cheeky bastard. This is me on a good day, these days."

"The years have not been kind," Ben remarked.

"No," Logan agreed. "No, they have not."

They stood in silence, the rain hammering away at the umbrella, and *plinking* into Logan's cup. Had it been anyone else, Ben would have offered to squidge up a bit and share the cover, but he knew the DCI's thoughts on them. He'd rather succumb to pneumonia than be seen beneath an umbrella.

Besides, the height difference would be a nightmare. Ben would be the one to end up soaking and, quite frankly, it was his bloody brolly.

The park had so many tents in it that it had started to resemble a festival campsite. There was one out on the street, too, and the cordon had been extended right across the road, meaning traffic was having to be diverted at both ends.

Palmer's Scene of Crime team were tiptoeing around in their gradually disintegrating paper suits. Palmer himself wasn't on duty tonight, which was some small mercy. He'd invoked the European Working Hours Directive, claiming he'd done too many hours in too short a period of time, and was refusing to come back out until the following morning.

Logan didn't know whether to condemn the bastard or applaud him. If you let it, the job would swallow up your whole life. He knew that better than most.

But a girl was dead. A killer was still out there. And rest was a luxury Logan couldn't afford.

"You spoke to the fella who was with her," Ben said. It wasn't a question, exactly, more of a prompt.

Logan nodded, still watching the paper suits do their stuff. "I did. Kel Conlyn."

Ben rifled through the internal filing system in his head.

"He was the last one to see Esme Miller alive, wasn't he?"

"He was," Logan confirmed. "He was also the only one out of over two-thousand members of staff not to get a mention in Clarissa McDade's email inbox."

Ben took a moment to think this through, but didn't get very far.

"Meaning?"

"Meaning, it's possible he deleted any reference of himself."

"Take a while that, wouldn't it?" Ben asked.

"No. Quicker that way than just removing anything incriminating. Search the name in the inbox, select all results, delete."

The rain pattered on Ben's brolly. Somewhere along the street, a Uniform turned away a car that had been approaching the cordon.

"Sounds like he was lucky he got stabbed," Ben said. "Or we'd have a new suspect."

"Very fortuitous, aye," Logan agreed.

"You seen the wounds?"

"Not up close, no. Stab injury to the right shoulder that missed anything vital. Slash marks on his forearms that suggest defensive wounds. I'm having Caitlyn go over it with the doctor who treated him at the moment. Tyler's staying to keep an eye on him. I think Conlyn has taken a bit of a shine to him."

"Seriously? Wow. Sounds like a wrong 'un, alright, if he's taken a liking to Tyler," Ben remarked. "We should probably haul him in now."

"Not quite yet," Logan remarked. He tore his eyes away from the SOC team, turned to Ben, and almost had an eye out on one of the brolly's spikes. "Jesus, careful with that bloody thing."

"It's no' my fault. I haven't moved."

Logan's expression said he was still very much holding the DI responsible. He made a gruff huffing sound, then glanced at his watch and winced. Later than he'd thought.

"I'm going to go check around at Conlyn's flat. Who's in the office?"

"Not sure. Hamza's away to get some sleep. There'll be CID around, though, why?"

"Find out who the landlord is. Get me a phone number. If they're local, get them to meet me there."

"Could take a while," Ben said. "If it's rented through a letting agency, it's going to be shut."

"Better get on it, then."

Logan set off walking into the rain, then stopped after a few paces. He closed his eyes and raised his head, the rain like a baptism on his face.

"In fact, on second thought, don't bother with that," Logan told him.

"Don't bother with the landlord?"

"No," Logan said. He looked back at Ben. A drop of rain hung suspended from the end of his nose for a moment, then *plinked* into a puddle at his feet. "I've got a better idea."

Logan waited until he was back at his car before taking out his phone. He tapped the Contacts app, scrolled down a few names, then hit dial. He was careful not to turn the car's engine on, in case the phone's audio suddenly came blaring out via the Bluetooth connection, broadcasting the conversation to everyone within earshot.

The phone was answered after a few rings. The voice on the other end sounded happy to hear from him. It wasn't, he knew, but it sounded it.

"Bosco," Logan said, cutting off the enthusiastic greeting. "How'd you like to get yourself in my good books?"

LOGAN FLASHED his warrant card as he approached the open front door of Kel Conlyn's flat, and a couple of neighbours stepped aside to let him through.

"That was quick," one of them—a woman in her forties—remarked. "We only called you a few minutes ago."

"I was in the area," Logan told her. He motioned to the door. "What happened?"

"Some big fella kicked it in. Just kicked it right in," the woman said. She nudged a tall, yet downtrodden-looking man beside her in the ribs with her elbow, bringing him to life.

"Just kicked it right in," the man agreed.

"We saw it, didn't we? Alan?"

"Yes," the tall man confirmed. "We saw it."

Alan's wife pointed to the block of flats directly across from Conlyn's. "We're over there. We heard a car screeching up, music blaring. I looked out, didn't I, Alan?"

"She did. She looked out," Alan said. "She just got up and looked right out."

"And there was this fella. Big. All in black. He had a balaclava on." She turned to her husband. "I'm saying, he had a balaclava on. Didn't he?"

"He did. Covering his face."

"A balaclava," the wife said. She gave Logan a meaningful nod, like he was supposed to be writing this down.

"Did he go inside?" Logan pressed.

"No! That's the funny thing. That's what I was just saying, wasn't I, Alan?"

"She was. She was just saying."

"He just kicked the door in, then ran off. Very strange behaviour, if you ask me. Very strange."

The woman shrugged and shook her head. "Anyway, we thought we should call you lot, since it doesn't seem like anyone's home. We didn't know what else to do. Did we?"

"We didn't know what else to do," Alan agreed.

"You did the right thing," Logan told them, which made

them both puff up with pride. "What do you know about the person living here?"

The woman screwed her nose up, like she wasn't a fan. "Eh. Not much. Keeps himself to himself, although he can be a bit... You know?"

Logan raised his eyebrows to indicate that no, he didn't know.

"*Flamboyant*," she said, whispering it like it was some sort of slur she didn't want anyone to overhear her uttering. "I mean, not that I've anything against that sort of thing, do I, Alan?"

"She doesn't have anything against that sort of thing," Alan said, as if operating on some sort of auto-pilot.

"Each to their own, I say. None of my business. It's just, some of them can be a bit... full-on. You know? Although, I must say, we haven't really spoken much to him since he moved in last year. Like I say, keeps himself to himself mostly."

Logan nodded. "Right, well I should—Wait. Last year?"

"Yes. He moved in... Ooh, God. When?"

"Now you're asking," said Alan, scratching his head. "September, maybe?"

"Not September. We were away in September," his wife reminded him. Quite aggressively, Logan thought. "How could it have been September if we weren't here?"

"Sorry, yes. I mean, no. Sorry," Alan gushed. "It couldn't have been September, you're right. She's right."

"It was August. I remember because the kids on the other side had just gone back to school."

A year. Fourteen months.

He'd told them he'd only been in a few weeks. He'd used that to explain his lack of furniture.

"I'd better have a look," Logan said. He could hear sirens

wailing in the distance now, and ushered the couple back towards their own front door. "Thanks for your help. If we need anything more, I'll let you know."

He didn't wait for them to reply. Instead, he turned to the door, already pulling on a pair of thin blue gloves.

You could say what you liked about Bosco Maximuke—and Logan often did—but the man was significantly quicker than a search warrant. Sure, he'd look for the favour to be returned at some point down the line, but Logan could deal with that then. Tonight, he'd needed a way into that flat, and Bosco—or, more accurately, one of his lapdogs—had provided it.

Creaking the door the rest of the way open, Logan stepped over the threshold and into the narrow hallway. The starkness of the place struck him, just as it had done on his first visit there. The bare walls. The exposed lightbulbs. The lack of carpets, furniture, and anything else that might make the place feel even remotely like a home.

He'd seen the hallway and living room last time, so he ventured into the other rooms. He found the kitchen first. It was similarly bare, although there was a fairly bog-standard selection of units and wall cabinets, and some dilapidated appliances that were probably included in the rent.

Logan checked the fridge and freezer. Both were empty, the power to them switched off. Most of the cupboards were empty too, although one turned up thirty or more tin cans, the labels all missing so it was impossible to identify the contents.

"The hell is all this?" Logan muttered, carefully lifting a can and turning it over in his gloved hands. The use-by date had passed recently, but there was nothing else remarkable about the tin, so he set it back down and checked the drawers.

The topmost drawer contained a selection of weathered cutlery, the metal dull, the plastic handles cracked and faded.

A scattering of utensils lay in the next one down, all with the same matching plastic as the cutlery, although less worn-looking, on account of having been used less.

The drawer below that was empty, aside from four placemats showing various Highland scenes, and a pack of three dishcloths still threaded through the cardboard they'd come packaged in.

The next door along in the corridor was a bathroom. It felt less uninhabited than the other rooms Logan had seen, thanks to a single towel and a toothbrush, but there was still something cold and impersonal about it. Nobody loved this room. They used it, perhaps, but only because they had to.

There was one door left. From outside, Logan could hear the howling of the sirens getting closer. One car, he thought, although possibly two. He could also hear the murmuring of the couple who'd made the call. With a bit of luck, they'd explain to the Uniforms who he was, and that he'd already gone inside, which should hopefully deter any of them from trying to arrest him on suspicion of burglary.

The bedroom door didn't budge when Logan turned the handle. Bending, he spotted a keyhole, and tried to look through it. Either the room beyond was in absolute darkness, or there was a covering on the other side of the lock. Either way, he could see precisely hee-haw.

"Bugger it," he muttered. Coughing to cover the noise, he put a shoulder to the door. The wood was thin and weak, and the door flew open without any resistance.

A single table stood in the middle of the bedroom, and there was a blow-up mattress in the corner. It sagged pitifully, most of the air in it clearly having moved on elsewhere.

It was the table that held Logan's attention, though. Or, more precisely, the laptop computer sitting on top of it. The lid was open, the screen lit-up. It showed the desktop, complete with a small selection of icons, and a wallpaper showing Keanu Reeves in a long black coat.

As Logan stepped into the room, two red lights started flickering on either side of the laptop's camera, then went solid. The screen flashed white, and Keanu was briefly replaced by a picture of Logan standing in the doorway.

Then, the display went black. Something inside the computer emitted a *paff* and a single flame sputtered up from the keyboard. It caught hold immediately, devouring the keys and licking up the screen before Logan could tear off his coat and throw it over the top. Some sort of accelerant. Had to be.

He slapped down on the coat, smothering and beating out the flames, but he knew it was already too late. Whatever forensic material the machine might have offered up was gone. Whatever was on the hard drive would be impossible to recover. Whatever evidence it could have provided was lost.

The fire caught hold inside the coat, quickly smouldering a hole the size of a ten pence piece through the outer material. The sudden inrush of air fuelled the flames below, forcing Logan to drop the coat as the fire tore through it.

Whatever accelerant had been used was on the table, too. Logan saw the fire go rushing down all four legs at once. The floor beneath his coat was already ablaze, and when the flames racing down the table legs met the bare wooden floorboards, they immediately ignited.

A fog of black smoke rose up from the flames, rapidly filling the top half of the room. Coughing, Logan clamped a hand over his mouth and stumbled out into the hallway, the billowing smoke chasing him through the door.

At the flat's entrance, he met two female uniformed constables coming the other way.

"Stay where you are," one of them barked, but he hurried towards them, ushering them both out.

"DCI Jack Logan, Major Investigations. Outside, now," he instructed.

Their eyes went to the cloud of black behind him, and the flames already licking floorboards of the hall. The fire seemed to leap across the threshold, whatever accelerant that was soaked into the floor of the bedroom clearly having been liberally applied in the hallway, too.

Logan emerged into the cool night air. For once, he'd have been grateful for a downpour to wash away the smoke residue and rinse his stinging eyes, but the rain had stopped on the way over, and pinpricks of light winked down on him from on high.

"Do you, eh... Do you have any ID?" asked one of the constables. The other had retreated a few steps and was talking urgently into the radio on her shoulder, calling in the fire.

"Aye," Logan said, bending double and hacking up a lungful of soot. He jabbed a thumb back over his shoulder. "It's in my coat. By all means, help yourself."

"God, Alan, look. It's on fire!"

"It is, and all. It's on fire," Alan confirmed.

Logan looked up at the two neighbours. They stood in the open doorway of their flat, peering across at the flames raging inside Conlyn's hallway.

"Is anyone upstairs?" Logan asked them, pointing to the flat above Conlyn's. The place was in darkness, but the fire was licking its way up the walls now, and anyone up there only had a few minutes to get out. "Is it currently occupied?"

"No. It's been empty for about... what, Alan? About a month?"

"About a month, I'd say, yes," Alan confirmed.

"About a month," his wife reiterated. "I was just saying that the other day, wasn't I? It's been empty a while. I was just saying that."

"You were."

"About a month."

Mercifully, Logan missed most of the exchange due to the fact he was hacking up a lung. The smoke had affected him quickly. It was lucky he'd left the front door open, or he may not have made it out at all.

"You alright, sir?" asked the closest constable, having obviously decided to take him at his word. "Maybe we should get you to the hospital."

Logan coughed again, then wiped his mouth on the sleeve of his shirt.

Shite. The hospital.

"Keys," he said, holding out a hand.

The uniformed officer briefly regarded the hand, then frowned. "Sir?"

"Keys. Mine are in my coat."

She backed away a step, glancing at her colleague for support. She was still on the call though, and only vaguely paying attention.

"I'm not sure that's... I mean, I don't know if..."

"Fine. It'll be quicker if you drive, anyway," he said, marching past her. He pointed to the other officer. "You, wait here, get everyone to a safe distance, and keep them away until the cavalry arrives. No one goes near."

"Uh..." she replied, but Logan was already past her, half-marching, half-jogging in the direction of the police car. Its lights were flashing on top, licking the front of the surrounding buildings in bright blue.

The first officer didn't seem to be moving. He beckoned to

her as he pulled open the front passenger door of the patrol car. "Well, come on then, we haven't got all bloody night!"

A look passed between both officers, then a shrug. The one with the keys hurried over to the car, shot a final look at her partner, then slid into the driver's seat beside Logan.

"Where to, sir?" she asked, firing up the engine.

"Raigmore Hospital," Logan said. He clipped on his seatbelt and rapped his knuckles on the dash. "Full blues and twos."

"Right, sir," the officer replied.

And then, with lights flashing and sirens screaming, the car screeched away from the kerb, leaving a growing column of fire behind them.

CHAPTER THIRTY-NINE

DC Neish staggered out into the hospital corridor to find Logan hurtling towards him. Blood oozed down the side of Tyler's face, filling his ear and staining his shirt. He clutched a wound somewhere above his hairline and leaned on the wall to stop himself dropping to his knees.

"Shite. Tyler, what happened?" Logan asked, skidding to a stop beside the DC. He threw open the door to the room that had previously contained Kel Conlyn, and was dismayed to discover that it no longer did. "Bollocks!" he ejected. "Where did he go?"

"Dunno, boss," Tyler admitted. He winced, like speaking brought a new wave of pain. "Some alarm went off on his phone. He checked it, then he just grabbed the vase and fucking brained me with it."

His eyes were swimming as he struggled to stay conscious. "Think he knocked me out."

"The camera. He must've seen me," Logan realised, looking left and right along the corridor. A nurse appeared at the far end, and almost jumped out of her skin when Logan bellowed at her. "You. This man needs help. Look after him."

"Is it him, boss?" Tyler asked. "Is it Conlyn?"

"Certainly looks like it, son," Logan said. He waited until the nurse was almost upon them, then gave the DC a pat on the shoulder. "But don't you worry about it right now. Get yourself taken care of."

"What on Earth happened?" the nurse asked, her voice shrill when she spotted the blood trickling from Tyler's head. "What's going on?"

"He'll explain," Logan told her. "Did you see anyone running past here? Kel Conlyn. Young guy. Twenties. Skinny. He's injured."

Logan was off and running as soon as the nurse had started to shake her head. He doubled-back almost immediately, and held a hand out to Tyler. "Phone."

Tyler screwed up one eye, like he was having to concentrate to figure out what was being asked of him. "Boss?"

"Give me your phone. Mine went on fire."

"Fire?"

"Later. Phone."

"Two-seven-two-one," Tyler said, handing it over. "That's the pin."

Logan took the phone, punched in the code, then set off again, already swiping through the contacts list.

He tapped a name, and was barrelling onto a ward when the call was answered.

"Tyler. To what do I owe the displeasure?" asked DI Forde.

"Ben. It's me. Long story, no time," Logan said. He threw open the door to one of the ward rooms. Five elderly women glowered at him from beds, while a sixth snored loudly in the corner.

After a quick check behind the door, he continued the call. "We need to put the hospital on lockdown. Nobody in or out."

"What? Why?" Ben asked.

Logan closed the door and hurried to the next one along. A storage cupboard this time. Empty, besides the stacks of toilet rolls, paper towels, and disinfectant gel.

"It's Conlyn. He's behind it, and he's done a runner."

"Shite. I thought Tyler was keeping an eye on him."

"He got the jump on him. Smashed a vase across the side of his head."

"Jesus, is—"

"He'll need stitches, but he'll be fine," Logan said. "Now stop talking to me and start talking to whoever can get this place locked down."

He hung up before the DI could reply to him, spotted a young woman with a stethoscope coming out of an office, and went striding over to her.

"Kel Conlyn. He's a porter, or an orderly, or whatever they're called," he barked.

Taken aback, the doctor could only stare.

"I'm polis. DCI Logan," he said, dropping his voice a few decibels. "A patient's done a runner. He's a suspect. We need to find him now."

"I thought... A patient? Who's the orderly, then?"

"Him. They're the same. The orderly is the... Forget it. I need to—"

An alarm blared. High-pitched. Urgent. Logan turned, looking back the way he came, where the alarm seemed to be emanating from.

"Fire alarm," the doctor said. "Shit."

Logan clenched his fists. "No, no, no. *Bastard.* They can't evacuate. It's him, he's set off the bloody alarm."

"They won't evacuate if there isn't a fire," the doctor assured him. "And even then, they'll start with the section the alarm was raised."

Logan spun to face her. "Is there a way to see where it was set off?"

"Sure. Over here," the doctor said, leading him to a panel on the wall. A red light winked at him, flashing an illuminated code.

"Where is that?" Logan demanded.

"That's... I think that's... Hang on."

She consulted a laminated list on the wall beside the panel. Behind them, half a dozen nurses went bustling into the various rooms to keep the patients calm.

"Outpatients," the doctor announced.

"Where is that?"

"That way, turn right, left, then straight on," the doctor told him, her hand gestures corresponding with the instructions.

Logan had started running at 'that way' mapping out the rest of the route as the doctor shouted her instructions after him. The phone rang as he skidded around the final bend and powered along the wide corridor that led to the Outpatients department.

At this time of night, the place was in half-darkness, the clinics all closed, the staff all gone home.

The doubts crept in as Logan huffed and wheezed the final few dozen yards along the corridor. The screaming of the alarm was ear-shattering here, each squeal stabbing like an icepick into his skull.

Why set off the alarm here? Using an evacuation as cover to escape would only work if there were people to evacuate.

How could you use a crowd for cover if there was no crowd to get lost in?

Logan's footsteps echoed off into the half-darkness ahead as he clattered to a stop. He turned back, chest heaving, and spat out a series of curses that were all drowned out by the sound of the alarm.

Tyler's phone buzzed in his pocket. Jamming a finger in his ear, he tapped 'answer' and pressed the phone hard against the other ear.

"Ben. Tell me you got him."

DI Forde's reply was too faint to make out.

"What? Speak up!"

"I said, 'Christ, that's loud,'" Ben shouted. "We're getting the doors locked now. Place should be secure in the next five minutes."

Logan groaned. "Forget it."

"What? I can't hear you."

"I said, 'Forget it.' It's too late," Logan said, looking back along the corridor in the direction he'd come from. "He's already gone."

THE COOL AIR hits him as he steps outside, chilling his lungs and nipping at his injuries. They were a mistake, he realises now. A silly idea. Pointless.

Like everything.

They were bound to figure it out eventually, but he thought he'd have more time. They'd hunt him down now. They still believed in all their little rules. They still believed it mattered. That anything *mattered.*

He had failed to make them see. To make them understand the utter pointlessness of it all.

It would be over soon. They'd find him. They'd stop him.

But not now.

Not yet.

Not quite.

There was still time for one more. He could still give them one final demonstration.

And this would be one they'd never *forget.*

CHAPTER FORTY

Logan stood in front of the Big Board, addressing his team, half of CID, and a dozen uniformed officers. He slapped a photograph with the back of his hand, more forcefully than was strictly necessary.

"Kel Conlyn. Twenty-two. Wanted in connection with the recent string of murders that I know we're all only too aware of. Some of you will have seen the video he made, and heard his... fucking... I don't know. Manifesto. He thinks nothing he's doing really matters. He thinks we don't exist. Well, we, ladies and gentlemen, are going to prove him very wrong on that."

Logan looked across the faces of the audience. They were crammed into the Incident Room, sitting on chairs and desks, standing where they had to. Most of them had been dragged out of their beds and brought in. Many of them had just gone off shift a couple of hours before.

Nobody had complained. Or, if they had, they'd at least had the sense not to do it within Logan's earshot.

Hamza, Ben, and Caitlyn were sitting right in the front

row, DC Khaled looking marginally more refreshed than the other two. Tyler had called from the hospital to say he'd be in after they'd finished stitching his head wounds, but Logan had told him to go home and get some rest.

"No offence, boss, but that's shite," Tyler had said. "I'm the one who let him get away. I should be in there."

Logan had ordered him to go home, and not to show face until next morning. At which point, with a bit of luck, Conlyn would already be in custody. Tyler had started to grumble about it, but Logan had shouted him down and ended the call. He'd almost have felt bad about it, if he hadn't been doing it for the boy's own good.

"This man has raped, and he has murdered, and he will do it again unless we catch him," Logan continued. He let that sink in for a moment, eyes narrowed as he observed the reactions of the audience. "And so, we are going to catch him quickly and efficiently before anyone else can get hurt. We're going to find him tonight. We're going to bring him in, and we're going to put him away for the rest of his miserable life.

"He's exposed, which makes him more dangerous than ever," Logan continued. "So, we need boots on streets. We need every shed, garage, and outhouse checked. We need people going door-to-door, even if that means waking up the whole bloody city."

A hand went up a couple of rows back. One of the guys from CID, whose name Logan hadn't yet learned. He asked his question without being prompted.

"What have we got on him? Family, past addresses, friends?"

"Not a lot," said Caitlyn, picking up on the nod from Logan. "We know—at least, we *believe*—he was kicked out by his parents on account of his sexuality, but we don't know where or when that was. We're still digging, but he's done a good job of covering his tracks. It looks like he's been planning this for a while. It's looking like he created the Kel Conlyn identity for himself."

She looked down at the pad she and Hamza had been scribbling notes on for the past hour. "There was a Kelvin Conlyn who shares the same date of birth, but he died a few months later. We think he assumed that identity using copies of the birth certificate."

"So, he could be anyone? From anywhere?" asked the CID officer.

"Basically, aye," Logan confirmed. "Accent's reasonably local, though. He could be putting it on, but my instinct is not. If we get his picture out there, we might get a match."

He looked to Hamza, a questioning eyebrow raised.

"It's gone out on social media, sir," DC Khaled said. "BBC and STV are going to include it in their bulletins, but we won't get much back from those until tomorrow." He stifled a yawn. Or tried to, at least. "Middle of the night. Not exactly big audiences."

"Right. I know we're all tired. We'd all like to be in our beds, not getting ready to go out in the cold and the rain," Logan said, addressing the crowd at large. "But we all signed up to the same job, and by Christ we're going to make sure we do it."

Another hand went up. A man in uniform, this time. "You said his family kicked him out because of his sexuality."

"We believe so, aye."

"So..." The officer looked around at the others. "He's gay? But he raped those women, didn't he?"

Logan managed to keep his anger in check. "Rape's rarely about sexual desire. It's about power. You should know that, that's hardly new information. He wanted to degrade those women and make them feel worthless. That's why he did it, no' because he fucking fancied them."

He let a couple of moments slide past while he waited to see if the officer was going to argue. The way the poor guy shrank down into his seat suggested he was not.

Logan gestured in Ben's direction. "DI Forde is going to be Office Manager on this. You'll report to your own immediate supervisor, who will report in turn to him.

"You do what DI Forde tells you, when he tells you. If he says 'jump,' you don't waste his time asking how high, you just do as you're told and hope it was high enough. Normally, I'm all in favour of questioning authority, but not now. Not tonight. No second-guessing him, no questioning his orders. DI Forde is the voice of God, and anyone who fails to follow his orders will find themselves struck down pretty bloody smartish. Is that clear?"

There was a general murmuring of agreement. It sounded reasonably positive, Logan thought. Most of them had worked with Ben before, or at least seen him in action. He was a *kent face* in a way that Logan wasn't. Everyone liked Ben Forde, and they'd do their best to keep him happy.

"What about you?" asked another of the CID boys. He was an older fella, sluggish-looking from too many takeaways and nights down the pub. "If Ben's running the show, what are you doing?"

"I'll be out on the streets with you lot," Logan said. "The more of us out there, the better chance we have of finding him quickly."

A hand went up. One of the Uniforms up near the back. Logan recognised her as the one who'd given him the lift from Conlyn's flat to the hospital.

"Yes, uh...?"

"Suzy, sir. Suzy Lewis," she said. "I was just wondering... What if we don't? Catch him quickly, I mean? What if he skips town?"

A hush fell, as everyone waited for the reply. Clearly, she hadn't been the only one thinking it.

"I don't care if he skips town," Logan told her. "I don't care if he skips the bloody country. I will hunt the bastard to the ends of the Earth if I have to."

He reached for the coat Hoon had loaned him. They were both similar sizes and shapes, although the coat was a little neat across Logan's shoulders, and the puce green was not a colour he'd have chosen—not even back in his alcoholic days.

"So, let's try and save me some bus fare, and let's catch him tonight, alright?" He pulled the coat on. "Any more questions?"

Everyone glanced around at everyone else. No more hands went up.

"Good, then let's get out there," he said. "And do our jobs."

LOGAN WAS ALMOST at the front door of the station when he met DC Neish coming the other way. His head was wrapped in a pristine white bandage, although there were a couple of darker dots on the gauze about his ear where blood was starting to seep through.

The DCI didn't know whether to chin the bugger for disobeying a direct order or shake him by the hand for the very same reason. Instead, he settled for something that lay somewhere between the two.

"Christ, if it's no' Rab C Nesbitt," he said, eyes flitting to the bandage. "What are you doing here, Detective Constable? I told you to go home."

"Aye, boss."

They both stood aside, letting nine or ten Uniforms pass them, followed by a couple of officers from CID.

"And yet, here you are," Logan continued, once the stampede had passed by.

"Sorry, boss," Tyler said, shifting uncomfortably. "It just didn't feel right, me being home. I should be here. I should be helping to catch the bastard."

There would be no talking him out of it, Logan could see that. He smiled inwardly but didn't let it show on the outside. The boy was full of surprises.

"Aye, well, you can help DI Forde coordinate things from here," Logan told him. Tyler started to protest, but the DCI cut him off. "Take it or leave it, son. You're injured. I'm not having you out traipsing the streets."

Tyler looked back over his shoulder at the station door, then sighed. "Right, boss. Fair enough. There's something I want to check up on, anyway. I think he might be from Nairn. Originally, I mean."

"What makes you say that?"

"Just... when we were talking, he was asking me about the job, and I mentioned being stationed in Nairn back when I was in uniform. He seemed to know the place pretty well. I'm sure there's a connection."

"It's a start. Go check it out," Logan told him.

"Right, boss."

Tyler's gaze followed the DCI as he marched on towards the exit. "Oh, and boss?"

Logan slowed and looked back, but didn't quite stop.

"If you see him, fucking lamp him one from me, will you?"

He got a half-smile and a nod in reply.

"I'll see what I can do," Logan promised.

And with that, he was gone.

CHAPTER FORTY-ONE

THE NIGHT CRAWLED PAST, THE DARKNESS OOZING LIKE treacle towards a dawn that seemed reluctant to show its face.

Doors were knocked, lock-ups searched, gardens examined. Dogs were brought in, and while a couple of them seemed to get Conlyn's scent around one of the side doors of Raigmore, they lost it again by the time they reached the main road.

CCTV from the hospital had picked him up as he was leaving, and confirmed the direction the dogs' noses had led them, but cameras were few and far between beyond the boundaries, and there was nothing to suggest which way he'd gone after leaving the grounds.

The station had phoned around every taxi company in town, but nobody had picked him up. He had abandoned his phone and other belongings when he'd legged it from the hospital, which meant there was no phone on him to trace and no bank cards he might be tempted to use. For all intents and purposes, he had vanished into thin air.

"Maybe the bastard doesn't exist, after all," Logan said, his fingers flexing on the steering wheel of the Volvo. He'd been given the spare key on the strict understanding that it was the only one they had and that, if he lost it, the cost of a replacement was coming out of his wages.

They'd given him a replacement phone, too. He'd spent ten minutes trying to get the bloody thing to connect to the car's Bluetooth, before giving up.

Ben's voice came from the phone's internal speakerphone. It echoed tinnily around the vehicle's insides. "If only. It'd have saved us a lot of bloody hassle, wouldn't it?"

Logan grunted in response. He was parked along the road from Conlyn's flat. It, and the flat above, were now nothing more than charred frames and a sagging roof. Even now, wisps of smoke drifted lazily into the air, dancing and swirling against the backdrop of the rising sun.

"You spoke to the neighbours there?"

"Aye. There's been no sign of him," Logan answered. "I didn't think for a minute that he'd come back here. And if he did, he'd have seen the state of the place and done an about-turn. He's not daft."

"No," Ben agreed, somewhat glumly.

"You turned up anything there?" Logan asked. It was a silly question—Ben would have let him know of any developments as soon as they'd happened—but he felt compelled to ask it, anyway.

"I'll give you three guesses," the DI replied. "And the first two don't count."

Logan heard him exhale. It was the sound of someone trying to put a brave face on defeat.

"We'll keep looking, obviously, but I reckon he's gone," Ben said. "Out of town, I mean. For all we know, he had a car parked right around the corner with keys in the ignition. He could be in the north of bloody England by now."

"Have you—"

"Circulated the details to the airports? Aye. Ferries, too. But if Kel Conlyn is a fake name, then he could be travelling under something else. They've got his photo though, and we're hoping for a hit on social media now that people are waking up."

Logan had never put a lot of stock in social media. Or people, in fact.

"Tyler get anywhere with the Nairn thing?"

"No. He's still looking into it. We're going to get in touch with the local schools there, but there'll be nobody in until after eight."

Logan nodded, but said nothing. It was proper polis work, he knew, but it felt like they were tinkering around the edges. Knocking on doors and getting on the phone had ended the careers of countless criminals over the years, but he didn't have high hopes of it leading to a collar this time. Conlyn—or whatever his bloody name was—was too clever.

Aye, maybe he had grown up in Nairn. Maybe they'd get a real name out of it, or a family they could talk to. But would it help them find him? Logan had grave doubts about that.

He listened to Ben yawning, tried to stifle one of his own, then gave up and went with it. It had been a long day yesterday, and the night had been longer still. Logan pulled down the Volvo's sun visor, checked himself in the little mirror, then shuddered and closed it all up again.

"You'll be knackered, Ben," he said. "You should get some rest."

"I'm grand," Ben said, but a follow-up yawn betrayed him.

"Aye, you sound it. You're no good to me if you're a zombie. How's Caitlyn doing? Did she get any kip?"

"A few hours, aye. I sent her through about half three. She

protested, of course, but I can be a persuasive bugger when I want to be."

"Good. Get her up and running the room. Go home, get yourself a few hours. Go see Alice."

Ben snorted. "You were making it sound quite tempting up until the very end there," he said, then he sighed. "No, you're right. You're right."

"You're no' as young as you used to be," Logan pointed out.

"Takes one to bloody know one, Jack," Ben replied. "And you could do with some kip yourself."

"Aye. We'll see," Logan said. "I'm going to take another drive by the hospital first and see if..."

His voice trailed off, unable to find an end to the sentence. Driving past the hospital wasn't going to do any good. They had footage of Conlyn leaving. There were cameras throughout the building, none of which showed him coming back in. They'd searched the building, combed the grounds, and there was still a heavy Uniform presence on-site.

Conlyn wouldn't be there. Ben was right, the bastard was probably hundreds of miles away by now. He was injured, aye, but they were superficial, and had already been treated. They'd hurt, but nothing a few over-the-counter painkillers wouldn't be enough to take the edge off.

If he had access to a car, then he was gone. Long gone. Almost certainly.

And yet, Logan couldn't shake the feeling that he wasn't.

"He's got a point to prove," said Logan.

Ben's voice crackled slightly from the phone's speaker. "Eh?"

"Sorry, thinking out loud. I'm just... I'm not sure he'll have done a runner. Out of the city, I mean. All this was to prove some point. If his point is that nothing matters, then running away and hiding so you don't go to jail sort of undermines that, doesn't it?"

"Well, we know he legged it from the hospital," Ben reminded him. "The state of DC Neish's napper is testament to that."

"Aye, true," Logan said. "But that's different. That was instinct. As soon as he knew I was in his place and had rumbled his set-up, he reacted. He didn't want to go to jail because he isn't finished. That's not the same as running away."

"So, you're saying you think he's still somewhere in the area?" Ben asked.

"I don't know," Logan admitted. He fired up the engine and the Volvo kicked into life. He flexed his fingers again, then tightened them, his big hands practically crushing the wheel. "But I certainly bloody hope so."

SOCIAL MEDIA TURNED out to be exactly as useful as Logan had anticipated, in that it wasn't helpful in the slightest. There were a few jokey answers from the usual internet arseholes, several hundred shares and retweets, but in terms of any information they could act on? Hee-haw.

The schools in Nairn were a bust, too, despite Tyler's insistence that Conlyn had known the place well. Uniform up there was knocking on some doors with a photograph of him, but nothing had come up so far.

They'd managed to get prints from the hospital, including off fragments of the vase he'd used to brain Tyler with, but they'd turned out to be another dead end. Whoever he was, he'd never had any run-ins with the law in the past.

Bills to the flat had all been in the name of Kel Conlyn. The landlord had dug out the original references Conlyn had provided when he'd taken the place on, but they'd turned out to be as fake as the rest of his identity, and none of the numbers worked, although the landlord had insisted that they had at the time.

Further investigation revealed they had been 'Voice Over IP' internet phone numbers rented through an anonymous online service. Conlyn had been out to cover his tracks from the very start, and had done a bloody good job of it.

According to his broadband provider, his internet traffic had all gone through a VPN, meaning they couldn't provide any logs of the sites he'd visited. His mobile phone was Pay As You Go, and a scan through it showed it had largely been used to phone taxis and takeaways, and not a whole lot else.

Dead ends, everywhere they turned.

The Incident Room was busier than usual when Logan returned, a couple of CID officers and some senior Uniforms having set up shop in there alongside the MIT. They all looked up as he entered, expressions heavy with expectation. A shake of his head was enough, and they all turned their attention back to the screens and documents they were working on.

"Caitlyn. Anything?" Logan asked, stopping by the desk DI Forde had been occupying when he'd left.

"Nothing, sir," the DS replied. "Sorry."

"Hardly your fault," Logan told her. He turned to where DCs Khaled and Neish were both tapping away at their keyboards. "You two got anything?"

Hamza made a non-committal noise, which was still a significant improvement on what Logan had been bracing himself for.

"Not sure, sir," Hamza said. "I've been searching through

forums. There are a few dedicated to Simulation Theory. It's mostly just Matrix memes, and links to news articles on the subject. That sort of thing."

"I hope there's a 'but' coming,' Logan told him.

"But, well... maybe. There's one guy, calls himself 'The Nowhere Man,' and he seems to be really into it. A lot of the language he uses in his post is similar to what we heard on the video. If we don't exist, why should we feel guilt or remorse for hurting people? Why should we follow rules? That sort of stuff."

"Hardly concrete, is it? Plenty of nutters out there," Logan pointed out.

"Aye, but if I search the same username in Google, sir, it takes me to some other forums and a Twitter account. On one of the forums, he's posted a link to the report on the Danni Gillespie attack. There's a photo of her injury—the 'FAKE' he carved into her—that I don't think we took."

"So, it's him, then?" Logan asked.

"Looks like it, sir," confirmed Hamza.

"How does that help us? Can we use it to find him?"

Hamza opened his mouth to reply, closed it while he thought this over, then winced. "Not really, sir. I mean, we might have been able to get his internet provider from the IP he posted from, and then get the address, but, well..."

"We already know his address," Logan concluded.

Hamza appeared to deflate before the DCI's eyes. "Aye. Still, there might be something I can turn up."

At the next desk, DC Neish sat up straighter. "Wait. Hold on a minute. Address," he said, mumbling the words in a broken staccato, like they were coming to him one at a time. His eyes met Logan's. "Them letters in Conlyn's flat. The ones I kicked over."

"What about them?" Logan asked.

"They all had the same name on them. He said they were for the last guy who lived there, but what if they weren't? What if they were for him?"

"Why wouldn't he open them? Why leave them in a pile in the hall?"

"Well, because..." The sentence started strongly, but quickly fell away. "I mean... Maybe he wanted to leave that identity behind or something?"

"Then why not just chuck them?" Logan asked. "Why keep them all?"

"Because he's..." The DC puffed out his cheeks. "...mental?"

It wasn't what you might call a thorough psychological analysis, but Logan couldn't really argue with it. Still, there was mental, then there was stupid, and what Tyler was suggesting fell firmly into the latter camp.

When they had so few other leads to go on, it was worth checking out, though. Everything was worth checking out at this stage, no matter how unlikely a lead it might seem.

"What was the name on the envelopes?" he asked.

Tyler's face froze. "Uh... sorry, boss?"

"The name. Who were they addressed to?"

Other than his mouth, not a muscle on the DC's face moved. "It was, eh... I think something like..." He swallowed. "Can't remember."

"For fu—"

Logan pinched the bridge of his nose, took a steadying breath, then continued.

"Get onto the landlord and see what you can find out," he suggested. "He'll be able to tell us who the previous tenants were. Maybe the name will give something a nudge in that head of yours. And get someone from Uniform round to check the house. It's possible some of the letters survived the fire, although I wouldn't hold out much hope."

"On it, boss," Tyler said, turning his attention back to the computer.

Logan took a seat and surveyed the Incident Room. DS McQuarrie was talking to a couple of Uniforms. They nodded intently, taking careful note of everything she was telling them. That was good.

What was less good was the general lack of energy in the room. After Logan's speech during the night, the place had been buzzing with excitement. They were going to catch the bastard, no one had been in any doubt.

Now that the night was over and the day was moving in on its turf, the energy had waned. Every minute that passed made it exponentially less likely that they'd find Conlyn. He could be anywhere in the country by now. With a fake passport—or a real one under his own name—he could be anywhere in Europe, in fact, and possibly even beyond.

And yet, Logan didn't think so. He was still here somewhere. Still in the city. He was going to show-face again, Logan could sense it.

It was just a matter of time.

CHAPTER FORTY-TWO

THE BREAKTHROUGH CAME JUST BEFORE LUNCHTIME, AND from the unlikeliest of sources, too.

"Boss, I've got it," Tyler announced, jumping up out of his seat with his notepad raised above his head. "I've got something."

All eyes were on the DC at once. Logan's legs raised him into a standing position without his brain having any say in the matter. He didn't want to get his hopes up, and yet he could feel a tingle across the skin of his arms, like electricity zipping between the hairs.

"I checked with the landlord, and aye, those letters were for the previous tenant. He told me the guy's name, and I remembered it was the same name on the envelopes," Tyler said.

Logan briefly contemplated sitting down again, but didn't. Not yet. Surely, the DC had more than that?

"Right. And?"

"And, it got me thinking. So, I got onto the Royal Mail and checked if they ever delivered letters to that address for anyone else. Any other names. They checked, and they do. Not often, but maybe once every couple of months."

Butterflies erupted into flight in Logan's stomach. "Who?"

Tyler, who had still been holding his notebook above his head like King Arthur with Excalibur, brought it down and glanced at the top page.

"David Oliver, boss."

"And did you—"

"Checked with the landlord, aye. He's never heard of him."

There was a flurry of typing from the next desk over as Hamza's fingers flew across his keyboard.

"OK, OK, let's not get too excited yet," Logan said, although he was struggling to follow his own advice. "We don't know yet if it's—"

Hamza let out a little yelp of something that may have been excitement, but could equally have been pain.

"Hamza?" Logan prompted.

"Got him!"

Hamza turned his screen so the others could see. A page from the *Press & Journal* website was open in the browser. It showed a picture of a young man wearing a university graduation cap and gown, smiling proudly as he held up a certificate. He was a couple of years younger, but there was no mistaking the man who'd been calling himself Kel Conlyn.

"Says he graduated from Glasgow Uni three years ago. MBChB in Medicine. He went in young. Some sort of child prodigy, by the looks of things."

Logan tutted. "Aye. You've to watch those bastards."

"Grew up in Nairn," Hamza continued.

"I fucking *knew it*!" Tyler cried, thrusting his hands above his head again.

"Home educated, though, so that'll be why the schools didn't recognise him."

Logan clapped his hands a few times, making sure he had the attention of everyone in the room. "Right, DC Tyler here has outdone himself and handed us a big win. We can all buy him a drink later, but for now, I want everything we can find on one—"

Logan pointed to Tyler.

"David Oliver, boss."

"—David Oliver. I want to know past addresses, friends, car registration, hobbies, shoe size, and what he had for his breakfast. You'll bring it to DS McQuarrie and DC Khaled, and they'll coordinate and decide what we're putting out to the press and social media."

He pointed to one of the CID officers at random, a redhead who looked like she knew what she was doing. "You. Sorry, forget your name."

"DS Elizabeth, sir. Hanna."

"Hanna. Right. I want you checking the airports, start local and work outwards. We need to know he hasn't left the country. Take who you need to get it done quickly."

"Right, sir," the DS replied.

"I want to see some initiative here from all of you," Logan said, addressing the audience as a whole. "DS McQuarrie can find you jobs to do if needs be, but you're here in this room because we think you can figure it out for yourself. Coordinate with each other and with your senior officers. Check everything. Leave no stone unturned. Get me everything you can on David Oliver, and let's flush the bastard out of hiding."

He clapped his hands again, signalling the speech was over. "Well? Come on. Jump to it."

The Incident Room immediately became a frenzy of activity, as officers got on phones, tapped at their keyboards, or got to their feet. The place had been whisper-quiet for the last few hours, but now it was alive with conversation, the anticipation of a collar suddenly palpable in the air.

"That was good work, son," Logan told Tyler. "I'd kiss you, if you weren't such an ugly bastard."

"I'd only have you for harassment, boss," Tyler replied. He took a breath that suggested he was going to say something more, but then just sat down.

"What is it?" Logan asked.

Tyler shook his head. "It's nothing. Don't worry about it."

"Jesus Christ, man, spit it out."

DC Neish wriggled uncomfortably in his chair. "It's just... This afternoon. It's, well, it's Sinead's wee brother's birthday."

Logan frowned and looked at the clock on the wall like it might be helpful in some way. It wasn't. "Is that today?"

"Aye, boss. But it's fine. I'll tell her I can't go."

Logan shook his head. "You've been on shift for a whole bloody day, Detective Constable," he said. "Go home. Get some rest. Clean the blood out of your ear, because—quite frankly—it's been annoying me all night. Go eat some cake and play Pass the Parcel, or whatever it is they do these days." He leaned over the desk and gave the DC a slightly awkward pat on the shoulder. "You did good, son. You did good."

Tyler blushed, just slightly. "Cheers, boss."

Logan turned to DS McQuarrie. "Caitlyn, you alright here for half an hour or so? I'll get Ben out of his bed and back in. He won't want to miss this."

"Fine, sir. Not a problem," Caitlyn said. "You off somewhere?"

"Aye. Hamza, you said he grew up in Nairn?"

"That's right, sir," Hamza confirmed.

"Good," Logan said, picking up his borrowed coat. "Then, get me that address."

CHAPTER FORTY-THREE

The house on Nairn's Millbank Street was notable for a few reasons.

It was newer than most of the other houses along the road, and set back a little at the end of a gated driveway. It had a hedge, which was badly in need of a trim, and a scattering of weeds had started to find their way through the bricks of the drive, making the place look somewhat unloved.

The most notable features of all though, were the windows, which had been completely whited out with dried Windowlene, and the 'For Sale' sign fixed to the fence. A 'Sold' sticker had been slapped on top, which explained the sense of abandonment the whole place was giving off.

"Damn it."

The gate was in good condition, suggesting the decay was all fairly recent. It opened with barely a squeak, and Logan's eyes scanned the front of the house as he approached. Big. Detached. Expensive-looking. Conlyn—*Oliver, he corrected*—had evidently come from a comfortable background. Financially, at least.

The doors were locked, as expected. The white coating on the windows made it difficult to see inside, but from what Logan was able to tell, the place was empty. There was a smallish shed around the back. It had been locked, but someone had broken the latch, splintering the wood where the screws had been torn out. It was empty now, aside from a lingering smell of turpentine and sawdust.

The back garden was all slabs and decking, and the weeds were making more of a statement back there. They'd squeezed through the narrow gaps at the edges of the paving slabs, and were positively flourishing between the wooden boards of the decking.

The kitchen window had less of a Windowlene covering than the others, and Logan was able to get a good look inside by clambering up on an upturned terracotta pot. The appliances were all fitted, so had been left in place when the occupants had moved out. There were a few other bits and bobs scattered across the worktops—an open pack of light bulbs, some junk mail, the instruction manual for something or other—but nothing to suggest the place was still being lived in.

"Moving in?"

The voice came from the other side of a tall fence that ran along the side of the building, separating it from the garden next door. It was too high to see over, but Logan spied some movement in the gaps between the upright boards, and it quickly translated into the shape of a man. He was shorter than Logan, but then that wasn't unusual. Older, too, judging by the flashes of white hair the detective could see.

"No. DCI Logan, Police Scotland Major Investigations," he said, automatically reaching for his warrant card. He hadn't had time to arrange a replacement yet though, and he found the inside pocket empty. "Sorry, ID was destroyed in a fire during the night."

"What, fire brigade on holiday, were they?" the neighbour asked, his voice so bright and chipper it had the same effect on Logan as fingernails scraping down a blackboard. "Having a job swap, were you?"

"Something like that," Logan said. He could see the man eyeing him up through the gap, and his appearance seemed to live up to expectations.

"You look like police, right enough. Is everything alright?"

"What do you know about the owners of this house, Mr...?"

"Dawson. Do you mean the old owners, or the new one?"

"Both."

"Not a jot about the new ones, I'm afraid. Never seen them. They bought it about... what? Six months ago, I think. All very sudden. Millie and John, they just upped and left one day, by all accounts. Neighbours for eighteen years, and not so much as a goodbye. Quite hurtful, if I'm honest."

There was a touch of anger colouring his voice, like he hadn't yet forgiven them.

"They didn't mention they were selling up?"

"No. By the time the sign went up, it already had a 'Sold' sticker on it. I went around to speak to them, but it was only David, the young fella, who was there. He was carrying boxes out to a van. I asked him what was going on and he said his parents were relocating to the east coast somewhere. Said they'd get in touch once they'd settled in. But nothing. Not so much as a postcard."

Through the gap, Logan saw the older man's gaze flit to the house. "Keep expecting to see someone moving in, but nothing yet. Shame to see it sitting empty like that. Lovely house. Lovely couple."

"What about the son?" Logan asked. "Have many dealings with him?"

"Not really, no. Kept himself to himself, mostly. Very bright, though," Mr Dawson said. "Home educated. I think he had some trouble with bullying in primary school. Millie mollycoddled him a bit, and he ended up being taught at home. She quit her job, and everything."

Dawson's gaze returned to Logan. "Why? Is something wrong?"

He was going to find out soon enough. It'll be all over the telly and the internet within the hour. May as well tell him face-to-face. Or face-to-fence, at least.

"We believe David Oliver may be involved in a recent spate of sexual assaults and murders in and around Inverness," Logan said. "We need to find him as a matter of urgency."

"Good God. *David*? But, I mean... He wouldn't, would he? He's always been a bit odd, but *murder*? I can't believe that."

"We're building a strong case against him, Mr Dawson. I've got very little doubt at the moment as to his guilt, and my priority is catching him before he can hurt anyone else," Logan said. He indicated the building behind him with a thumb. "Have you seen anyone coming and going in the last few days?"

"No, not a thing. Quiet as the grave, and I'm a very light sleeper, so I'd have heard anyone coming during the night. I heard you from my kitchen," Dawson said, looking quite pleased with himself. "I was thinking of giving the estate agent a ring though, to get them to contact the buyer. There's a bit of a whiff coming from the place some days. I think the drains must be starting to back up. They'll have to get that seen to."

Logan felt his mouth puckering and his eyebrows falling

into a frown. He hadn't smelled anything, but then it was cold today, and there was a bit of a wind to keep the air moving.

"Mr Dawson, I don't suppose you have a spare key for the house, do you?"

"Yes. God. Somewhere. John left me with it when I was looking in on their old dog—rest her soul—when they were away for the weekend a few years back. Told me just to hang on to it in case of emergencies. I'd have to look for it, though."

"Right. Can you go and find it and then meet me round the front?" Logan asked. "I just need to make a quick phone call."

THE ESTATE AGENT on the sign was legitimate, the phone number taking Logan straight through to the main reception. There, the authenticity of the whole thing ended. They'd never listed a property for sale on Millbank Street, much less sold one. Whoever had put the sign up, they said, it was nothing to do with them.

That had sealed it. When the neighbour turned up with the key, Logan took it, thanked him, then sent him back to his house with instructions not to come out until he'd been told otherwise.

Dawson had almost questioned the order, but the smell was more noticeable around the front, and Logan had seen the moment when the realisation had hit him. His hand had shaken when he'd passed the DCI the key, and he'd quickly turned and walked back to his own garden, without once looking back.

There was no mistaking the smell when Logan turned the key in the lock and pushed open the door. It was the same cloying, acrid stench he'd smelled so many times before. It was similar to the aromas that lingered in the mortuary, only rawer and more intense.

Matured.

It was tinted with other smells, too. Lavender, he thought, and other flowery things. His eyes went to the electrical sockets, and the air-fresheners plugged into every one. Presumably, the intention had been for them to mask the smell, but they mingled with it, amplifying it, and making it even more stomach-churningly nauseating than it would otherwise have been.

He called it into the office before he went any further. They'd need Forensics in here. He declined the offer of an ambulance. Based on the smell, they were months past that stage.

The downstairs was empty, stripped of all furniture, just like the flat that had gone up in flames. Logan *creaked* his way into four bare rooms and a small bathroom, then steeled himself as he made his way to the stairs.

The carpet had been removed, and each footfall *thunked* like a drumbeat on the exposed wooden steps. The emptiness of the place carried the sound, echoing it back to him as he made his way up to the top.

The higher he got, the thicker and more pungent the smell became, until he was forced to bury the bottom half of his face in the crook of his arm.

It wasn't until he reached the very top step that he heard the flies. Their murmuring drone guided him to the second of the four doors that led off from the upstairs landing. The pocket of Hoon's coat was completely devoid of the protective gloves Logan usually carried in his own, so he covered his hand with his sleeve and carefully pushed down the handle and let the door ease open.

The room erupted in movement, as hundreds of flies took

to the air, fully exposing the corpses on the bed. They had putrefied badly, to the point that Logan couldn't quite tell where the bodies ended and the bedclothes began. The floor was carpeted with dead insects, suggesting most of the feasting had happened some time ago, and the flies that were still hanging around were scavenging what little was left.

John and Millie—because Logan had no doubt that was who he was looking at—had both been naked when they'd died, their hands wrenched in front of them, their wrists bound together. The exposed bones of their arms were linked, so that with their wrists tied they would have been unable to separate themselves.

Locked together, until the end.

Cause of death was impossible to determine from that distance, and Logan had no intention of getting any closer without protective gear. Ideally, an airtight rubber suit and a diver's helmet. Even then, the bodies were so far gone it might never be possible to figure out what had killed them.

Who had killed them was less of a mystery.

Two more victims to add to the tally. Two more lives taken by that sick bastard. His own parents, too. How many others were out there? How many would they never know about?

"No more," Logan said, announcing it like some sacred vow. He pulled the door closed and made for the stairs, the smell worming through his defences.

He made it to the front step before the urge to vomit almost became overwhelming. Had it not been for the police van screeching to a stop at the end of the driveway, he'd have thrown up right there on the driveway, and it was only through sheer stubbornness and force of will that he was able to keep the meagre contents of his stomach where they should be, and his self-respect intact.

"I wouldn't," Logan said, stopping the uniformed officer halfway up the drive. "Just keep the door closed, wait for the SOC team to get here. If you can avoid going in, I'd advise you to do that, and be bloody grateful for it."

The Uniform, who clearly didn't recognise him, started barking questions. Logan ignored them, and looked back at the house. At the whited-out window. At the flies crawling up the inside.

"No more," he muttered. "No more."

CHAPTER FORTY-FOUR

DC NEISH STOOD FROZEN TO THE SPOT, HANDS RAISED, almost all of his weight on one leg. He didn't dare move, didn't dare blink, didn't dare breathe. He could only stand there, stock-still, or it would all be over.

Come on. Come on...

Pink's *Get the Party Started* kicked back in and Tyler continued dancing. Sinead had her back to the living room, but smirked at Tyler in the mirror as her finger hovered over the 'stop' button on her Spotify app.

Truth be told, musical statues wasn't going down all that well with Harris and the other kids, but Tyler was having the time of his life. He wasn't going to win, of course—he wasn't a monster—but he was determined to at least get to the semi-final stage. At that point, he'd throw the game, safe in the knowledge that he *could* have won it if he'd really wanted to.

The party wasn't exactly jumping. There were six kids, including Harris. They all seemed nice enough for nine and ten-year-olds, although one of them—Grant something or other —had the potential to be a right wee dick. Grant was still in the running for Musical Statues, along with Harris, the girl next door, and Tyler himself. Tyler just needed to survive one more round and—

The music stopped unexpectedly. Tyler tried to freeze, but he was midway through a *Saturday Night Fever* style finger-point, and he'd been caught off guard.

"Tyler," Sinead said. "You're out."

DC Neish resisted the temptation to point out that Grant was clearly moving, too, and to call for a Steward's Enquiry, and accepted the defeat with relatively good grace.

"Aye, it's a fair cop," he said, squeezing past the frozen kids until he was standing next to Sinead. "I'll be the lookout, if you like. Eyes like a hawk, me."

"All that investment in police training was money well spent, eh?" Sinead teased, as she tapped the 'play' button and Pink came blasting from the Bluetooth speaker.

He hummed along quietly as the kids shuffled awkwardly on the spot. They'd all passed the age when they could dance freely without embarrassment, and mostly now looked like they wanted the floor to open up and swallow them.

He'd helped Sinead drag the kitchen table into the living room, and she'd spent half an hour covering it in party food. Tyler snaffled a sausage roll while he watched the kids dancing. He'd already made a substantial dent in the sausages, cheese, and pickled onions on sticks, and had taken to stashing the cocktail sticks in his pocket so no one could see how many he'd eaten.

The music stopped as he was halfway through chewing.

"Grant," he said immediately, spraying pastry crumbs down his front.

"What? I wasn't moving!"

"You were," Tyler said. He swallowed the sausage roll and turned to Sinead. "He was."

"Grant, you're out," Sinead said.

"This is bullshit," Grant muttered, stomping past the other kids. He dug a sweaty hand into a bowl of Smarties, and helped himself to several dozen. "Total bullshit."

Sinead and Tyler both watched the kid go *thudding* over to the couch, where he threw himself down next to the other three who had already been eliminated, took out his phone, and started tapping away at the screen.

"And it's down to the final!" Tyler announced. "Harris 'Hot Shoe Shuffle' Bell, versus..."

Shit, shit, shit. What was her name?

"Emily 'Michael Jackson' Boardman!" Sinead finished.

They hit the music and the kids returned to dancing unenthusiastically on the spot. Now that there were just the two of them left, they turned their bodies away from each other to ensure nobody could make the mistake of thinking they were dancing together.

"Michael Jackson?" Tyler whispered.

Sinead bit her bottom lip. "I know. I panicked."

"Fortunately, they're all probably too young to have any idea who he is," Tyler said. "But if word gets back to the parents that you've been flinging 'Michael Jackson' around the place, you're going to have Social Work at your door."

Sinead grinned and gave him a playful thump on the arm. "Yeah, yeah. Shut up."

She stopped the music again. Both kids froze. Tyler's eyes narrowed, tick-tocking between them both as he really tried to ramp up the tension.

"Sorry, Jacko. You're out," he said, shooting the girl an apologetic look.

"Fix!" bellowed Grant from the sidelines. A few of the other kids giggled, and Harris looked absolutely mortified as he shuffled over to collect his prize.

"Skittles. Brilliant," he said. You could probably argue that he was trying to look enthusiastic, but his heart clearly wasn't in it.

As Harris took the bag of sweets, Grant called over to him. "Here, Bell," he said, dropping his phone in his lap and opening his hands.

Harris only hesitated for a moment, before chucking the Skittles in the bigger boy's direction. Grant caught them with a hand clap, his eyes blazing greedily. "Nice. I love these."

He ripped open the bag, spilling half a dozen of the colourful candies down the gap between the cushions. The kids on either side-eyed the sweets expectantly, but Grant was making no signs of sharing. "Can we go play Fortnite now?" he asked, masticating his way through a mouthful of Skittle-mush.

Harris looked hopefully up at Sinead. "Can we?"

"Not Fortnite, surely?" Tyler groaned. "It's full of—"

He looked around the room at the faces of the children who were all now glaring at him, waiting to see what he was going to say.

"—bugs," he said, rather than the 'bloody nine-year-olds' that had been his original intention when he'd first opened his mouth.

Harris tutted, then very pointedly looked away from the DC and back to Sinead.

"What about the other games?" Sinead asked. "We haven't done Pass the Parcel yet."

"I'm not five," Harris told her.

Sinead looked down at the carefully wrapped parcel sitting

on the table. It was balanced right on the edge, the only space available after she'd set out the buffet.

"I spent ages wrapping that," she muttered, although it was more to herself than to Harris. She looked at Tyler, who offered a half-smile and a shrug in reply, then she sighed. "Fine. If that's what you want, you can go and play—"

There was a knock at the door. Heavy. Solid. Threatening, almost. The sound of traffic came rushing in from the hall as the front door was opened. Tyler and Sinead both tensed, and were halfway across the room when a hulking figure came striding into the living room. Behind them, back at the buffet table, Harris gasped.

"Right, then," said DCI Logan, rubbing his hands together. "Where's this cake?"

HARRIS STOOD in front of the other kids, holding court. Logan stood beside him, a paper plate in one hand, a fork in the other, and half a pound of chocolate cake already lining his stomach. Like Tyler, Logan was also partial to a little sausage on a stick. Like Tyler, he also now had a pocket full of cocktail sticks, and a slightly guilty conscience.

"It was amazing!" Harris said, more animated than he'd been all day. "The guy had a knife to my throat, right? Like, properly to my throat. Like, he was going to kill me. And then, *boosh*! Chief Inspector Logan comes in and just smacks him. He just totally smacks him and then goes chasing after him."

Over by the buffet, Sinead paused with a mini-Battenberg halfway to her mouth. "That's not how it happened," she told Tyler. "If there was any *booshing* being done, it was me."

"You were the principal *boosher*?" Tyler asked.

Sinead laughed. "I was *boosher* number one."

"No way," Grant sneered. "You didn't really have a knife to your throat. Did he?"

"Oh aye," Logan confirmed, chewing on another forkful of cake. "Handled it perfectly, too. Better than I could've. From where I was standing, he didn't even look worried. I actually thought he probably had it all under control himself. We almost just turned around and left him to it."

Harris drew several admiring looks from the others, not least of all from Emily.

"Did you catch him?" she asked, her eyes flitting up to Logan then quickly diverting away again, like the sight of him made her nervous. "The bad guy? Did you catch him?"

"Aye. More or less," Logan said, glossing over the details. "But I wouldn't have without Harris's help. It was thanks to him we cracked the case."

"No way," Grant snorted.

Logan stopped chewing. He took the paper napkin from his plate and dabbed at his mouth, his gaze locked firmly on the boy with the Skittles.

"Are you calling me a liar, son?" he intoned. "Is that what's happening here?"

Grant appeared to sink into the cushions. His face, which had still been red from the effort of slowly shuffling from foot-to-foot during Musical Statues, lost all its colour in one sudden flush.

"Uh, no."

"No what?"

"No... sir?" Grant squeaked.

Logan stabbed his cake with the plastic fork. "Better," he said, then he shovelled another bite into his mouth and got back to chewing.

Across the room, Tyler watched on. Harris was practically bouncing with excitement, and would look up at Logan every few seconds like he was afraid he might vanish into thin air.

"He seems to really like him," Tyler remarked.

"God, aye. He hasn't stopped going on about him since they met in Fort William," Sinead said. She caught the slightly wounded expression on Tyler's face. "He likes you, too."

Tyler shot her a sceptical look.

"I mean, he will. Once he gets to know you better."

"Right." Tyler half-turned his body towards her. "And... is that going to happen? Am I, you know, allowed to show my face round here again?"

"I don't know." Sinead smirked, her eyes darting across his features. "It's pretty horrifying. Maybe if you wore a paper bag..."

"Oy!" Tyler protested. "Bit harsh."

Sinead smiled and leaned in closer. Tyler began to lean in too, his eyes closing. But then Sinead plucked a sausage roll from the plate behind him, popped it in her mouth, and grinned.

"That was just nasty," he told her.

Sinead nodded. "Yeah. I know."

"Is this man bothering you, constable?"

They both turned to find Logan standing beside them, his plate now empty.

"Because, I can have him forcibly removed from the premises, if you like."

Sinead smiled. "Let me get back to you on that, sir," she said. "And thank you *so much* for coming."

Logan held up the plate. "Well, I realised I hadn't had breakfast or lunch, and I was in the area, so..."

Sinead looked past him to where Harris was still answering questions. "How did you get away from them?" she asked.

"Hmm? Oh, they asked me if I wanted to play Fortnite."

"And what did you say?"

"I said, 'What the fuck is Fortnite when it's at home?'" Logan replied.

Tyler and Sinead both stared at him, mouths open.

"Of course I didn't say that. Jesus Christ, what do you think I am? I said I'd maybe play another time."

The other two officers relaxed.

"I have no intention of following through on that, by the way. So we're clear. I don't know what Fortnite is, and I don't want to know. I was being nice."

"First time for everything, eh, boss?" Tyler said.

"Bold statement that, for a man who's only here out of the goodness of my bloody heart," Logan pointed out.

"Fair point, well made," Tyler conceded. He glanced at Sinead. "We didn't think you'd be able to make it."

"Any news?" Sinead asked.

Logan sighed. Never a promising start. "Car was picked up on a camera on the A9 earlier today, headed south near... what's that place? They do the adverts on the telly. All the toffs go there."

"House of Bruar?" Sinead guessed.

"Aye. Just past there," Logan said. "They found the car itself abandoned in a layby this side of the Forth bridge a couple of hours ago. The thinking is that he's in Edinburgh, so central belt has taken over the hunt for him."

"That's... good?" Sinead said. The faces on both men said otherwise. "Isn't it? We know who he is, what he looks like, and all that stuff. We're bound to get him sooner or later."

"Aye. I suppose you're right," said Logan, helping himself

to a chocolate-coated marshmallow. "Still, I didn't think he'd run. Bit disappointed in him, if I'm honest. Least the bastard could've done is let us nab him ourselves."

He grabbed a handful of crisps from a bowl and cupped them in one hand. "Right, I'd better get off. Hoon wants an update, and I need to persuade DI Forde to handle the paperwork. I'll go say bye to the wee man and his pals."

Leaning in closer, he dropped his voice to a whisper. "I'd watch the lad with the Skittles, by the way. The old arsehole alarm is going off, and it's rarely wrong."

"Yeah, we're all over him, boss," Tyler said. "I'm just waiting for an excuse to crack out the handcuffs."

"Good man," Logan said. He crunched a couple of crisps. "Right, back to it, then. I'll see you both later. Enjoy the rest of the party."

He shot Sinead a warning look. "Don't let him wangle his way out of the dishes."

"No chance," Sinead said, smiling.

"Cheers for that, boss."

Logan looked between them both. For a moment, it looked like he might be about to say something, but then he just nodded. "Right. That's me," he said, then he tossed the rest of the crisps in his mouth, turned on his heels, and went to say goodbye to Harris.

Sinead and Tyler both watched him as he bent to talk to the boy, then begrudgingly accepted a round of high-fives from everyone except Grant, who just sat in the same spot, eating the Skittles and trying to look disinterested.

"He's full of surprises, isn't he?" said Sinead.

"Aye. You can say that again," Tyler agreed.

They both waved as Logan turned and shot them a final farewell look, and then he was out in the hallway, and the sound of traffic filled the room again as he opened the front door and stepped outside.

"You think he's happy?" Sinead wondered, once he was gone.

Tyler frowned. "Yeah. I think so. Aye. More or less. I mean, not 'happy' exactly. I've never seen him actually *happy*, but... Aye. He's fine, I think. Why?"

Sinead watched the door. From outside, there came the sound of a car engine starting.

"No reason," Sinead said. "Just wondering."

Harris's voice pipped up as he and the others started heading for the door. "We're going upstairs to play Fortnite!"

Sinead rolled her eyes. "Fine. If that's what you really want. On you go."

She waited until they were all clumping up the stairs before sagging and exhaling in relief. "Thank God for that. I thought they were never going to leave," she said, then she reached under the table and produced a bottle. "Wine?"

Tyler's face split into a grin. "I thought you were never going to ask."

CHAPTER FORTY-FIVE

"Now, technically, this isn't the best time of year to watch this film," Tyler explained. "*Technically*, it's a Christmas movie, but I'm so appalled that you haven't seen it that we're breaking with tradition."

Beside him on the couch, Sinead shook her head. "Of course he hasn't seen it. He's nine."

"Ten," Harris and Tyler both corrected at the same time.

"OK, well you've *been* nine," Sinead said.

"We've all been nine, Sinead," Tyler pointed out. "What's your point?"

She slapped him on the arm and swirled the final few dregs of wine around in her glass. She was curled up with her legs beneath her, Tyler on her right, Harris leaning against her on the left.

She'd eventually managed to kick the other kids out before she had to feed them, and had ordered dinner from the Chinese for the three of them, which Tyler had insisted on paying for. Pride had made her argue, but three glasses of red wine had made her somewhat more pliable and open to negotiation than usual, so she'd eventually relented.

"It doesn't look like a Christmas movie," Harris remarked. On-screen, a close-up of a young Bruce Willis eyed up the exploding Nakatomi Plaza. The film's title—'Die Hard'—was emblazoned in red at the bottom of the image.

"That's the beauty of it. But trust me," Tyler told him. "It's the *Miracle on 34th Street* of action movies."

"What's *Miracle on 34th Street*?" Harris asked.

Tyler leaned past Sinead, stared at Harris to make sure he wasn't on the wind-up, then shot Sinead a reproachful look. "Have you given this boy *any* film education whatsoever?"

"*Up!*" Sinead announced, a little giggly.

Tyler frowned and glanced down at the couch, in case she'd spilt something and was telling him to move. "Eh?"

"The film. *Up!* With the dog and the balloons," Sinead said. She turned to her little brother. "We watched that last week, didn't we?"

"Well, I did. You fell asleep," Harris said.

"Did I?" Sinead asked, seemingly shocked by the accusation.

"Yes. You always fall asleep."

Sinead took a sip from her glass, draining it. "Fair point. I will give you that one," she admitted. "Still, the first fifteen minutes were *amazing*."

Tyler picked up the remote. "Right, well it's physically impossible to fall asleep during *Die Hard*, so no worries there. Everyone ready?"

"Ready," Harris confirmed.

"Go for it," said Sinead, then she immediately contradicted herself. "Wait. No. Not yet. I'll go get us more drinks first. And should we do popcorn? We have popcorn. It's in one of those microwave thingies."

She looked from one to the other. "Yes? No? Popcorn?"

"I never say no to popcorn," Tyler replied.

"Yeah, I'll have some," Harris agreed.

"Right, then!" Sinead said, unfolding her legs from beneath her. It took her a couple of attempts to get to her feet, then another few seconds to figure out where everyone's glasses were. "So, wine, wine, Irn Bru."

"And popcorn," Tyler reminded her.

"And popcorn." A troubling thought struck her. "It might be out of date, though, that's the only thing."

Tyler shot Harris a sideways look, then shrugged. "We'll take our chances. Want a hand?"

She waved the suggestion away. "It's fine. You stay here. I can figure it out."

Tyler watched her head through to the hall, swaying ever so slightly as she went. It was only when he heard her open the kitchen door that he realised Harris was looking at him.

"Alright?" Tyler asked.

Harris nodded, but said nothing.

"You're going to love it. This film, I mean. It's a classic. Just cover your ears at the sweary bits."

Harris nodded again. "Jack said it was you who worked out who's been killing them people," he said.

It took Tyler a moment to process this. "Jack? Oh, the boss? Aye. He lets you call him Jack, does he? Reckon my arse'd be out the window if I tried that." He put a hand over his mouth. "Bum'd be out the window, I mean. Sorry."

Harris half-smiled at the fake apology. "Did you?"

"Did I what?"

"Figure out who the bad guy is?"

The boy was staring at him, waiting for his response. From the kitchen, Tyler heard the *beep-beep-beep* of the microwave being programmed, then the whirring hum as it activated.

"Because Jack said you figured it out. The killer's name and stuff. He said it was you."

Tyler puffed out his cheeks. "I mean... I suppose so. Aye. I suppose it was."

Harris's eyes, which had been narrowed in suspicion, widened just a fraction. They flicked up and down, giving the DC a quick once-over.

"Cool," he said, then he faced the telly again, a satisfied smile playing on his lips.

"Thanks," Tyler said, sitting up a little straighter. "I guess it was."

They sat in a silence that wasn't entirely comfortable, but wasn't particularly awkward either, listening to the *pop-pop-popping* from the kitchen.

They hadn't said much, and yet in just those few words, Tyler had felt the atmosphere between them thawing. He wouldn't say that the boy now liked him, by any stretch of the imagination, but he at least looked like he might be prepared to tolerate the DC's existence, which was a start.

Aye, the boss was full of surprises, right enough.

The popping had all but stopped now. Tyler glanced at the hall door and picked up the remote again, his finger hovering over the 'play' button. *Die Hard* was one of his top ten favourite films of all time, and his favourite Christmas movie by far. He'd first seen it when he was around Harris's age, and if he was completely honest, it had played a big part in his decision to join the police.

It had been a few years since he'd seen it, and he wasn't

sure who he was more excited for—himself, or the boy who was about to witness its brilliance for the very first time.

Assuming Sinead got her finger out.

"Popcorn nearly ready?" Tyler called through. He could still hear the microwave *whirring*, but the popping had stopped now, aside from the odd occasional *paff* as one of the more reluctant kernels finally succumbed to the heat. "Sinead?"

There was no answer from the kitchen. No movement in the hall.

"You're going to burn it again!" Harris called. "Like last time."

Tyler smiled at him and rolled his eyes, but then his attention went straight back to the door, his ears straining for any sign of movement.

"Sinead?"

"She probably went for a pee," Harris said.

"Aye. Yeah. Probably," Tyler agreed.

He settled back on the couch, trying to get comfortable. A black and white Bruce Willis stared back at him from the screen. Through in the kitchen, the microwave's droning ended with a *ping*, and a stillness fell over the house.

Tyler couldn't keep his gaze from making its way back to the door. He kept his voice as light and natural as possible as he got up from the couch. "I'll go see if she needs a hand. You wait here, OK?"

"OK," Harris said. "It's fine if it's burnt. She felt really guilty about it last time. I don't really care about the popcorn, anyway."

"I'll tell her that," Tyler said, making for the door. "I'll be right back."

The hall was empty, but that wasn't unexpected. He

stopped at the bottom of the stairs and called up into the darkness. "Sinead? You up there?"

Nothing.

A swirl of cold air circulated in through the gap in the open kitchen door. Tyler nudged it the rest of the way and stepped through. The smell of burnt popcorn hung in the air. The inside of the microwave was filled with a cloud of grey-white smoke, visible even with the oven's light now out.

The back door that led out to the garden stood open. From somewhere not too far away, Tyler heard the sound of tyres crunching on gravel and the sharp, sudden *shriek* of a wheelspin. He reached the door in three big paces, was outside and onto the path in five.

The red glow of a set of tail lights vanished around the corner at the end of the road. Along the path, the back gate *clacked* as the wind blew it open and closed.

He heard movement behind him, back in the house. He ran up the path, bounded up the steps and skidded to a stop in the kitchen.

Harris stood there, looking confused. "Where is she?" he asked.

"Hey. I thought I told you to wait through there?" Tyler said. He closed the back door behind him, then started in the direction of the hall. "I need to go check the bathroom. She's probably in there."

"What's that?" Harris asked. He pointed to the fridge, and Tyler had to bite his lip to stop himself stating the obvious.

He realised immediately that the boy wasn't asking what the fridge was, and instead saw where he was pointing. Earlier, the front of the appliance had been covered in magnets—holiday mementoes, mostly, but a selection of letters and numbers, too.

Now, all but four of them were on the floor. Those that remained were all letters.

Four of them, all chillingly familiar.

F. A. K. E.

"Oh God," Tyler whispered, as the bottom fell out of his world. "Oh God, no."

CHAPTER FORTY-SIX

Ben Forde finished fastening the buttons on his coat, then placed a hand on the Incident Room's light switch. "I'm warning you. I'll lock you in, Jack," he said. "You should be getting yourself home."

Across the room, Logan glanced up from his computer and mustered up a smile of acknowledgement. "Aye. I won't be long. Just checking to see if they've caught him."

"You've been refreshing that bloody thing for the past three hours," Ben pointed out. "You're exhausted, man. Get your arse home to bed."

Logan's eyes flicked back to the screen. HOLMES was back up and running, which was something. He'd been hoping for an update on there—or preferably, a phone call—to say that David Oliver had been nabbed.

He'd been hoping it for a while now. So far, those hopes had been repeatedly dashed.

"Aye. Aye, you're right," Logan admitted. He jabbed the monitor's power button more violently than was strictly necessary and got to his feet. "We should hear something in the morning."

"Exactly. No point killing yourself."

He waited while the DCI pulled on the coat he'd borrowed from Hoon, then clicked the light switch as he approached the door.

Logan waited in the corridor while the DI locked the door, then they both wandered along it, automatically falling into step, neither man in a massive rush to leave.

"You straight home yourself?" Logan asked.

"Chance'd be a fine thing. Alice wants me to swing by Tesco for—and I quote—'a few things,'" Ben said. "A few things my backside. She's sent me a whole bloody shopping list."

He shook his head despairingly, and Logan could sense a rant coming on.

"That's the problem with the world these days," Ben began.

"What, Alice?"

"No! Well... No. Twenty-four-hour supermarkets."

"That's the problem with the world, is it?" Logan asked. "No' all the murderers and war criminals, and what have you?"

"That's the thing. Twenty-four-hour supermarkets are driving the problem. They're *creating* these bastards," Ben said. He caught the look on Logan's face. "Aye, you might laugh, but it's the sense of entitlement they're creating. Nobody can wait for things these days. It's all *now, now, now*.

"Back in the day, if you wanted a tin of beans at three in the morning, you were shit out of luck. You had to wait. Now? No problem, swing by the twenty-four-hour supermarket, and it's right there. Instant gratification. Beans on demand!"

"You think having round the clock access to baked beans is turning people into murderers?" Logan asked. He was exhausted, hungry, and his whole body felt slightly broken, but he couldn't fight the smirk that tugged the corners of his mouth upwards.

"No' just beans, obviously."

"Spaghetti hoops?" Logan guessed.

"Everything. It's the instant gratification thing. It's turning people greedy. *Want, want, want. Now, now, now*. What was wrong with waiting, eh? What was wrong with a bit of patience?" Ben asked. "And another thing, I just know I'll go in there and there'll be at least one person wandering around in their bloody pyjamas. At *least*. I mean... If that's no' a sign of the end times, then I don't know what—"

His phone rang, and he immediately stopped talking, like he was afraid the person on the other end might somehow hear him.

"That'll be Alice," he said, dropping his voice to a half-whisper, and reaching for his phone. "For Christ's sake, don't tell her I said any of that."

He answered the phone without looking and pressed it to his ear, suddenly all smiles. "Hello, dear! I'm just on my—"

The words faltered to a stop. His expression changed. From a few feet away, Logan heard the voice on the other end. He couldn't make out the words, but the tone was unmistakeable. Urgent. Panicked. Afraid.

"Tyler, Tyler, calm down, son, calm down," Ben said. He raised his eyes to Logan, brow crinkling in concern. "Take a deep breath, and tell me what's happened."

LOGAN STOOD in Sinead's living room, looming over Tyler, who was sat in the middle of the couch, his head in his hands. He and Ben had reached the house just after a couple of squad cars. He'd dispatched the Uniforms to check the street behind the house, and to start canvassing the other buildings across the road to see if anyone had spotted the car, or seen Sinead being bundled into it. There had been no other phone calls, which suggested the abduction had gone unnoticed, but it was worth a double-check.

The word replayed itself in his head after he'd thought it. *Abduction*.

Jesus Christ.

"She was only through there for a couple of minutes, if that," Tyler said. "Like, that was it. She went through, put the popcorn on, and then that was it. She didn't stop the microwave, and she wasn't answering, so I went through to look for her, and..."

He tightened his grip on his head and rocked forward. "She was gone."

"He must've doubled back," said Ben. "Abandoned the car to throw us off, then made his way back up."

"Where's Harris?" Logan asked.

"Next door. With the neighbour. She said she'll look after him. He's in a right state, though," Tyler said.

"Aye, well, we don't need you in the same state," Logan said. His tone wasn't exactly gentle, and it drew a raised eyebrow from DI Forde. "Get it together, son. We won't find her if you're a basket case."

A flash of something like betrayal flitted across DC Neish's face, then he sniffed, nodded, and stood up. "You're right, boss," he said, his voice wobbling. "Sorry, boss."

"Better," Logan said. He glanced back over his shoulder at Ben. "Hamza and Caitlyn on their way?"

"Be here shortly. Got CID and Uniform coming from all over, too. Scene of Crime will be along at some point."

"And what then?" Tyler asked. "When they turn up, what then?"

He looked at both his superior officers in turn, eyes wide and pleading. "What are we going to do?"

Logan's hand clapped down on the younger man's shoulder. "We're going to find her, son. Even if we have to turn this whole bloody city upside-down."

CHAPTER FORTY-SEVEN

PAIN. IT JOLTED THROUGH HER, SNAPPING HER AWAKE with disorientating suddenness.

Her head was filled with it, consumed by it. It was a pressure, a weight, pressing sharply down, leaning on her skull and pinning it to the bed.

Bed?

Gritting her teeth, she fought back against the pain enough to lift her head off the mattress.

The room was dark, lit only by the faint orange glow of a nightlight somewhere over by the door. It didn't help that her eyes were coated with a sleepy white film. It gradually cleared as she blinked it away, and as her vision adjusted to the gloom, she saw a *My Little Pony* poster looking back at her from the wall, a purple unicorn winking like it had just let her in on a secret.

The rest of the room was similarly themed, from the toys on the shelves to the quilt beneath her on the single bed. A child's bedroom, clearly. But whose? Where was she?

And how the hell had she got here?

The pain seared through her head again, forcing her to drop it back down onto the bed. Through the brain-fog, she remembered the kitchen. The microwave. The *pop-pop-pop* of the popcorn kernels.

She'd poured another glass of wine. Her third? Fourth? And then...

And then...

A hangover? Was that what this was?

No. No, it couldn't be. She'd had hangovers. This was different. This was—

She remembered the sound in the kitchen behind her. The creaking over by the door. The soft *thup* of a footstep on lino. The brief-but-blinding agony that exploded like a bomb-blast against the back of her skull.

Some deep-seated primal instinct screamed at her, ordered her to get up, get out, get away. She rolled towards the edge of the bed, not ignoring the pain but fighting it, resisting it.

A rope cut into her wrist, jerking her to a stop. She turned, room spinning in uneven loops around her, and saw the restraints for the first time. One on each wrist, binding her to the bed frame. Her legs, too. She was spread in an X-shape, secured in place. Pinned. Helpless.

She wanted to scream, to shout, to cry out, but bit down on her lip to stop herself. What if he was out there? What if he was listening, waiting for her to wake up? What if he—

A leering white face rose up from behind the footboard at the bottom of the bed.

For a split-second, she thought it was something ghostly and supernatural, but then the truth of it hit her. It was a mask. Similar to the one Clarissa McDade's killer had worn in the video, only this time the mouth was twisted into a cruel mockery of a grin.

Eyes studied her through two oval holes in the plastic. They were deep in shadow, but she could just make out the moving reflection as he looked her up and down.

From behind the mask came a falsetto giggle, then a voice began to sing.

"*Lazy bones, sleeping in the sun...*"

He raised a hand. The blade of a scalpel *glinted* in the glow of the nightlight.

"*How you 'spect to get your day's work done?*"

Sinead almost screamed then. What harm was in it? He was already here. There was nothing left to lose.

But something kicked in, keeping her mouth shut. She had plenty left to lose—everything, in fact—and screaming was only going to panic him or make him angry. She didn't want him panicked, and she definitely didn't want him angry.

She could get through this. Somehow, she could get through this. She just had to stay calm.

"It's good that you're awake," he said, the mask shifting slightly as he spoke. "I prefer it when they're awake."

"What do you want?" Sinead asked. "What are you going to do?"

David Oliver, Kel Conlyn, or whatever the man behind the mask was currently calling himself, ducked down out of sight again. Sinead raised her head, straining to see where he'd gone. She craned her neck to the right, searching for him, then yelped in panic when she whipped her head around to the left and found him squatting beside her, the mask just a few inches from her own face.

"Anything I want," he whispered, the scalpel clutched between finger and thumb. He placed a hand on her face. His fingers were soft and smooth as they caressed her. His thumb rubbed across her cheek, wiping away a tear. "Are you scared?" he asked.

There was no point trying to pretend otherwise. "Yes," Sinead told him.

The shout was so loud it almost blew the mask off. "WRONG!" he bellowed, his fingers snaking through the hair at the side of her head and tightening. "You're not scared. You're not *anything*. Fear. Anger. Lust. Those emotions, they're not real. They're implanted."

He yanked harder on her hair, forcing her head down onto the bed. "They're fucking *digits*. That's all. Numbers and code, like the rest of you. Like the rest of everyone."

"P-please," Sinead sobbed, the pain burning through her scalp and lighting up her brain. "Stop."

"What does it matter if I stop?" Oliver asked, his voice dropping to a low murmur, the mask moving closer to her ear.

She could smell his breath wafting through the gaps. It smelled of mint and strong coffee. Combined with the sour stench of his body odour, it made her want to gag.

"Hmm? What does it matter?" he demanded. "What does anything matter? You're not real. You don't exist. What can I *possibly* do to you that's worse than that?"

"I am real," Sinead told him. "You are, too. Everyone is."

"NO!" he roared, his hand untangling from her hair and clamping onto her throat, instead. "That's a lie. You're a *fucking liar*, just like the rest of them!"

He leaned his weight on her, pushing down onto her throat. Sinead's eyes bulged as she coughed and spluttered, her body instinctively fighting for air. Her head tingled. Darkness crept in, shadows closing at the edges of her vision.

Just when she thought she was about to pass out, he eased off enough for her to gulp down a breath. She wheezed in and out, eyes streaming, chest heaving, breath coming in frantic, uneven rasps.

Oliver waited until the breathing had steadied a little, before continuing in a low, matter-of-fact voice.

"I'm going to show you what happens to fucking liars like you."

"THIS IS MY FAULT."

Logan glanced over from the driver's seat, to where DC Neish was gazing out of the Volvo's side window at the streetlights passing outside.

"It isn't."

"It is," Tyler insisted, not turning. "I told him about her. In the hospital. I was trying to see if I could get him to open up, and I told him about me and Sinead."

Logan's hands tightened on the wheel, but he said nothing.

"I actually told him her name."

"You weren't to know. We weren't sure he was a suspect at that point."

"Bollocks, boss," Tyler said, turning to look at the DCI. "We had our suspicions. I should never have told him her name."

He went back to gazing out the window. His reflection stared accusingly back at him. "This is all my fault."

"We're going to make it right, son," Logan told him. "We're going to find her."

"How? Where? We don't have any idea where he took her!" Tyler snapped. "Not a fucking clue."

"Then we figure it out," Logan barked back.

It was just the two of them in the car, the rest of the team having split up to lead searches of their own. The streets were awash with blue, officers coming in from all over the area to help with the search.

They'd run through the obvious places first, with teams checking his parents' house, the ruins of his flat, and combing the hospital from top to bottom.

Caitlyn had led a team to scope out the empty shop where he'd first taken Danni Gillespie, but it was a doughnut place now, and none of the locks had been tampered with.

Squads were checking out other empty commercial properties across the city, but the internet and years of austerity measures had taken their toll on the High Street, and there were a lot of empty shops to search through.

How much time did Sinead have? Not much, going by the bastard's past performances. Not enough for them to fine-tooth-comb the whole city, certainly. They had to be smarter than that. They had to think like he would.

"He'd have to get her somewhere quickly. If he knocked her out, he wouldn't want her waking up before he got her to where they were going. If he didn't, and had just restrained her in some way, he'd be worried about her attracting attention," Logan said.

"God. If he's hurt her..."

"Come on, Tyler, help me out here," Logan scolded. "Stop feeling so bloody sorry for yourself and help me figure this out."

Tyler sat up straighter in his seat. "Right, boss. Aye. So, he wouldn't have gone too far. Is that what you're saying?"

"That's what I'm saying," Logan said. "He'd want to take her somewhere she wouldn't be discovered. At least, not until he was ready to show off his handiwork."

Tyler swallowed like he was about to be sick.

"Sorry, son, but if we're going to get her, we need to be polis, not her friends."

The DC nodded, swallowed twice more, then managed another contribution. "He had a car, so he could've taken her anywhere. They could be miles away."

"Too risky," Logan said, pulling up at a set of traffic lights on red. "For all he might talk about there being no consequences, he goes out of his way to avoid them."

He drummed his fingers on the wheel, waiting for the lights to change. A taxi and a baker's van crossed the junction ahead of them, going about their business.

Somewhere he knew. Somewhere close. Somewhere he wouldn't be disturbed.

"Jesus!" Logan ejected, leaning forward. "I might know where he is."

He crunched the Volvo into gear and floored it through the lights, earning a *honk* from another driver who was forced to screech to a stop.

"Where?" Tyler demanded. "Where is he?"

"Somewhere he knows is empty," Logan replied. The car surged along the street as he pushed his foot all the way to the floor. "Now, hold on. And be ready for anything."

CHAPTER FORTY-EIGHT

CLACK.

Sinead watched as Oliver placed the scalpel down on the bedside table. He'd moved it deliberately so it was in her eyeline, and hummed quietly as he set out his tools, the sound muffled slightly by the mask.

He'd taken a larger knife from a rucksack and set that down first, the serrated blade pitted with rust or dried blood.

Next, he'd brought out a stick. It was a little shorter than the knife, but thicker, with eight or nine jagged points where twigs had been hacked off. She didn't know what he planned to use that for. She didn't want to.

A roll of masking tape had been next. He'd set it down with a *clunk*, then thought better of it and pulled off a strip that he'd then placed over Sinead's mouth and slapped firmly to make sure it stayed stuck.

"Do you think they're watching?" he asked, straightening the line of implements on the bedside table so they all looked neat and *just-so*. His eyes went to the ceiling, then down to the woman on the bed. His voice dropped to just above a whisper.

"The coders. The creators. Do you think we've got their attention yet?"

Sinead couldn't have replied, even if she'd wanted to. She found her gaze returning to the serrated knife, then creeping sideways to the stick.

"Your boyfriend spoke very highly of you," Oliver said, his tone becoming relaxed and chatty. "He's quite a catch. You did well. If he'd been real, I'd have almost been jealous."

He reached for the knife, then hesitated.

"You know what?"

He pushed the mask up onto the top of his head and flashed Sinead a smile. "There. That's better, isn't it?"

Removing it completely, he turned the mask over in his hand. "I don't really know why I did that. What was I trying to hide? *This* mask?"

He caught his cheek between finger and thumb and pulled sharply. "Hiding one mask behind another. It makes no sense, does it?"

His eyes bulged, his brow furrowing. He crushed the plastic mask in his hand and leaned over Sinead, suddenly furious. "*Does it?*"

Sinead shook her head, tears streaming down her cheeks.

That seemed to satisfy Oliver and he leaned back, straightening. "No. Exactly. Hiding a mask behind a mask. What was I thinking?"

He looked to the ceiling again, as if in apology, then went back to humming his tune.

With his attention back on his tools, Sinead twisted her right hand. She'd been working away at the knot for the past few minutes and felt there was a chance—a slim one—that she could pull it free. It would hurt, and it would take time, but it was possible.

Please, God. Let it be possible.

"The camera," Oliver said, slapping the heel of his hand against his forehead. "I forgot the camera. People went nuts over that last video. They loved it. It really helped spread the message, you know? And that's one of the reasons we're doing this, isn't it?" he asked, like she was a willing participant in it all. "To spread the message. To let everyone know what they really are."

He placed his hand on her face again, ran it down over the purple bruising on her neck, then brushed it lightly against one of her breasts.

"You wait right there," he told her, smiling at the way she flinched at his touch. "I'll be right back."

She waited until she heard him making his way down the stairs, then tugged and wrenched at her arm. The rope tore at her wrist, each twist burning her skin and sending shockwaves of pain racing all the way up to her shoulder. She ignored them, heaving and pulling, knowing that her life almost certainly depended on it.

Downstairs, Oliver hummed quietly as he made his way through to the living room, and over to the table where he'd left the camera equipment. The GoPro hadn't been cheap, but it came with a free head mount, and the 4k footage would look incredible.

He glanced briefly at the framed family photographs on the wall, winked at a smiling Esme Miller, then started to make his way back to the stairs.

Halfway there, the front door flew open, revealing a heavy-set figure framed in the glow of a streetlight. Oliver recognised the detective at once, hurled the camera equipment at him, then flew to the stairs in a panic.

"Fuck, fuck, fuck!"

"Stay where you are!" Logan bellowed, powering across the room with DC Neish hot on his heels.

Oliver scrambled up the stairs on hands and feet, then launched himself upright at the top. He barrelled into the bedroom, hands grabbing for the larger of the two knives.

Gone. What the hell?

He looked up and jumped back in time to avoid a scything swipe of the blade. Sinead leaned on one elbow, the other arm free, the knife clutched in her trembling hand.

No, no, no!

He grabbed the scalpel, briefly entertained the notion of stabbing the living shit out of the meaningless bitch on the bed, then concluded that her knife was bigger than his.

Instead, he turned and ran back to the stairs, swishing the scalpel in front of him and driving back the detectives who had been headed in the opposite direction.

"Back off! Fucking *back off*!" he warned, slicing furiously at the air just a few inches in front of Logan's face.

The DCI put a hand behind him, stopping Tyler in his tracks.

"Where is she?" Tyler demanded. "*What have you done to her?*"

Oliver swiped with the scalpel again, coming dangerously close to Logan this time. The DCI raised an arm and heard the *sshkt* of the blade cutting through the sleeve of his borrowed coat. He retreated more quickly down the stairs, forcing Tyler back until they were both standing by the foot of the stairs, one on either side.

"It's over, David," Logan said. "Put the knife down. You're only making an arse of yourself."

"Shut the fuck up!" Oliver spat, visibly recoiling at the use of his real name. He had the surgical knife held out in front of him, his knuckles white as he gripped the handle. "You don't matter. None of this matters. You think you're so fucking important, but you're nothing."

He laughed, his shoulders shaking with silent, hysterical guffaws. "You're literally nothing at all."

"Then, there's no reason not to hand over the knife," Logan countered. "I mean, if you're right, it doesn't even exist, so why are you waving it about like that if it's not real?"

Oliver's eyes went to the blade, then back to Logan.

"You know what I think?" Logan asked. "I don't think you really believe any of that shite. Not deep down. I think you've been using it as an excuse, so you can act out whatever messed up fantasies you've got going on in that sick head of yours. If it was really about this simulation shite, why only take women? Why the sexual assaults? Why degrade and humiliate them?"

Logan's eyes narrowed. He jabbed a finger in Oliver's direction, ignoring the risk the knife posed.

"I'll tell you why, David. Because it's not about who exists and who doesn't. It's about power, same as every other rapist out there. It's about a small, pathetic wee man trying to make himself feel big and strong. That's all it is. That's all it ever is."

"Shut up! Shut up!" Oliver hissed.

A floorboard creaked beneath Tyler's feet. Oliver whipped the knife hand towards him, the blade pointed directly as his face. "Don't fucking move!" he screeched. "Last warning!"

"Oh, grow up, David, ye daft bastard," Logan spat. As diplomacy and negotiation strategy went, it wasn't exactly textbook stuff. "It's over. We've got you. This place is going to be swarming with angry polis any minute, who're all holding you responsible for getting called out of their beds two nights running. Put down the knife and I might be able to protect you from them. *Might*, mind. No promises."

Oliver gritted his teeth, the scalpel shaking in his grip. For a moment, it looked like he might be about to consider it, but then he saw Tyler's eyes flick briefly to the stairs behind him and heard the faint suggestion of a footstep.

Logan was closest, so Oliver lunged for him, slashing and swiping with the blade. The DCI raised his arms to protect himself, and the coat sleeves were sliced to ribbons. At least a couple of the swipes found skin, and Logan hissed in pain as blood bloomed through the material.

Oliver was suddenly behind him, the knife pressed against the detective's throat. Halfway down the stairs, Sinead froze, the combat knife in her hand, a rectangle of red around her mouth marking where the tape had been.

"You stupid bitch! You stupid fucking bitch! I'll kill him. I'll fucking kill him."

"DC Neish, take Constable Bell outside. Make sure she's OK," Logan instructed. If he was scared, there was nothing in his voice to indicate it.

"What? No!" Sinead said.

"No can do, boss," Tyler agreed.

Logan grimaced as the knife was pressed more firmly against his skin. Blood oozed down his neck. A trickle, for now, but a promise of much more to come.

"Do what he says. Get out," Oliver snapped. "And make sure everyone stays away, or I slit him open. He'll be dead before he hits the ground."

Tyler's jaw clenched. His gaze flicked from Oliver to the knife, then up to the DCI's face.

"You heard him. Go," Logan urged. "Both of you, get out."

Sinead passed the knife from hand to hand, sizing up her chances of making it to the murderer before he could draw the blade across Logan's throat. There was no way she could close the gap in time though. It was hopeless.

"That's an order, Detective Constable," Logan said. "Get out. Both of you. Now."

"Come on," Sinead whispered, taking Tyler by the hand. "We have to go."

Tyler stood his ground for a few moments, then let out a little groan of anguish. "We'll be right outside, boss," he promised.

Sinead opened the door, and the wailing of sirens reverberated around the room. Backup was close, but probably not close enough.

The door closed, muting the volume of the world outside.

"Right then, Davey-boy," Logan said. "What now?"

"What?" Oliver hissed.

"The plan? What's the plan, now that you've got me all to yourself?" Logan pressed. "You do have a plan, aye? What is it? You going to just vanish us into thin air, maybe? Or hack the fucking Matrix or something? You must have some sort of plan, surely? This can't be it."

"Shut up, shut up, I'm thinking," Oliver said. "You had to ruin it. You had to *fucking ruin* it. You had to interfere!"

"Is that what your parents did? Interfere?" Logan asked. "Or was there some other reason you tied them up and killed them? They must've pushed you hard, did they? You a child prodigy, and all that. I bet they never gave you a minute's peace."

"Be quiet! Fucking shut up!" Oliver snapped.

"Still, killing your own maw and da," Logan tutted. "What kind of headcase does that?"

"I said *shut up!*"

The hand holding the scalpel was shaking badly now. Logan could feel the blade digging deeper into his skin.

"Calm down, David. I'm no good to you if I'm dead," Logan pointed out. Unnoticed by the knifeman, he slowly slid a hand into a trouser pocket.

"I'm *calm*," Oliver said, the words coming out as something close to a sob. "I'm perfectly fucking calm. It's not real. Emotions aren't real. It's numbers. Just numbers. Ones and zeroes. That's all!"

"Whatever you say," Logan told him. "But if you want my advice, you'll move us away from the window before the snipers arrive."

"They won't shoot if I've got a hostage."

"Normally, aye, but none of them like me very much," Logan said. "So, better to be safe than sorry."

Oliver hesitated, then the knife relaxed just a fraction on the DCI's throat. "Right. Here's what we're going to do. We're going to go through to the kitchen, and you're going to pull the blinds shut."

"Now you're thinking straight," Logan said. "But, how about instead of that, we do this?"

He jabbed sharply backwards with his right hand, while grabbing for Oliver's knife arm with his left. A scream erupted by Logan's ear as half a dozen cocktail sticks were embedded in the thigh of the man behind him.

The knife hand jerked, but Logan yanked it away before it could slice his throat. He twisted, squeezing Oliver's bandaged forearm, then drove a punch right into the centre of the bastard's face.

Eyes blurred by tears, and choking on blood and snot, Oliver grabbed the scalpel with his free hand and lashed out with it. Logan shoved him, sending him tumbling to the floor.

He lay there on his back, coughing and wheezing, with the DCI looming over him like the spectre of Death.

"Put it down, David. It's over."

"It doesn't matter. Nothing matters. Nothing's real," Oliver whispered. He raised the knife, turning it so the blade was pointed straight at his own throat. "None of it is real!"

Logan made no move to intervene. He didn't have to.

"You don't really believe that, do you, son?"

Oliver's hand shook. Tears and snot and blood covered his face like a mask.

And then, with an animalistic roar of helplessness, despair, and a dozen other all-too-real emotions, he let his arms drop to his sides, and the scalpel fall freely from his grip.

Logan placed a foot on the knife, pinning it in place. Blood trickled down his arms and dripped from his fingertips. Hoon's coat was ruined. He'd never hear the bloody end of this.

"David Oliver," he said, not savouring the moment, exactly, but drawing some grim satisfaction from it. "You, sunshine, are nicked."

CHAPTER FORTY-NINE

THE MORNING PASSED. WOUNDS WERE STITCHED UP. Statements were given. Press announcements were made.

Some harsh words were exchanged about 'the state of that fucking coat,' but compared to the past few days, things were relatively uneventful.

It was almost noon by the time Logan was ready to go home. Ben and Caitlyn had offered to take on most of the paperwork duties, leaving Logan and Tyler free to go and get some rest.

Very few words had passed between the DCI and the DC since they'd returned to the station. Those that had been exchanged had been enough though, and most of the meaning had been there in the silences.

"You'll be sleeping the next week away, I'm assuming?" asked Ben, escorting Logan towards the Volvo. He'd been harping on at him to 'bugger off home,' for the past couple of hours, and was determined to make sure he actually left the premises.

"Something like that, aye," Logan said. Loathe as he was to

admit it, he was utterly exhausted. Even the drive home seemed like some Herculean effort he wasn't convinced he had the energy for.

He clambered into the driver's seat, closed the door, and pressed the button to wind the window down. "If anything comes up—"

"Away and shite," Ben told him. "Go. Home. Rest. The world can limp by without Jack Logan for a couple of days."

Logan chuckled drily. "I suppose so."

"And you're going straight home. Right?"

Logan tapped the button to raise the glass between them. "Aye," he said. "Something like that."

THERE WAS one more thing to do. One final loose end to tie up.

He met the uniformed constable at the gate of a neat little semi-detached, explained the situation, then led him up the path and rang the doorbell.

A series of musical chimes rang out somewhere in the house. It was followed almost immediately by the barking of a small dog, then the muttering of a man as he tried to shut the animal in another room.

The door opened. Logan noted the way the man's face instantly crumpled when he saw the officers standing on the step. He knew. The game was up.

"I'm sorry," said the nurse, Bob Brews. "I'm so sorry. I don't know what came over me."

Logan just stared, saying nothing, giving the man all the rope he needed.

"When I took the tape off Esme, I just... I don't know. It

felt... important. I didn't mean to keep it. Not really. It's just... It was something, I don't know. Interesting. Exciting."

He met Logan's eye for the briefest of moments, before the intensity of his stare became too much. "I shouldn't have taken it. I should've left it. I'm sorry. I'm so sorry."

Logan didn't even bother to reply. There was plenty he could've said, of course—how he'd withheld evidence, how he'd potentially jeopardised a murder investigation—but he mentioned none of it. There'd be time for that later.

Instead, he addressed the officer beside him.

"Constable, charge Mr Brews, would you?" he said, and then he turned away from the man in the doorway and strode off along the path before his anger could get the better of him.

LOGAN'S LEGS protested as he heaved himself up the stone steps of his block of flats. Never had the nickname 'the plod' been more accurate, he thought, dragging himself up onto the first landing, and turning towards the second flight of stairs.

The door to Tanya's flat opened, and Logan's nostrils flared as Bud appeared in the doorway. He leaned against the frame, a pair of grey jogging bottoms on his lower half, a variety of poorly done tattoos the only thing covering him from his waist to his neck.

He grinned, showing off his yellow teeth. "Afternoon, officer," he said. "Rough night?"

Logan took a step towards him. "I thought I told you to—"

"It's fine," said a female voice from the hallway. Tanya appeared at Bud's back, then squeezed past him and ushered him back into the flat. Logan could see him standing further along the hall, watching them, the grin still plastered on his face.

"What are you doing?" Logan asked her.

"It's fine. We sorted everything out," Tanya said. She smiled, and Logan got the impression that she almost believed the words coming out of her still-bruised mouth. "It's not going to happen again. We talked it through."

Logan wanted to argue, but what was the point? He'd seen the same thing play out over and over again. He'd be talking to a brick wall, and right at that moment, he didn't have the energy.

"Well, I hope it works out," he said, then he went back to dragging himself up the stairs.

"Uh, Mr Logan? Jack?"

Logan stopped, leaning on the metal bannister for support.

"You'll, um, you'll be around, won't you?"

Logan scraped together something close to a smile. "Aye," he told her. "I'm always around."

He waited until she had waved and closed the door, then muttered something under his breath, and fumbled for his keys.

There was a sour smell in the flat when he shambled inside, and he remembered he hadn't put the bin out in days.

It could wait. There was no way he had the energy to tackle those stairs again today.

He slumped onto the couch, and the springs *sproinged* in complaint. His head had just fallen backwards so it was resting against the top of the cushion when the phone in his pocket rang.

Logan groaned. It was a new work phone—a replacement for the one that had gone up in flames—and no one but the MIT and Bob Hoon had the number. If they were calling, then his dream of a solid seventy-two-hours of sleep would be well and truly out the window.

With some effort, he traced the ringing to the left front pocket of his trousers. *Unknown* was displayed on-screen. Hoon, then, probably. Everyone else was programmed in.

"Logan," he said, bringing the phone to his ear and letting his head fall back onto the cushion again.

His own voice echoed back at him down the line.

"Hello?" he said.

Silence.

Logan sat forward, ignoring the aching it triggered.

"Who is this?" he asked.

The reply, when it came, was a soft giggle. A *whisper*.

"Oh, Jack," it said. "You know *exactly* who I am."

And then, the line went dead. Logan stared in disbelief at the screen until it turned dark, then let the phone fall onto the couch beside him.

It was him. That voice. That damn whisper. It was *him*.

But there was nothing he could do about it. Not yet. Not right now. He hadn't slept in days and exhaustion was moving in to claim him, turning the edges of the room into a haze of darkness.

He stretched out on the couch, kicked off his shoes, and lay staring up at the ceiling.

The events of the past few days had almost killed him. People he cared about, too.

And yet, as his eyes closed and the world slipped away into darkness, a knot in his stomach told him that things were about to get much, *much* worse.

READY FOR MORE?

DCI JACK LOGAN AND HIS TEAM RETURN IN...

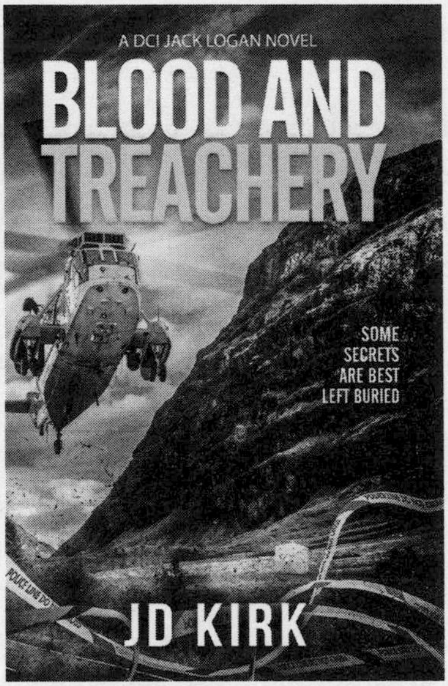

Blood & Treachery

JOIN THE JD KIRK VIP CLUB